a PORTHKENNACK
CONTEMPORARY

LOVE AT FIRST HATE

JL MERROW

RIPTIDE
PUBLISHING

Riptide Publishing
PO Box 1537
Burnsville, NC 28714
www.riptidepublishing.com

Love at First Hate

Cover art: Garrett Leigh, blackjazzdesign.com
Editors: Rachel Haimowitz, Veronica Vega
Layout: L.C. Chase, lcchase.com/design.htm

ISBN: 978-1-62649-833-4

First edition
September, 2018

Also available in ebook:
ISBN: 978-1-62649-832-7

a PORTHKENNACK
CONTEMPORARY

LOVE AT FIRST HATE

JL MERROW

TABLE OF
CONTENTS

CHAPTER ONE

"Bye, Uncle Bran!" Gawen's voice had finally settled into a deep baritone that was hard to credit, coming from the slight, tousle-headed figure waving by the front door. "And thank you for *The Gorg*—uh, the book."

"*The Gormenghast Trilogy.*" Chuckling, Bran waved back from the vast distance of four feet away, having barely made it a couple of paces down the path. "You're welcome. And don't stay up all night reading it. School tomorrow, remember."

"But I haven't got any interesting lessons. It's just English, French, and History. And *double games.*" Gawen's tone made it clear what he thought of that.

Bran could empathise. But only silently. "Physical education is important for your health. And you need to pass your exams in *all* your subjects, not just the interesting ones." Gawen's mother Kirsty being something of a free spirit, this sort of gentle nagging was often left to Bran.

"I *suppose.*" Gawen's mouth turned down comically. Bran managed not to laugh as he said a final farewell.

As he walked through the garden towards the road, the faint light from the open door threw eerie shadows from Kirsty's driftwood sculptures. Bran had never managed to get used to them. He could see they were art, and good art at that, but they weren't his kind of art. Too . . . unrestrained.

He'd stayed later than he'd planned. Kirsty had cooked, Gawen had begged, and Bran could remember being thirteen himself—wanting his father to spend time with him, and the crushing disappointment of being refused. So he'd allowed himself to be persuaded. He'd got a more-than-decent meal out of it, and all in all it'd been a definite improvement on the rest of the day. Pennock & Hardy were proving annoyingly obstinate over the Constantine Bay property, and Bran had had sharp words with a visitor to Roscarrock House. Too many of them seemed to be under the impression that "Private: No Entry" only applied to other people. Sometimes Bran hated living and working in a house that was open to the public.

Still, the house was his heritage. And Gawen's too. For a boy who lived for maths and physics, Gawen was gratifyingly interested in Bran's retellings of Roscarrock family history. Everyone said, of course, that that was down to Gawen's father, but Bran liked to think he deserved at least some of the credit. After all, he'd been more of a father to the boy than his brother had for the first ten years of Gawen's life. Jory was doing a better job of fatherhood now, though—Bran had to grant him that. He'd moved back to Porthkennack just over a year ago, and looked likely to stay for good. Bran had worried, at first, that Jory's presence would mean Gawen would have less time for Uncle Bran, but apparently his affections were made of sterner stuff than that.

It was a warming thought, and Bran found himself smiling as he walked back through the town. The sun had set a while ago, and a soft breeze was blowing in off the sea. It brought with it the scent of brine and seaweed, and the cries of gulls as they foraged around town for the rich pickings left by careless tourists—not so many of them, this early in the season, but enough for a noticeable increase in avian activity. Bran imagined pitched battles fought over discarded bags of chips or half-eaten sandwiches, then wondered when he'd become so fanciful. Gawen's influence, no doubt.

The direct route from Kirsty's house led him through a quieter part of town, away from the pubs, restaurants, and amusement arcades of the centre. Bran's shoulders relaxed. He'd never been one for raucous entertainment, even in his teens, and he couldn't help finding it a little tacky. On the other hand, a thriving local economy was nothing to be sniffed at.

The street lamps were set farther apart here, and just ahead of him, one flickered. On, off, on—and then off for good, or so it seemed. Bran would have to report it. He fumbled in his pocket for his phone, then tried to remember how to turn on the torch app like Gawen had shown him a month or so ago. There. Bran shone the surprisingly bright light at the post, and made a note of the number.

When he switched off the light again, the darkness seemed three times as stygian. Bran was damned, though, if he was going to use a torch to get through streets he'd known all his life. The next street lamp wasn't all that far away.

As he looked towards it, Bran saw the silhouette of a man coming towards him with unhurried tread, and tensed for a moment before firmly telling himself not to be such a child. There was something familiar about the half-seen figure, wasn't there? Hardly surprising, of course, in Porthkennack. Bran squinted, but couldn't make out who it was—and of course, with every step nearer, he was shrouded further in darkness.

Bran's face, by contrast, would be faintly illumined by the glow from the far street lamp. He hated being at a disadvantage. Still, if it was an acquaintance, presumably the man would greet him verbally, and hopefully he'd recognise the voice. Bran walked on, trying not to be too obvious about examining the advancing figure. The man had his head down and his hands in his pockets. Bran frowned. Surely he knew that figure?

They were only a few feet from one another when, perversely, the faulty street lamp sparked back into life. Pale light fell across them both, making Bran blink as much in surprise as in the sudden brightness.

The man looked up. "*You.*" It was a vicious snarl borne on alcoholic fumes. "Bastard!"

Eyes wide, Bran drew in a breath—and then a fist drove into his stomach and all breath fled, leaving only a tight knot of pain.

He stumbled. Struggled not to fall.

Then his head exploded in agony, and the darkness was absolute.

CHAPTER TWO

"You sure this is right?" It was followed by an earsplitting belch. Sam managed not to sigh out loud. Or wince at the reek of beer as he bent down to go over the bill for table eight. "You had the banquet meal for four and up, yeah? And there's seven of you. So that's that total." He underlined it in pen.

"What's all that other guff, then? How come you charged us for all them other meals?" The guy who'd apparently been designated the mathematician of the group frowned. He was a big, beefy bloke in his early twenties, and Christ knew why he'd got the honours given his total lack of comprehension of simple addition.

"That's because three of you wanted chips with it, and then the gentleman over there"—Sam pointed to the biggest bloke at the table, currently swaying worryingly in his seat—"decided he didn't like curry and he wanted an omelette instead. And then there's drinks."

"We never had all them lagers. You sure you didn't get the number wrong?"

"Wrote them all down as you ordered them," Sam said patiently.

"Yeah, but you could've made a mistake. Wrote it down wrong."

I have a PhD. In medieval history. Which you probably can't even spell right now. "Trust me, I didn't make a mistake. I'll show you the chits if you like."

"Nah, don't bother." Maths Genius raised his head to address his mates. "You lot of wankers are a bunch of bloody pissheads."

"I only had water," Omelette Guy complained.

"*Water?*" One of his mates burst out laughing. "You fucking poofter."

Maths Genius pushed back his chair so suddenly he almost knocked Sam flying, and stood up to bang on the table. "You leave him alone, you wanker."

"And mind your fucking language!" one of the others yelled out, to raucous laughter.

"Don't feel well," Omelette Guy mumbled, swaying some more.

Bloody hell. "Cash or credit card?" Sam tried to keep them on track.

"Oi, lads, who's got cash?" Maths Genius bellowed.

There was a chorus of, "Dunno," "Let me check," "Who's had my wallet?" and "Cashpoint wasn't working."

"Yes, it fucking was," Maths Genius answered to the last one. "I got mine out all right."

Someone cackled. "You got it out in the restaurant? You filthy bugger."

"Takes one to know one, mate," someone else said. "I saw you dipping your wick in—"

"Credit card, then?" Sam raised his voice, desperate to be heard. Omelette Guy had gone a horrible yellowy-grey colour. "And you can settle up with your mates when you get out of here?"

"Oi, hang about, hang about," Maths Genius grumbled. "Give us a minute, here. Or do you not want a bloody tip?"

Give them a minute? Didn't they have beds to go to? It was nearly 1 a.m., and Sam was *this* close to telling them where to shove their tips, if he hadn't needed the money so badly. "Sorry. But I think your mate needs some fresh air." He nodded at Omelette Guy.

The two lads either side of Omelette Guy seemed to notice for the first time that he wasn't looking too good. One pushed his chair so far away he banged into a girl in platform heels just getting up from a nearby table. "Whoops—sorry, love."

"Bloody hell, mate, you watch what you're doing," she squawked, tottering. "I nearly ended up in your lap."

He leered. "You can sit in my lap anytime, gorgeous."

"Oi, watch it, chum, she's with me." Heels Girl's boyfriend puffed his chest out.

Chair Guy got to his feet.

Sam *really* wished he wasn't on his own upstairs tonight.

Then one of the other lads from table eight showed a bit more fellow feeling—not to mention total obliviousness to the threatening atmosphere—by patting Omelette Guy on the shoulder. "You all right, Rob? You're not gonna chuck, are you?"

Omelette Guy gagged.

Sam's heart stopped.

Chair Guy jumped three feet away. "Oi, watch it, I got new trainers on."

Heels Girl and her bloke scuttled away.

Sam met Rob's mate's eye. "Think we'd better get him outside." Taking an arm each, they hauled the big guy out of his seat and, sweating, down the narrow stairs, past the queue still waiting for takeaway, and out onto the street.

Where he finally hurled. Massively.

At least it was outside. Thank God for small mercies. Sam looked down and realised with a sinking heart he'd caught some splatter. He'd have to clean that off in the loos. Luckily one thing this place wasn't short of was disinfectant.

"Rob, you big girl!" A shout in his ear alerted Sam to the rest of the group stumbling out of the restaurant.

Shit. Had they paid? It'd be coming out of his wages if they did a runner. "Uh, guys, did you settle the bill?"

Maths Genius clapped him on the back. "Don't worry. Even left you a tip, cos Pete reckoned it'd be racist if we didn't, you being a Paki and all. Oi, you are a Paki, right? Or have you just been at the spray tan?"

"Tel, you tosser, you can't call him a Paki."

"You did!"

"Yeah, but not when I was talking to him. Sorry, mate." He gave Sam an apologetic smile. "Pig-shit ignorant, some people are. You have a good night."

Finally, *finally* they left, walking off unsteadily down the street. Sam breathed a sigh of relief, and headed back into the restaurant to clean himself up.

"Sam?" his boss called. "Why haven't you got the mop out? We can't have that mess out there putting people off."

"Sorry, Al, doing it now." Sam sighed and got moving. "They did pay, right?" he couldn't help asking.

"Of course they did. But I don't think they were impressed with your service. They left a very small tip. You'll have to do better than that in future."

And there, in a nutshell, was the story of his life.

CHAPTER
THREE

"MR. Roscarrock?"
A woman's voice. Soft and competent. It reminded him of Bea.

Bran wished she'd leave him alone. His head ached terribly, and he was nauseous. Had he been drinking?

"Mr. Roscarrock? Are you with us again?"

Bran blinked his eyes until they focussed on a middle-aged female face wearing a concerned frown. "What?" It came out sounding rusty, as well as brusque.

"You've had a bump on the head, Mr. Roscarrock. Do you remember what happened?"

His thoughts were like slurry. He'd . . . been visiting his nephew, hadn't he? "Gawen?"

"Is that your partner? Someone you'd like us to contact?"

"No." Bran struggled to order his brain. Why did they think that? But no. It was just a . . . thing. Reaction. Because he'd said a male name. But how could they know—*did* they know? "Bea . . . My sister. My twin." It seemed important to add that, although once he'd said it, Bran was no longer sure why.

"She's been informed, and she's on her way."

Bran blinked at her. "Where?"

"You're in the Royal Cornwall Hospital in Truro. You were brought here by ambulance."

Ambulance? Had there been an accident? "Why?"

"You've had a bump on the head. Do you remember?" It was said with endless patience. How many times had she asked him this already?

"What happened? Is Gawen all right?" Bran struggled to sit up, but a vicious, sawing pain in his chest felled him almost before he'd moved.

Gentle hands eased him back down. "It's all right. Nobody else was hurt."

"What happened?" he asked again.

"You were found lying unconscious in a Porthkennack street."

Hot shame at the indignity tightened Bran's chest, causing a physical pain. To make matters worse, he heard himself make a sound that was unmistakeably a whimper. As if it wasn't bad enough that he'd been lying in the street like a drunkard.

But it didn't make *sense*. Why couldn't he remember? He'd been at Kirsty's, talking to Gawen about . . . he wasn't sure what. Schoolwork? Family history? He couldn't remember leaving.

"Mr. Roscarrock? Do you need some more pain relief?" Her voice had the patient emphasis of someone who'd said it at least once before.

"No." He didn't need to be coddled.

"Well, if you're sure. But don't try to move; you've got a couple of cracked ribs. Just try to rest now, and your sister will be here soon. Let me know if you're too uncomfortable, and we'll see what we can do to make you feel better."

Bran did as she said. It wasn't like he had any other option. He lay there and blinked at his surroundings. A hospital room—yes, she'd said he was in hospital. At least it was a private room. Wasn't that unusual? Perhaps Bea had insisted.

Bea. He wanted her desperately. She'd make sense of everything. She always did.

Bran wasn't sure how long it was after that when Bea arrived, but at least his thoughts were no longer swimming through treacle. She looked stressed. Probably hadn't appreciated having to drive all the way out to Truro at such a late hour. Not that Bran could see a clock, but the sky outside the window was pitch-black. He had an uneasy idea he'd lost time again.

"Bran," she said, then stopped, her lips tight. Her nostrils flared as she took a deep breath. "Who did this?"

"I . . ." He was appalled to realise it hadn't occurred to him to wonder about it. "It was an accident?"

"They told me you were mugged. Your wallet was stolen. If you hadn't been recognised by the people who found you . . ." She stopped again, blinking. "I wouldn't even have known you were here."

"Bea?" Bran hated feeling so helpless to comfort her.

"You're *all I have*," she said fiercely. "So we are going to find out who did this, and they're going to *pay*."

She sat down in the chair beside the bed, and extended a cool hand to cup his face as if he were a child. The touch was unaccustomed, and he almost flinched, but stopped himself in time. It wasn't *unwelcome*. Neither was seeing her so fierce on his behalf, but right now he felt completely unequal to thoughts of vengeance. His wretched uncertainty about himself, about *anything*, was overwhelming. "They said I had cracked ribs?"

Bea nodded. "Broken. That's what they told me. It means the same thing, anyway. Just that calling them *cracked* sounds as if it's not so serious. They think you hit your head on the wall as you fell. And then that *bastard* kicked you. Do you remember any of it?"

Bran made to shake his head, and immediately regretted it. "No."

"We'll find out. Don't you worry."

The policewoman who came to talk to him the next day looked around Jory's age. Her dark, curly hair was cropped aggressively short at the sides and a little longer on top, probably an attempt to counteract the soft prettiness of her face, with her light-brown skin, large, dark eyes, and full lips. She was vaguely familiar—someone Bran had seen around town, but had never spoken to.

Bran's head still ached horribly, and it hurt to breathe too deeply but, his mind having cleared from the mental sludge of last night, he was by now so bored he was actually glad to see her.

"Mr. Roscarrock? I'm Constable Sally Peters. Do you feel up to answering a few questions?" Her voice was jarring—not the warm,

West Country burr he'd expected, but something more like Essex with a faint echo of Jamaica.

"You're not local?" he found himself asking in surprise. "I'm sorry. That was rude."

She shook her head. "Don't worry. I get that every time I open my mouth. I was born and bred in Chingford. Moved down here when I got married."

He glanced automatically at her left hand, which was bare.

She caught his glance, and smiled. "Stayed when I got divorced. You know you're the one who's supposed to be answering the questions, right?"

"Then you should probably ask them." It came across as brusque, he was aware. But he already knew this was a waste of time. "Although I'll tell you now, I can't remember a single thing about what happened to me."

She pulled out a notebook and pen. "Let's start with your movements yesterday. You live in Roscarrock House, up on the promontory at Big Guns Cove?"

"As I'm sure you already know."

"Must be nice, big house on the cliffs like that." Her tone was neutral, conversational. "So you went for a walk into town?"

"I went to visit my nephew. Gawen Roscarrock." An uneasy thought struck. "He's thirteen, so I hope you won't be bothering him about all this."

She ignored the implied question. "And you saw him at the house he shares with his mum . . . Kirsty Fisher? Your brother's ex-wife?"

"Correct."

"And is that a regular thing for you, going down there?"

Bran bristled at the suggestion he might not take his responsibilities seriously. "I see him frequently, yes. He's the heir to the estate."

The constable made a note in her book. "Always at his house?"

What an odd question. "No, of course not."

"But when you do go down there, is it always on a Thursday night?"

"No . . ." Bran frowned in thought, having realised what she was getting at. "Well, more often than not, I suppose. He has activities he does other evenings. And Friday nights are spent with his father.

And his father's partner," he added, because apparently Malory Thomas was now a permanent family fixture. Bran could hardly ignore his existence, much as he was an indirect reminder of unpleasant things.

"That's Jory Roscarrock, your little brother?"

Bran snorted. It hurt his chest, and his next words came out embarrassingly strangled. "Hardly *little*."

She laughed. "Yeah, I've met him. They had me round to speak to the kids at his school. Community-relations thing. Got a crick in my neck just talking to him."

Bran found himself liking Constable Peters. He didn't *want* to like her. He wanted to be angry and indignant, and rail at her for wasting time with trivial questions instead of getting out there to bring his assailant to justice.

"Right. So you'd quite often be walking back through town at that time on a Thursday night?"

"I suppose so. I don't always stay for dinner."

"But most times you do?"

Bran realised he couldn't actually remember a time in recent months when Kirsty hadn't offered, or he hadn't accepted. It was unsettling, to see how much of a routine he'd fallen into without noticing. "Yes."

"Always the same route?"

"Generally . . . yes. It's the quickest way."

She nodded and made a note.

"I can see where you're going with this," Bran said, his throat tight. "You think someone was lying in wait for me."

"Just exploring the possibilities, sir. Can you think of anyone who might have wanted to harm you?"

Bran swallowed. Since Bea had visited him, he'd been able to think of little else. "I'm sure you're aware a man in my position must inevitably come into conflict with other local businessmen from time to time. Purely in a commercial sense, obviously."

"Your position as . . .?"

Bran had a strong feeling she already knew who he was, but wanted to hear how he would phrase it. "As the major local landowner in Porthkennack," he said, careful not to sound as though he were bragging.

"Is there anyone in particular you've come into conflict with recently?"

"The Edes. And the Andrewarthas. They're the only ones who've borne a grudge." The only ones who'd been vocal about it, at any rate.

"What, all of them?"

"If you're newly arrived in Porthkennack, you may not realise how clannish it is. Family feeling runs deep."

She cocked her head. "I've lived in Porthkennack a few years now. And I've never seen any trouble coming from either of those families."

Bran snorted. "No? Perhaps you should consider that Jago Andrewartha had the nerve to run my brother out of the Sea Bell last year, and tell him he was barred from going back. For no fault of Jory's, I might add. And Jago was thick as thieves with Gerren Ede."

"Gerren Ede?"

"A tenant of mine, now deceased. His family objected to my perfectly legal actions in taking back possession of the house he was renting at the time of his death. Apparently the concept of property ownership means very little to them."

She made another note. "Have any of them ever threatened you?"

"No, or you'd have heard about it."

She raised her eyebrows. Perhaps he *had* been a little vehement. "And might there be anyone with a more personal motive to wish you harm?"

"No."

"And . . ." She flipped a page in her notebook. "You're single?"

"Yes."

"No recent relationships that might have ended badly?"

"No," he said, as firmly as he could. He was uncomfortably aware of the contrast with his previous statement. It was true enough, though. Craig and he hadn't been in a relationship. Merely an arrangement.

"You're sure about that?"

Christ, was she reading his mind? "Quite sure." Bran refused to believe Craig would ever hurt him, despite the circumstances of their parting. And in any case he was miles away in Newquay.

"And your sister?"

"What about her?"

"She's single too?"

"I don't see what that has to do with anything. But yes."

"Just getting the full picture." Her smile took away his irritation at the overly intrusive questions. Not for the first time, Bran wished he was able to be attracted to someone like her. Life would have been so much simpler. Happier. Women were kinder, as a rule, weren't they?

An image of Bea flashed into his mind to give the lie to that generalization. He swallowed.

"Everything all right, sir?"

"Yes. I'm . . . just tired." He realised how true it was as he said it, and closed his eyes.

"I'll let you rest, then. But if you think of anything else that might identify your attacker, give me a call, okay?"

CHAPTER
FOUR

S am knew it was going to be a bad day when he bumped into Maria in the corner shop.

His eldest sister was, like all the female members of Sam's family, a small woman, but she made up for her size with the strength of her opinions—also like the rest of them. She was seven years older than he was and, as she liked to remind him, a proper doctor, a GP in a local practice who helped real live people instead of poking her nose into the affairs of dead ones. She had three children. Her husband, Ray, a bank manager, liked to joke they'd wanted one of each: a doctor, a lawyer, and an engineer. It was only one of the reasons Sam had never got on with him.

She had her youngest with her today. Santa was straining against the straps of her buggy—already fighting to escape her parents' narrow view of her destiny? Her stubborn expression turned into a shy smile when she saw her uncle Sam.

Maria's face, by contrast, settled into grim determination. "Mum's been asking about you. She said she hasn't seen you for weeks."

Nice greeting. Well, if she was going to be rude, so was he. Sam ignored his sister and focussed on his niece. "Hey, Santa-pants." He waggled his fingers at her, and she giggled.

Then he turned to Maria. "Fancy meeting you here. What with you living the other side of town and all. A more suspicious bloke might think you were stalking him."

"Then the more suspicious bloke should start answering his phone. Not to mention his front door. I knocked three times, you know. And rang the bell. Not ten minutes before you came in here."

"I was out," Sam lied, feeling guilty. He'd just assumed it was someone calling for one of his housemates.

Or, well, someone he didn't want to see.

Maria looked him up and down. "Pyjama party, was it?"

Shit. He'd *known* he should've made the effort to put his jeans on, instead of coming out in the checked flannel lounge pants Mum had given him for Christmas. But for Christ's sake, he'd only wanted a pint of milk for his breakfast. Seeing as one of the gits he lived with had drunk all his.

"You realise it's nearly lunchtime." Maria's disapproving tone was all too familiar from when she'd tried to mother him as a child.

"So? I didn't get off work until gone two. I've gotta sleep sometime."

"I hope you're planning to get properly dressed tomorrow. You *are* going to be there for Sunday lunch at Mum's, aren't you? You've missed at least three weeks. She's doing roast lamb," Maria added with a pointed look.

"I'll think about it, 'kay?" Mum's roast lamb was to die for. And the whole family knew it was his favourite. "Saturday's my worst night, though."

Her face softened. *Very* slightly. "I don't know why you keep working there. All that education, wasted. Are you even applying for proper jobs? I don't mean academic ones," she said quickly. "But there must be something better you could do than clearing up after drunks."

"Yeah, right. Cos the interview would go *so* well, wouldn't it? 'Come in, Mr. Ferreira. Oh, it's Dr. Ferreira, is it? Tell me, why aren't you looking for work in your field? Failure of due diligence . . .? I *see*.'" He could hear his voice getting louder and more bitter as he went on. "Thank you, Dr. Ferreira. That'll be all. Don't let the door hit you on your way out.'"

Santa started to grizzle, and he felt like a total bastard.

Maria glared at him. "It's like you've just given up." She bent to her daughter, speaking softly and giving her a sippy cup that stemmed the tide of tears but didn't stop those wide, sad eyes tugging on Sam's heartstrings.

He didn't say anything. What was there to say?

"Now, are you coming to lunch tomorrow or not?" Maria asked briskly, having straightened up. "Mum says she's got a load of letters for you too. Who's writing to you at Mum's?"

"Don't know." He could guess, though. Thank God he could trust Mum not to open his post. He crouched down to ruffle Santa's thick black curls and, not incidentally, hide his face from his way-too-perceptive sister. "I'll think about it," he repeated.

He already knew he wouldn't go.

He didn't mean to, but when he got back into his room, Sam somehow found himself opening up the betting site on his mobile and having a bit of a flutter. He even won a small amount, first off. Then he lost the lot, and more. Christ, he had to stop giving in to temptation like that. It was just . . . if he got a proper win, a big one, he'd be able to wipe out all his debts. Start fresh.

Surely one day the odds would have to work in his favour?

CHAPTER FIVE

Home at last. Bran climbed painfully out of the taxi and paid the driver, feeling exposed and vulnerable out in the fresh air for the first time since the . . . incident. Perhaps he should have let Bea pick him up from hospital after all—God knew she'd tried hard to persuade him to accept her offer. But it would have taken time out of one of the few days she didn't work, and he was a grown man, not a child in need of a nanny.

It was a warm, bright day, the sun glinting off the sea with a painful, piercing intensity. Bran closed his eyes, but the throbbing ache remained. He'd been told the headaches might linger for a while, and to consult his doctor if they hadn't gone away after three months.

Three months. Thank God for the peace of Roscarrock House, set high on the cliffs that bounded Mother Ivey's Bay from Big Guns Cove, and far from the madding crowd of Porthkennack proper. At least, outside of opening hours. Bran sighed.

As he lingered by the gate, the figure of a man appeared, walking up the cliff path towards him, and Bran drew in a sharp breath. The starburst of pain in his chest was nauseating.

Inside. He had to get inside. With an unsteady hand, he opened the gate, wishing it were ten feet high and he could padlock it behind him. A dog barked, startling and reassuring him in one. A dog walker. Not his mysterious assailant from the other night.

Probably. Although it could have been anyone, couldn't it? Bran turned to look back.

He didn't recognise the man with his dog. A tourist, then, in all likelihood. Not anyone he knew.

Safe.

Bran was still sweating, his heartbeat painfully loud in his ears, by the time he'd closed the front door behind him.

Constable Peters had made it quite clear she doubted the attack on him was random. As if he couldn't have told as much from his injuries. Two broken ribs from a kick when he'd already been on the ground. Already unconscious, he imagined. He could have died. If they'd kicked him harder, maybe punctured a lung . . .

It was all strongly suggestive of either a personal grudge, or a hate crime. The theft of his wallet and phone had undoubtedly been an afterthought, a clumsy attempt to obscure motive.

Can you think of any reason you might be targeted for a hate crime? she'd asked.

She might as well have asked outright if he was gay. Straight white men didn't suffer hate crimes, did they? *No,* he'd said.

It was possible, he supposed. Someone might have seen him in Newquay with Craig, although even there, he'd been discreet. But why, then, come after him in Porthkennack?

No. This was personal. Someone in Porthkennack hated him enough to physically assault him. It was horrendous. He'd spent years telling himself it didn't matter whether he was liked or not, so long as he was respected. Now, just thinking about the sheer level of animosity this . . . *person* must have for him made him ill.

He couldn't face the stairs, so he dragged himself to his study and sank into the comfortable chair by the hearth, its familiar red leather hardly more worn now than when Father had used to sit in it. Unlike the desk chair, which he'd had reupholstered twice since then.

Christ, he wanted a drink. But it was only midday, and he'd been told not to mix alcohol with the painkillers they'd given him. And in any case, he needed to get back to work. God knew how many emails would be in his inbox regarding the exhibition centre alone, and there was the Constantine Bay property dispute still to be dealt with.

He should switch on the computer and make a start on it. He would. Just a little more rest before he faced the storm.

Bran jumped badly at the sound of the back door opening and closing, the movement sending fire through his rib cage even as terror danced along his spine. *Someone's in the house.*

"Bran? Are you home?" Bea's voice.

Foolish relief making him queasy, Bran opened his mouth but couldn't manage to get out a word before she poked her head around the door.

"There you are. How are you feeling?"

A hastily drawn breath caught in his throat, and he barely managed to stifle the reflexive cough in time. "Fine."

"You don't look well." She strode into the room and stretched out a hand as if to feel his forehead, but drew it back without touching him. Perhaps his skin looked damp. Certainly he *felt* unpleasantly clammy. "Have you been home long?"

Bran darted his eyes to the carriage clock on the mantelpiece. It was past six. He must have been asleep. The idea was embarrassing, but not so much as the alternative: that he'd spent all those hours staring into an empty grate.

He just wished he felt in the slightest degree rested. For God's sake, things were supposed to be getting back to normal now he was at home. But he'd felt better in hospital, with all the noise and the clatter and the determinedly cheery nurses jollying him into eating bland, institutional meals. "A few hours."

"Do you want something to eat?"

He should, shouldn't he? But the thought of what she was likely to offer him, some premade meal thawed in the microwave, appealed not in the least. "Some toast, maybe."

"Well, come on, then. You're supposed to keep mobile." Her voice was terse. Was she angry with him?

Bran frowned but heaved himself painfully out of the chair and followed her into the kitchen, where she began opening and closing cupboards with unnecessary clatter. "Do you have to be so loud?" he snapped.

Bea turned to give him a searching look. "Your head still aches."

It wasn't a question, so he didn't bother with an answer.

"I'm making you some soup. You can't just live on toast." She opened a tin and dumped the contents into a pan, then switched on the gas. "Here. Come and stir this."

It was some kind of beef broth, with chunks of overcooked carrot and potato and spots of grease floating on the top. The sight turned his stomach even as the smell made it rumble. Bran suddenly wished Jory were still living with them. He'd have cooked something decent, using fresh ingredients.

Jory had visited him in hospital twice—the first time, Bran had assumed, to make sure he didn't look too terrifyingly battered for Gawen to face, as Jory had brought the boy the very next day. Bran had braced himself for a torrent of questions and requests to see his bruises, but Gawen had been unusually subdued. Bran still wasn't sure what that was all about. Fiercely glad his unknown assailant hadn't left marks on his face—surely the hardest thing for concerned relatives to deal with—he'd assured them both he was fine, and would be out of bed in no time.

And he had been, hadn't he? He was home now, and everything was back to normal.

Something hissed and spat, and Bran jerked his hand away, the wooden spoon splattering the stove top with thick droplets. His sharp intake of breath sent splinters of pain through his chest.

Bea darted to turn down the flame, and the bubbles in the soup pan subsided. "Bran?" she said sharply. "You just let it boil over?"

"I . . . I'm not hungry." Hot and uncomfortable, he dropped the spoon on the counter and fled for his study.

Bea appeared five minutes later with a bowl of soup, a couple of slices of moderately burnt toast, and a tight-lipped expression.

Bran couldn't meet her eye. "Thank you," he said, and was careful to eat it all.

Bran felt worse, rather than better, the next day. On top of everything else, he seemed to be coming down with a cold, and it'd made his night even more of a misery. He'd woken up repeatedly, his ribs aching, feeling as though he were suffocating. It was almost a relief to drag his weary body out of bed.

It was a Monday, so Roscarrock House was closed to visitors, thank God. Bran wasn't sure he could have borne strangers invading his home today.

He choked down some toast and coffee—Bea had already gone to work by the time he'd risen—then trudged to his desk and switched on his computer. His email inbox was so ridiculously full he didn't know where to start. For God's sake, it had been less than a week. Could nothing function without his input? Redevelopment work on the old cannery site had come to a standstill, the contractor claiming vital equipment had been stolen. How the hell had that even happened? Some of those machines weighed twenty tonnes. He should call the police and demand to know what was being done. Make it plain he expected this blatant disregard for the laws of property to be treated as a priority.

But that would leave them less time to spare on the matter of his . . . Bran attempted to swallow, his throat dry. Perhaps he'd leave them to it. Constable Peters had seemed competent enough. He took up his paperknife to make a start upon the stack of post Bea had left neatly on his desk.

He was only halfway through when the telephone rang, breaking the still of Bran's study with its cacophony and causing his hand to slip, the paperknife jabbing painfully into his palm. Bran cursed as he glanced at the number displayed. The solicitor's office, again. He'd call them back when he was ready, damn it. Did they have to keep bothering him? He let it ring, and put down the paperknife with a hand that wasn't quite steady. Emails first, perhaps.

Thank God the new exhibition centre hadn't been targeted by the thieves. If, indeed, there *were* any thieves and it wasn't just some ridiculous excuse cooked up by the contractor to explain the works falling behind schedule. Bran rested his eyes on the painting of Edward of Woodstock, the Black Prince, that hung upon the wall opposite the fireplace. It was an excellent copy of the nineteenth-century portrait by Burnell, showing the prince as dark-haired, dark-eyed, and determined, in armour, coronet, and heraldic colours. He'd been thrust into an adult world at an early age, as had Bran—although of course Bran's campaigns involved far less bloodshed.

Bran could still remember first reading about the prince in a book he'd found in the library, back when he'd been a child and Jory an unruly toddler. It wasn't, of course, the first book he'd read about knights of old, but it'd been the first book he'd found that actually explained what chivalry *meant*: bravery in war, courtly behaviour to ladies, and courtesy to one's enemies. As long as they were of noble rank, of course. No one gave a damn about the peasants.

He'd been very glad he wasn't a peasant, for all that he lived six hundred years and more after the prince's time. His imagination had been captivated by the stories of the sixteen-year-old general who'd won campaigns in France. The Prince of Wales who'd never lived to be King of England.

It'd seemed so unfair that because Edward was known to history as the Black Prince, everyone assumed it meant he'd been wicked. He'd been brilliant—at least, in his early years. Perhaps not so much in his later years, but he'd been ill then, hadn't he? Illness changed a person. Even at ten, Bran was well aware of that. It made them less than they were, and it changed everyone around them too. Father hadn't been so . . . He'd been different, before Mother became ill.

It wasn't fair, he'd thought, with a child's keen sense of justice. Why did Jory have to come and make Mother ill?

Odd, how childish misconceptions continued to colour attitudes long after they'd been overthrown. Bran was quite aware, these days, that Jory's birth hadn't been the cause of Mother's illness, and that even if it had been, it would hardly have been Jory's fault. But still he had to watch himself for signs of lingering resentment.

Did Bea feel the same? She had when they were children. He knew that. But now he found it so hard to tell how she felt.

Twenty-Seven Years Ago

"This is Alan," Bea said with a blush.

Bran stepped up to accept the offered handshake, wishing it wouldn't be terribly obvious if he wiped his palm on his trousers first. He was mesmerised by a pair of deep-brown eyes that seemed to see right inside him.

Oh God, he was probably blushing as red as Bea. But he'd never known a man could be . . . there was no other word for it.

Beautiful.

If it hadn't been for the colour of his skin, Alan could have stepped straight out of one of those TV shows where impossibly good-looking American teenagers lived impossibly glamorous lives. He was wearing faded, well-fitting jeans Bran would bet his whole year's allowance were designer, and a crisp polo shirt with an exclusive logo. It showed off strong, well-shaped forearms and a hint of biceps with deep-mahogany skin. His tousled hair was so black it shone.

Bran had never felt the urge to run his fingers through anyone's hair before. It probably wouldn't be as wonderful in reality as in his imagination—Alan almost certainly used mousse or gel or something to style it like that—but Bran wouldn't mind finding out, even so. Alan was tall, stylish, and confident, like some of the upper-sixth-form boys at Bran's school, only more so. He looked like he belonged on a yacht in . . . Bran almost thought the south of France, but maybe that was too *establishment* for someone so modern, so trendy.

So unmistakeably nonwhite, his father's voice muttered sourly in his mind.

Bran made a rude gesture at his father. Also, of course, entirely in his mind. Father didn't understand the modern world. He didn't understand that things were changing, that it wasn't all about *people like us* these days. Not that Father was a racist, obviously. He would never call Alan any of the offensive names Bran heard regularly thrown across the school playing fields. He tried to ignore the voice whispering in his ear that Father never used any hateful words for gay people either, but that didn't mean anyone was left in any doubt as to how he viewed them.

"So you're Bea's brother?" Alan asked, flashing white, even teeth directly in Bran's eyeline. He towered over Bea. His accent was a disappointment, though—flat and northern beneath the overlay of public school polish.

Bran was about to speak, but Bea broke in, her voice loud and excited. "Yes. This is Bran. Short for Branok."

"Another of those Cornish names, is it? Like yours." Alan cast a clearly approving gaze over Bea's figure that made Bran want to punch him. And then run far, far away, although he was much too old to *cry*, for God's sake.

How old was Alan, anyway? Older than their fifteen years, that was for certain. Was he even still at school?

"You're here on holiday?" Bran forced himself to ask politely.

"Oh, didn't Bea tell you? I'm spending the summer here with friends. Working on my surfing." He smiled again. "Please *don't* come and watch me. I must look like a right prat to a local like you, falling in the water every five minutes."

Suddenly Bran wasn't annoyed at him anymore. "I'm sure you'll pick it up in the end."

"Alan's studying politics at Oxford," Bea said as proudly as if she'd coached him for the entrance exams herself.

"Reading, not studying," Alan corrected her. "And it's PPE—philosophy, politics, and economics."

Bea *knew* that, surely? "It must be fascinating, learning all about power," she said, smiling back at Alan.

"It is. You should consider it when you're applying for a place—unless you've already made your choices? I'm sure you'd have a good chance of getting in."

"You really think so?"

Why was she *being* like this? Letting him patronise her, as if she were just some silly little girl?

Alan turned to Bran. "And what about you? You look more like a scientist. Or mathematician, maybe?"

"Maybe," Bran conceded. He did like science, but it wasn't where the money was, was it? Everyone said so. "Not engineering?" he asked, just because it was the sort of thing his teachers were always telling him to think about. He'd already discounted it himself, but he found he wanted to hear what Alan would say.

Alan stared at him for a moment, his head cocked. Bran hoped he wasn't blushing under the scrutiny. "No. Too hands-on for you."

Bea laughed. "That's *exactly* what Bran always says."

"Oh, didn't I tell you? I can read minds," Alan said, then offered her his arm like an old-fashioned gentleman. "And I just heard *you* thinking you're dying for an ice cream. Shall we?"

Bran watched them go—his sister and the tall, sophisticated stranger—and had never felt so alone.

CHAPTER
SIX

Present Day

Jory came to visit in the evening. He walked into Bran's study wearing the concerned expression that hadn't seemed to leave his face since the . . . incident.

The first thing he said was, "Are you sure you should be out of hospital? Shouldn't you at least be taking it easy in bed?"

"I'm fine," Bran snapped, then regretted it. It'd made his head throb more fiercely, and worse, he was fighting the urge to cough. Knowing it would hurt like hell if he gave in, Bran took shallow breaths in the hopes it would subside, and gripped the smooth, leather arms of his chair by the fire.

"We need to talk about the exhibition." Jory loomed beside the mantelpiece, making Bran's neck hurt and his headache worse when he looked at him. "I've spoken to Dr. Banerjee—"

"*You've* spoken to her? Why not Sanderson or Trenowden?" They were, after all, his fellow sponsors of the exhibition. Not that they'd shown any great inclination to take an active role, but in the circumstances, they could damn well step up. He'd been quite clear with them as to his vision. Surely they should be the ones to persuade Dr. Banerjee to withdraw her resignation and come back and curate the exhibition?

Jory grimaced. "They said—well, Sanderson did, and Trenowden agreed—that they didn't think it was their place to get involved with staffing. They seemed to feel you'd made it plain they weren't going to get any say in that sort of thing. You being the major investor and all."

"Idiots." Perhaps he *had* asserted his control over the direction of the exhibition a little too strongly, but damn it, it wasn't all to do with money. Bran was the only one of them who actually knew the first thing about Edward of Woodstock, and it had been important they realise he wouldn't be dictated to. He wasn't going to let anyone turn his lifelong dream into a garish, Disney-like theme park just to maximise the profits.

"Anyway, she's adamant she's not coming back. She says she doesn't need the stress." The disapproval now showing in Jory's expression was hardly an improvement on the concern he'd shown earlier.

Bran disliked feeling under attack from his little brother almost as much as he hated being an object of pity. He heartily wished he was at his desk. "She should grow a thicker skin, then."

He reached for his glass of water. It seemed to take an inordinate amount of effort. Having taken a sip, which did little to calm his throat, Bran rested the glass on his lap in the hopes Jory wouldn't notice how much his hands were shaking.

"It's been nearly two weeks now with no curator," Jory went on, "and if we don't get someone in soon, the exhibition won't be ready in time for the official opening."

Bran was *aware* of all this, damn it. "I'll deal with it in due course."

Jory's eyes narrowed. "You don't look well enough to deal with anything right now."

Bran was rapidly losing patience. "Then you'll have to curate it."

"What? Me?"

"You've done it before. That mermaid exhibition at the museum."

"That was *tiny*. The Black Prince exhibition is orders of magnitude bigger. And I've got a full-time job now. Are you expecting me to do it in my spare time?"

"Your working day finishes at three, for God's sake."

"Three forty, actually. And that's just lessons. Or did you think state school teachers didn't bother with things like after-school clubs, or marking, or lesson plans?" Jory's tone was one part righteous indignation to three parts sarcasm.

Bran's head was killing him. He wished Jory would just go away. "Then take a sabbatical."

"At this end of the school year, with no notice? Teaching doesn't work like that. And nobody gets a sabbatical in their first year of the job."

"Then what do you suggest we do? Cancel the opening?" Bran's voice had risen to match his brother's, and the strain of it tipped him over into a miserable coughing fit. He spilled his water in his lap, and spilled it again as he tried to put the glass back on the table.

Jory at least had the decency to look contrite as he took the glass from Bran's shaking hand, and when he spoke again, it was softer. "Of course not. But we need to get on and find someone."

"I told you. *In due course.*" Bran's voice was hoarse and painful. Christ, it was cold in here.

"Why don't you ask Jennifer Solomon to put out some feelers? She could—"

"*No.* It has to be someone I can trust." Jennifer Solomon was the last person he'd ask to find him a new curator. Bran might be wrung out and exhausted, but he'd be damned if he'd let his exhibition be thrown away on some trendy historian who'd probably want to present it all from the French point of view, for God's sake.

"I'm sure Jennifer would take your views into full consideration." Jory leaned towards him, frowning. "Are you sure you're okay? You look sweaty."

"I'm *fine.*" Damn it. He'd set off that *bloody* coughing again. Bran fumbled for his handkerchief, then snatched at the one Jory pressed into his hand. He held it to his mouth through racking coughs, sick with the pain in his throat and chest.

"Bea? *Bea!*" Jory was shouting.

His vision blurry, Bran felt more than saw his sister come into the study.

"I think we need to call a doctor." Jory sounded panicked. "He's coughing up blood."

To hell with it all. Bran wanted to tell him to stop being such an idiot, but he couldn't stop coughing. And he was just so tired . . .

Later that night, Bran lay propped up in bed in the same hospital room as before, tethered by a cat's cradle of lines that stripped him of all sense of bodily autonomy. He was only faintly aware of Bea's strident voice as she told Jory to "Just get it sorted out, and don't bother him with it anymore."

He wondered what and who she was talking about. But not for very long.

Drug-fuelled oblivion beckoned, and Bran was only too eager to heed its call.

Twenty-Seven Years Ago

Bran was getting tired of being left behind. He'd caught up with Bea and Alan in the Square Peg Café, which was a newly opened, touristy place they'd never normally go to.

It would be paranoid to think they were trying to avoid him—wouldn't it?

Then again, Bea didn't smile when he joined them at their table. Alan did, but there was something *wrong* about it. One of the masters at school would smile like that whenever a boy made an excuse for not having got his prep done. He always gave the worst punishments too.

Bran's own smile froze on his face, but he sat down anyway. He could hardly *not* at this stage. "Have you been having fun?"

"Yes. We have been," Alan said, still with that horrid look on his face, and was there just the slightest, insulting emphasis on *have been*?

No. Bran was being paranoid and imagining it, he was certain. "Where were you? I looked for you on the beach." Bea had said they were probably going there, and she'd taken her swimming things with her. Bran had checked.

He'd been annoyed with her for not waiting for him. Bran was good at swimming, far better than Bea was, and he'd wanted to show Alan how fast he was, how fearless in the water. It would have been good to have someone to lark about with. Bea didn't much like getting splashed.

Bea roused herself. "We changed our minds."

So he hadn't missed his chance. That was good. "Well, maybe we could all go this evening? It's hot enough that the water won't be too cold, and there won't be so many people ar—"

Alan interrupted him. "We're going clubbing tonight."

"Oh. Okay. That would be fun too." Bran wasn't so sure. He hated dancing—but it would be worth it to see Alan dance, wouldn't it?

Bea and Alan shared a look, and then she got to her feet. "Excuse me. I won't be a moment." She headed off into the café.

Alan watched her walk off, then turned to Bran, his tight, empty smile still in place. "Look, I don't want to be rude, but it's probably best if you don't come along tonight. I really don't think you'd enjoy it."

"I— Why wouldn't I?" Bran hated himself for stumbling over his words.

"Well, even if you make it in the door, it's not like any barman in his right mind is going to serve you, is it? No offence, but you look about twelve."

Bran flushed. "I'm not bothered about drinking. I can do that at home."

"Oh, for God's sake . . . Fine. Rude it is, then. I don't want you there. It's Bea I'm interested in, all right? Nothing against poofs, but I'm not one, and I'm buggered, pun not intended, if I'm going to spend my evening being drooled over by one."

Bran jerked to his feet, knocking over his chair with a crash that had every pair of eyes in the place turning to stare at him. He felt hot and sick. "I'm not . . ." He couldn't say it.

Alan's smile was, humiliatingly, sympathetic. "Course you're not. My mistake. Still, three's a crowd, isn't it? You'll understand one day. Now run off and play with somebody else's annoying little brother."

As if he were a *child* and needed to grow up. Was that what Alan thought of him? It wasn't fair. He didn't treat *Bea* like that, and she and Bran were the exact same age. His chest so tight it hurt, Bran forced himself to walk, not run, out of the café.

Once out of sight, he abandoned all restraint and ran for home, his eyes stinging.

Bea crept into the house after midnight like a guilty cat bringing in its kill, her high-heeled shoes dangling from one hand. Mother had been in bed for hours, and Father shut in his study. They probably hadn't even known she'd been out.

Her face was red and blotchy, and her makeup smeared. She didn't look calm, or in control. She didn't look like herself at all. She could have been any teenage girl who'd sneaked out for a summer's night on the town and was now regretting it.

Bran was glad her night hadn't gone well. He'd been miserable, stuck at home on his own. Fearing that that was how his life would be from now on.

"Don't let Father see you," he said urgently. Father would throw a fit, and somehow, they'd both be in trouble.

Bea blinked at him but didn't speak.

"Bea?"

Bran moved closer, and drew in a sharp breath that he immediately regretted. She reeked of alcohol. He wasn't all that good at distinguishing different varieties by smell alone, but the aroma was nothing like the wine they had at dinner, or even Father's heady, expensive whisky. Father had let him try it once, on his and Bea's birthday, and it'd gone down smoothly at first, but then the burn had hit his throat and he'd choked. Jory had laughed, the little toad. Bran had thought about giving him some to drink one day when Father wasn't watching, and seeing how *he* liked it, but in the end, he hadn't quite dared.

What Bea reeked of now was cheap and sour, and reminded him of the bottle of gin Alderton had smuggled into the dorm one night and got sick on. "Do you feel ill?" he asked.

Bea shook her head with a jerk.

"You'd better clean your teeth before anyone else sees you. Or smells you, rather," he added pointedly.

She hugged herself with a convulsive motion. "I'm going to have a bath."

"That would probably be a good idea too," Bran said, unsure why he felt uneasy. *That man*—he wasn't going to call him *Alan* in his head now, not after the way he'd made it plain he wasn't the least bit interested in Bran's company—had clearly upset her somehow, which was good, wasn't it? It meant Bea wouldn't be spending time with him anymore.

Things would go back to the way they'd used to be.

Bran had time to think about things in the forty minutes it took Bea to come out of the bathroom, her face scrubbed clean of makeup and expression alike, and her hair in a towel. Too much time, and too many thoughts he didn't like. Not at all.

His stomach churning, he followed her into her room.

"Bea, did that man . . . Did he do something?"

She darted a glance at him, but he couldn't see anything in her eyes in the split second before she looked away again. "No. Of course not. But I'm not going to be seeing him anymore."

Bran smiled, relief making him light-headed. "Good. I mean, it can be just us again, then, can't it? And . . . and that's better."

Bea still wasn't looking at him, but her words made everything all right. "Yes. That's better. Just us."

CHAPTER
SEVEN

Present Day

S am nearly didn't bother to answer his phone when he saw the unknown number. It was almost time for his shift at the restaurant, and it wasn't likely to be anyone he'd want to talk to. Then again, it didn't look like any of the numbers he was avoiding, and Christ knew he hadn't spoken to another person all day. He picked up.

"Yes?"

"Um. Hello. Is that Sam?"

"Yes. Who's calling?" Sam sat down on his bed, directly facing the fist-shaped depression in the plasterboard left by some previous tenant. Having lived here for six months, Sam was pretty sure he knew how they'd felt.

"It's Jory. Jory Roscarrock. From Edinburgh University, if you remember? Sorry—I was given a new phone, and never got around to switching the number over."

Jory Roscarrock. Like he'd have forgotten *him*, even though it'd been well over a year since they'd last been in touch. Warmth flooded through Sam. It'd been too long without a friendly voice. "Jory, mate! It's been ages. How are you?"

"Good, good. And you?"

"Uh, yeah. Good. So everything's okay now? With your family, and that?" Sam had never been totally clear why Jory had left Edinburgh in such a hurry—he'd had a vague idea it was some family emergency—but he was pretty sure it hadn't been to go to another job.

"Yes. Fine." There was a breathy laugh. "I got a house of my own, and you'd be amazed how much better I get on with my brother and sister now."

"Yeah, no. I've got sisters myself. So how's Rafi?"

"Er, we split up."

Shit. He should have thought of that. Other people had moved on with their lives, hadn't they? Instead of down. "Sorry."

"Oh, don't worry about it. You couldn't have known. It's not like I advertised it on Facebook."

Yeah, Jory had always been crap at social media. Then again, Sam had pretty much dropped off the internet in the last year. Anyone he was likely to want to hear from had his phone number.

Not that many of them had used it, until now.

"I'm with someone else now, anyway," Jory went on. Sam could hear the smile in his voice, and found himself smiling fondly in return, with barely any envy souring the taste of it. "Mal. He's from London, used to drive a Tube train, but we're living together now. In Porthkennack. He works at the local museum." Jory drew in a breath. "So, um, I heard you'd left Edinburgh too?"

The warm feeling that'd been wrapping itself around Sam like a blanket dropped away, leaving only the flat chill of his dingy room behind. Of *course* Jory had heard about his disgrace. *Everyone* had heard about it. Which was why he was currently holding down a job as general dogsbody in an after-pub curry house.

"Yeah. Back in Luton."

"And . . . are you working?"

Sam tried to make it light, but he couldn't keep the bitterness out of his tone. "Depends what you call working."

"Um, well, if you're already set up, don't worry about it, but I was just wondering . . . The local castle, you know it's got a connection with the Black Prince? Well, my, um, I mean a local group is planning a major exhibition about him in conjunction with the castle. It's due to open in July. English Heritage are putting on a tournament, and there are going to be some other events, but the curator's had to drop out suddenly. Ah, illness. He—they asked me, but obviously I'm not really qualified, and anyway I'm teaching now . . . But I remembered you'd had that internship at the National Museum of Scotland, and I wondered if you'd be interested? Seeing as it's your area?"

Sam could hardly speak for a moment. The Black Prince. One of the key figures in the Hundred Years War. Sam had done his dissertation on the medieval conflict between England and France, had been starting to make a name for himself on the subject, before . . . Before. "That sounds brilliant. Uh, do they want my CV?" He'd have to get a bit creative about the last year. Maybe he could pretend he hadn't had time to update it? "I guess they'll want to interview me." That could be the sticking point. He wasn't sure he could lie to people's faces.

"Oh, you won't need to bother with any of that." Jory gave a little laugh. "I mean, I already know you."

Bloody hell. Jory had told him back in uni about being a Roscarrock, and what that meant in Porthkennack. Sam hadn't been sure whether to believe him, but apparently the feudal system really was still alive and kicking in darkest Cornwall. It made him feel almost guilty for taking advantage of it—but wasn't it about time the Old Boy Network did something for someone who wasn't white, Anglo-Saxon, or protestant? He swallowed. "When do they want me?"

"As soon as you can get here." The smile was back in Jory's voice. "To be honest, they're having kittens. They've secured sponsorship from local businesses and lottery funds, got English Heritage on board, and committed publically to opening in July, and now they're left with no one to curate it. How soon do you think you can realistically come down?"

Sam bit back his instinctive response of *Tomorrow, or tonight if I give it some welly down the motorway*. Best not to look too keen.

Ah, sod it. "Jory, this is . . . Thanks. Thanks so much for this. I won't let you down. Uh, any chance I could doss down on your sofa for a few days while I find somewhere?" Shit, he hadn't said when he was coming, had he? He thought quickly. He should finish out the week at the restaurant. Probably. Although it was tempting just to jack it in straight off, even if it meant losing a couple of days' wages. "If I come down at the weekend, would that be okay?"

"That's great. It'll be good to catch up with you. And it's no problem putting you up. We've got a spare room. It's a bit rough and ready—we're still doing the place up—but, you know. There's a bed, and you can stay as long as you want."

"Thanks, mate. But just till I find a place." He didn't want to sound like some charity case, or desperate or anything.

Then again, if he hadn't been desperate, he'd probably have asked about salary, wouldn't he? Sod it. This was Jory.

Sam didn't have to pretend with him.

CHAPTER EIGHT

Three days later Sam parked his Mini in front of a grey stone cottage and wiped his hands reflexively on his jeans. This was it. First time seeing Jory in ... Christ, it must be nearly eighteen months now. Weird, thinking about seeing him again. Sam had thought he was over that little crush, but now he wasn't so sure.

He'd just have to hope it wasn't too embarrassingly obvious. Especially not to this Mal bloke. That'd be well awkward, that would. *Hi, mate, nice to meet you. You don't mind if I invade your house and drool over your boyfriend, do you?* Hopefully he wasn't the jealous sort. Tube driver from London, Jory had said, hadn't he? Seemed a bit, well, blue-collar for a bloke like Jory. Not that Sam was an intellectual snob or anything, but Jory's last bloke, Rafi, had been an academic like him. What did he and Mal have in common? How had they met?

Come to that, what was Mal even short for? Malik? Malachi? Maleficent? Sam stifled a chuckle that was more of a snort, realised he was wiping his hands on his jeans again, and told himself to get a grip. He hadn't driven three hundred miles just to sit in his car outside the house.

Sam gave himself another few seconds' grace by checking his phone for messages (there weren't any—at least, not any he wanted to read before deleting them) and then got out of the car. He slung his backpack on one shoulder, walked through Jory's small front garden, and knocked on the door.

The bloke who answered it wasn't at all what Sam had expected. He was a lot younger than Jory and Sam, for one thing. And for another, he was holding a rat in his arms.

"All right, mate? You're Sam, yeah? I'm Mal, 'spect Jory told you about me? Come on in. This is Myrtle, by the way."

"Myrtle the rat? Shouldn't she be a turtle?" She was black and white like the cows he'd seen in the fields on the way down, and was squirming and snuffling in Mal's grasp. Her tiny pink hands—they were too humanlike to call paws—clutched at his fingers.

"Heh, nice one. Yeah, fussy eater, ain't you, babe? Always moaning about her food."

Sam followed him in, leaving his backpack by the door and looking around nervously for any signs of further rodent infestation. They'd had a rat in the restaurant once, and the manager had gone DEFCON 1 on the poor furry little sod. Sam had felt bad for it at the time, but even he wouldn't have considered picking the thing up and giving it a cuddle.

The living room they walked into was a surprise too. From what Jory had said about fixing the place up, Sam had been expecting beanbag chairs and packing-crate tables, but this room at least seemed pretty much finished. The paint on the walls and ceiling was fresh and gleaming white, showing off the age-blackened ceiling beams. Sam wondered if that was to remind Jory to duck so he wouldn't keep bumping his head on them, or if they were just high enough that he didn't have to bother.

A large old fireplace drew the eye at one end, with a couple of serious-looking swords mounted above it. Replica fourteenth century, by the looks of them. "Burglars a problem around here?" Sam couldn't help asking.

Mal blinked, then followed his gaze and laughed. "Not anymore, they ain't. Dragon attacks are well down and all. You into swords? I'll get one of these bastards down for you if you want to give it a swing."

He wasn't speaking figuratively. Both weapons had the relatively short blade and longer grip of a sword designed to be used easily either one- or two-handed. Interesting that Mal knew they were often called bastard swords—then again, it wasn't something easily forgotten.

"Uh, maybe later." Sam was worried a yes might mean him being asked to hold Myrtle.

"Yeah, course. Sorry. You want to get settled in, dontcha? Your room's upstairs, first door on the right. You can't get lost. Bathroom's next to it, and me and Jory are the other door. Take your stuff up, and I'll get the kettle on." He flashed Sam a grin, then strolled off towards the kitchen, still holding Myrtle the rat.

Looked like eating out might be a good idea. Or was that just being rattist?

Sam hauled his backpack onto his shoulder and headed for the stairs. And okay, here was where he could see the house was still a work in progress. The staircase was bare wooden boards, and so was the upstairs landing—in fact, Sam could see through doors left casually ajar that none of the rooms upstairs were carpeted. They hadn't been painted either, with blotchy white patches showing where cracks and blemishes had been filled in but not yet sanded down. Well, that was good. Gave Sam something to offer to do, and maybe pay off a little of what he owed Jory for giving him this chance—not to mention a roof over his head.

His room was small, but no smaller than the room he'd been living in back in Luton, in the shared house with damp in the bathroom and slug trails downstairs. Most of the space was taken up by the double bed, but there was room for a small wardrobe and a bedside chest of drawers. An actual rag rug in shades of blue took up the rest of the floor area, and was surprisingly soft underfoot. None of the furniture matched—the bed was age-darkened pine, and while both the wardrobe and drawers were painted white, they were very clearly not from a set. It was reassuring, somehow, that Jory's house wasn't all magazine-perfect.

The view from the window was a hell of a lot better than the one he'd had in Luton. It overlooked a large, overgrown garden—another thing Sam could help with—and beyond the fence were unbroken fields. The skies above them were filled with swooping birds whose raucous calls Sam could just hear through the open window. He drew in a deep breath. It felt, all at once, like he *could* breathe, like he'd been living on half rations of oxygen in Luton.

Well, that was air pollution for you. It was going to take him a while to get used to the quiet again too, without planes flying low overhead every couple of minutes before coming in to land at Luton Airport. Or police sirens every night. Or one of his housemates having a screaming row with her boyfriend. That'd been what'd hit him, going back to his hometown to live after the years in Edinburgh. The noise. Yeah, Edinburgh could be busy and loud too—especially around August, when the festival was on and you couldn't move for tourists—but that was different. That was the sound of people having fun, not living grinding lives of desperation.

Of course, moving back home in disgrace to find his mum had let out his room and he'd have to fend for himself had probably coloured his perceptions a bit.

Sam sat down heavily on the bed, which creaked to remind him it wasn't as young as it'd used to be and probably ought to be treated with more respect. He hoped Mal and Jory's bed was in better nick. Lying awake at night listening to the rhythmic creaking of them shagging would just be the icing on the cake.

Enough of that, though. Sam jumped up again with all the energy he could muster. Fake it till you break it, right? He dug around in his backpack until he found his phone charger and the book he'd been reading—*The King That Never Was*, because it couldn't hurt to make sure he had all the facts at his fingertips—and bunged them on the bedside table.

There. Moved in.

Then he jogged back down the stairs.

Mal looked up from his English Heritage magazine and bounded to his feet. "Found your room all right?"

Sam couldn't help contrasting Mal's obvious energy with his own. "Yeah. Thanks. Listen, I really appreciate all this. You and Jory putting me up, 'specially when you don't even know me."

"Oi, it's no big. Not a problem. You're Jory's mate, and you've gotta look out for your mates, right?"

"What did he tell you about me?"

"Uh, he met you in Edinburgh, but you're not Scottish. Oh, and not to get you started on the historicity of the Arthurian legends."

Sam laughed. "You mean, the lack of it?"

"Moving on, now. Moving on. Cup of tea?"

"That'd be great. Cheers."

It was a bit awkward, being here on his own with Mal. Sam kept wanting to apologise again for putting him out, but if he did that, Mal would have to go on saying it wasn't a problem and they'd be stuck in an eternal loop of politeness.

"So, uh, Jory's out, then?" Sam asked, partly because he'd been wondering where the bloke was but mostly just to make conversation.

The rat had disappeared somewhere—hopefully into a cage—so there wasn't even that to talk about.

"Oh. Yeah, sorry, mate, didn't I tell you? He's gone to see his nipper."

"His what?"

"His son. Gawen." Mal spun round and whipped a photo off the top of a bookshelf. He shoved it under Sam's nose. "This is a recent pic. He's a good lad, he is. Well bright."

Shell-shocked, Sam stared at the photo, which showed a blond, tousle-headed boy in his early teens—his *teens*?—proudly holding a lizard and grinning at the camera. "That's Jory's son? How flippin' old was he when he had him?"

"Nineteen."

"Bloody hell, he kept that quiet."

"Uh, yeah." Mal was looking worried now. "Prob'ly shouldn't have told you about him, come to think about it. I mean, Jory prob'ly wanted to tell you himself." He scratched his head and gave Sam a rueful smile. "You any good at acting?"

It didn't sound like a serious question, so Sam laughed. He could see why Jory liked the guy. "Sorry. But we could say I saw the picture and asked, if you like."

"Nah, I'm crap at lying. Right, you want this cuppa? Or a coffee, if you like? We've got decaf and all. Both kinds." Mal threw out his arms as if to say the world was Sam's coffee shop.

"Coffee with caffeine, if you've got it, please."

"Right. One cup of instant anxiety coming up. White?"

Sam grinned. "Nah, I'm Indian, mate."

Mal laughed. "Wanker. Just see if I offer you any sugar."

Jory turned up half an hour later, which was a bit of a shame as Sam had been about to get the story on how Mal had first met him.

He loped into the living room with that earnest expression on his boyish face that Sam remembered so well. "Sam, so sorry I wasn't home when you got here. Did you have a good trip?"

Christ, it was good to see him. "Yeah, not bad, thanks. And don't worry. Mal's been taking good care of me."

Mal grinned. "Yeah, I've been telling him all your dirty secrets. How's JJ?"

"He's okay. And stop calling him that. His name is not Jory Junior, and Kirsty hates it." Jory bent down to give Mal a kiss, then joined him on the sofa.

"She ain't here, is she?"

"No." The two of them shared a weirdly intent glance that left Sam baffled.

Jory turned to Sam. "Um. I expect Mal explained about Gawen?"

"Uh, yeah. He looks a lot like you," Sam said, because *Oi, what's all this about a secret family?* wouldn't have been very polite. "Doing well at school?"

It was clearly the right question to ask. "Very. We've got high hopes for his GCSEs, and his teachers are already talking about Oxbridge."

"That's great. Going to have another academic in the family, then?"

"That's up to him. When he's older." Jory made a face. "My brother's keen for him to go into the family business, and Gawen looks up to him quite a lot."

"Yeah, how's Gawen doing about that whole thing, anyhow?" Mal put in.

Jory sighed. "Better, I think. Although it's possible he's only saying what he knows we want to hear, and doesn't actually believe it himself. My brother was attacked just over a week ago," he added to Sam.

Sam stared, going from confusion to concern in nought point six seconds. "Seriously? Is he all right?"

"He's been better. A couple of cracked ribs and a concussion, and now he's come down with pneumonia as well. They had to readmit him to hospital in Truro—he'd only been home a day or two."

"Bloody hell. But he's going to be okay?" Pneumonia was serious. All Sam could think of was how they used to call it the old man's friend, because it killed you off nice and quick.

But that was before antibiotics were around, and Jory's brother wasn't *that* much older than him, was he?

"He should be. Yes, I'm sure he'll be fine. He's in good shape generally, and he doesn't smoke. Although his diet could be healthier." Jory's mouth turned down.

Sam tried to be reassuring. "A bit of extra weight can't hurt at a time like this."

"Um, well, if anything he's too thin."

Mal clapped Jory on the shoulder. "He'll be fine. You wait. Bran ain't the sort to let a little thing like pneumonia slow him down. He'll be back home in no time."

"I suppose . . ."

"Stop *worrying*. And stop feeling bloody guilty, all right? You're as bad as Gawen."

Jory must have caught Sam's baffled expression. "He was on his way home from going to see Gawen when he was assaulted, so of course Gawen's been blaming himself. You know what kids are like— he kept asking Bran to stay a little longer, and Bran did, and now Gawen's convinced it's all his fault his uncle got hurt. And it's made him nervous about walking around on his own, as well."

"Jeez. Poor kid. You don't expect that kind of thing in a place like this." Sam hadn't, anyhow. He'd thought he was leaving the seedier side of life back in Luton. Then again, people were the same everywhere, weren't they? "S'pose at least there weren't any knives involved in the attack. So what was it? Mugging? Gangs?"

"Gangs? Do we have those around here?" Jory glanced at Mal, who shrugged. "Nobody knows who attacked him, and Bran can't remember."

"Rough."

Mal snorted. "If you ask me—"

"Nobody did," Jory said.

"—they ought to check out who he's evicted lately." Mal gave Jory a defiant look. "What? I know he's your brother, and Gawen likes him, but seriously, he ain't exactly Mr. Popular around here. *You* don't even like him."

"I care about him!" Jory protested. "And he's . . . better than he used to be."

Mal clearly wasn't buying it. "You only think that cos you don't see as much of him as you used to. Now you've moved out of the stately home and all."

Sam goggled. "Stately home? What, you escaped from Downton Abbey or something, mate?" Another thing Jory had never got around to mentioning while they were at Edinburgh together.

It was Mal who answered. "Nah, more like Toad Hall. And guess who's Mr. Toad?"

Jory rolled his eyes. "I suppose that makes me Ratty."

"Nah, don't be daft. That's me, innit? You're Mole. I mean, come on. First date we went on, you took me down a flippin' tunnel, dintcha?"

"That wasn't the *first* date," Jory protested. He made a face at Sam. "On our actual first date, we went to the pub. Which I then got thrown out of and barred from."

"Yeah, and that was all your bruv's fault too," Mal said darkly.

"Blimey, what did he do? Start a bar fight?"

Sam stared, bemused, as Jory and Mal started to laugh.

"Sorry," Jory said, straightening his face with a visible effort. "But, um, no. Very much not."

Mal was still cackling. "Bloody hell, I would *love* to see Bran's face when he hears he's been accused of being drunk and disorderly."

"So what *is* so bad about the bloke?" Sam asked, confused.

"You mean apart from the stick up his arse the size of Land's End?" Mal drew in a breath, like there was going to be more, but stopped when Jory nudged him.

"He's just . . . old-fashioned, that's all. He means well." Jory looked uncomfortable.

Mal looked like he had something to say about that too, but cut himself off with a glance at Jory's face. "You'll find out, anyhow. Right. Are we eating tonight, or what?"

"Food would be good," Sam agreed quickly. Last thing he wanted was to be a spare wheel in a domestic. "Anything I can give you a hand with?"

This Bran bloke couldn't be *that* bad, Sam reflected ten minutes later as he chopped onions with a manly sniffle. Jory's kid liked him, and Mal was obviously expecting Bran to be around, else how would Sam find out what he was like?

Maybe Bran just didn't approve of Mal, who, from the way he talked, was a fair few rungs down the social ladder from posh-boy Jory. Course, the same could be said of Sam, so maybe he should brace himself for some arsey behaviour.

Maybe it wasn't the class thing at all. Maybe *old-fashioned* was a euphemism for *homophobic*. Then again, if Big Brother Bran was a bigot, would Jory have defended him?

Maybe it was just the rats. The poor sod could have read *1984* or *The Rats* at an impressionable age, or something.

Sam grinned to himself. He couldn't help feeling sorry for Bran if that was the case.

CHAPTER NINE

Bran loathed being back in hospital. The nurses had all turned into tutting schoolmarms—including the male ones—who scolded him incessantly for failing to do his physio (it hurt), failing to eat his dinner (he had no appetite), just generally . . . failing. Even in his private room he barely seemed to get a moment to himself. God knew how patients on the public wards managed.

At least, the larger, more laudable part of him loathed it. There was a shameful fraction of him that felt safe here. Cocooned from the world in harsh sheets and stiff cotton blankets. And it was shameful, because there was so much he needed to be doing. He couldn't even call his solicitor about the Constantine Bay property, as Bea had neglected to bring him his phone and there wasn't one by his bed. Apparently there'd been an outcry over excessive charges and it'd been got rid of. Bran was all for stopping people preying upon the vulnerable in principle, but he wished those principles hadn't left him entirely cut off. There was, presumably, a payphone somewhere in the hospital—Bran doubted they'd entirely got rid of the things, given that mobile phones had to be kept switched off in some departments to avoid interfering with the machinery—but it might as well have been on the moon. Even going to the bathroom exhausted him.

Bran hadn't expected another visit from PC Sally Peters, and was pathetically pleased to see her. His fever had gone down, leaving him with bone-deep tiredness and an aching frustration over this new setback. He had so much to do.

"Have you caught him?" he asked brusquely, desperate to get the words out before they made him cough.

She waited until his hacking had subsided before answering. "No joy, I'm afraid. Have you managed to remember anything else?"

Bran shook his head. "CCTV?"

"It'd be nice, but no. The nearest areas with coverage to where you were attacked . . ." She shrugged. "That close to the centre of town, there are way too many people milling around to single anyone out. And there's nothing to suggest anyone was going your way."

"Residents?"

She seemed to catch his meaning. "I went door to door, but at that time of night everyone had the curtains drawn and the telly on. Nobody saw or heard a thing. Not until the gentleman who found you raised the alarm."

"Who was it?"

"Mr. Harper. On his way home from the Sea Bell public house when he pretty much tripped over you."

"Harper? He's married to Gerren Ede's daughter." And the Sea Bell was Jago Andrewartha's pub, as she must know. Unease prickled along Bran's spine.

"I had a word with Mr. Harper and Mr. Andrewartha. I'm satisfied they didn't have anything to do with your assault."

Easy for her to say. Bran looked away from her and stared out of the window at gulls swooping in the sky.

"Mr. Roscarrock?" Her voice was gentle. "Whoever attacked you can't have counted on you suffering a loss of memory about the attack. They'd be expecting arrest, and it's not easy to conceal that." She paused. "Although granted, there was a street lamp out. It's possible they were hoping you hadn't seen them clearly enough for identification."

It gave Bran vindictive pleasure to think of the perpetrator living in fear of reprisals. They must have been in agony, waiting for the official knock on the door, and racking their brains as to why it hadn't come. Did they assume he was playing with them? Bran liked to think so.

Equally likely, of course, they were now sitting at home congratulating themselves on having got off scot-free. Perhaps even planning a further attack? His chest tightened painfully, and the coughing began again.

Twenty-Seven Years Ago

It was months before Bran realised something was wrong with Bea. He'd been at his boarding school, naturally, and she'd been at hers, so it wasn't until the Christmas holidays that he knew.

He'd written to her, of course. But she hadn't written back. And besides, he'd had his own worries, after what . . . *that man* had said to him. Everyone said that Meadows in the fourth form was a poof, but Bran wasn't like him, with his girlish laugh and his uselessness at games. He *wasn't*.

Everyone looked at other boys in the showers when they could get away with it, didn't they? It was only natural to . . . to compare. It didn't mean anything.

His first sight of his sister when he got back home was like a punch to the stomach. She was a tiny, shapeless mound on the sofa, her legs curled underneath her the way she'd used to sit when she was a little girl and her legs were too short to reach the floor. She had on a big, baggy sweater and ski pants; her face looked pale and too thin above her unnaturally lumpy figure.

"What's wrong with you?" he asked sharply.

She gave him a sour look. "Happy Christmas to you too."

"Are you ill?"

"No."

"You haven't got an eating disorder or something, have you?" Leighton's sister had been hospitalised for making herself sick after meals. It had been all over school, mostly because Leighton was on the large side himself and had knocked another boy's tooth loose for suggesting he ought to try following her example.

"Don't be an idiot. I'm pregnant, that's all."

"But . . . how?" He blushed, realising how stupid he sounded. How naïve. "I mean, I know *how*, obviously, but—"

She huffed. "You *do* remember Alan, back in the summer?"

"Alan?" It came out too quickly, too loud, his voice too high. Bran's chest felt as though she'd plunged a knife into it. "You mean he— I'll bloody kill him!"

"And how are you going to manage that? You don't even know his last name."

"Do you?" he snapped back.

"Of course I do."

"Why didn't you tell me?" It hurt, that this had been going on for months and he hadn't known. She was his sister. His *twin*.

She shrugged. "It's not like you could have done anything about it."

"Are you . . . Are you going to marry him?" That was what would have happened in one of Mother's books. Bran liked to read them in secret—*she* might not mind, but Father certainly would. Tales of days long ago when men were strong and decisive, and duels were fought for honour. If a girl got in the family way, her father forced the man to marry her. Or her brothers did.

Of course, in the books her brothers were always handily taller, stronger, and more numerous than the vile seducer and his cronies.

"No. He's going to marry someone else." Bea said it with no emotion Bran could make out.

"Then why was he doing *that* with you? And if you knew he was engaged, why did you—"

"Because he didn't tell me until afterwards!" Bea's voice broke.

Oh. Oh God. That *bastard*. Then another thought struck. "We should have him arrested. He was over eighteen, wasn't he? And you were underage. He could go to jail."

"*No*. Don't be an idiot. Everyone would find out about it then. And anyway, I told him I was seventeen. And yes, I know it was stupid of me. I *know*." The hurt in her voice piercing the hot bubble of his anger, Bran sat next to his sister on the sofa. He wanted to give her a hug, but she'd never liked it much when he'd hugged her as a child, so he didn't.

"But . . . what are you even going to *do* with a baby?" he asked softly. "How will you finish school, go to university . . ." He trailed off. Would their parents raise it? It'd be just like having another Jory all over again, crying and breaking things and having to be minded when he had far better things to do.

Bea rolled her eyes. "I'm not going to *keep* it. It's going for adoption as soon as it's born."

Oh. Well, that was probably best, wasn't it? Bran couldn't really see Father welcoming a dark-skinned little stranger into the family fold. Then he frowned as another thought occurred. "Why not just . . . you know. Get rid of it."

"No." Bea snapped it out.

"But—"

"*Don't*, all right? I've had all this with Mummy and Father." She drew in a shaky breath. "I'm not going to run from my mistakes. It's my own fault I'm in this situation, and I'm not going to just flush a baby down the toilet to get out of it."

Did she have to be so blunt about it? Still, Bran didn't envy her those conversations one bit. "What does Father think?"

"He didn't like the idea at first, but he agrees now it's the honourable thing to do. I'll just have to study at home from now until it's born, and then I can go back to school. We'll say I had glandular fever."

Honourable. That was clever of her, getting Father to think of it in those terms.

"What's it like?" he asked after a moment.

"What?"

He gestured at her stomach, still veiled by her heavy sweater. "Being pregnant."

She shrugged. "It's not like anything. It just is. And in four or five months, it won't be."

Present Day

Kirsty came to visit Bran in hospital later that afternoon. She brought with her not useless flowers, inane reading material, or fruit he had no appetite for, but something more useful: photographs of her emerging sculpture of Edward of Woodstock. Carved from a single, massive tree trunk, the statue would stand larger than life outside the exhibition centre. It would weather, yes, but it was designed to do so— Kirsty had spoken of her wish for it to be organic, subject to change.

It was already far more impressive than Bran had dared to hope. "This is really good. It's not your usual style," he couldn't help adding with a touch of accusation.

She laughed. "You think I don't know I only got the job because Gawen begged you to let me do it? I thought you'd appreciate something less abstract than the usual. And I've got a good model for him. He's a rugged, outdoor sort, like a prince would have been in those days." Kirsty rambled on about the young man, Euan Mayhew, whom Bran strongly suspected she was involved with romantically. She didn't say, and he didn't ask, a hangover from before she and Jory had divorced, back when they'd preserved between them the polite fiction that the marriage was more than just a device to legitimise Gawen's birth.

Bran had even less reason to pry now. But then again—"He must be spending a lot of time at your house. Does Gawen get on all right with him?"

"Gawen doesn't see a lot of him. Euan's mostly around while Gawen's at school. The light's better then." She gave Bran an arch look. "Jory's met him, and they get on fine."

So stop worrying about Gawen. Bran tried to follow her unspoken advice. "When will you have the statue finished? It looks almost done." In fact the finer detail of the face gave way to a rougher, more blurred outline as the eye moved down to the statue's feet, but Bran was fairly sure that was intentional.

"In plenty of time," she said airily, then laughed again. "Gawen's got his half-term holiday coming up, remember? So I won't be working on it much then, but it should be ready a week or two after that. But how's the exhibition itself going?"

That was the question, and one that had been dogging his sleepless nights. Bran drew in a breath and was plunged into a coughing fit. *Damn* it.

CHAPTER
TEN

S am woke up early on Sunday morning, unused to the light that shone directly in his face through the thin cotton curtains at his window. He lay in bed for a while, eyes closed against the brightness, listening for any signs of movement in the house. His stomach rumbled, but it'd be a poor way to repay Jory and Mal for their hospitality by waking them up clattering around their kitchen.

It was weirdly comfortable, lying in this strange bed in a strange room. Not at all like waking up in his grotty room in Luton. Maybe it was just the early-summer sunshine, made warmer in tone by the ochre-yellow curtains, but the place seemed full of optimism.

After ten minutes or so, Sam realised he *could* hear Jory and Mal moving about, but it wasn't breakfast they were making. Feeling a melancholy pang of arousal, he got up quickly, used the bathroom, and headed downstairs. Luckily, helping out in the kitchen last night had given him a rough idea of where everything was. He made himself a plate of toast and a mug of instant coffee without too much trouble, and took them into the living room to eat in front of the telly.

Sam's spirits rose as he ate. This could be a fresh start for him in all kinds of ways. Jory and Mal had found each other here, right? Maybe he could find someone too. Someone who wasn't closeted, or married, or both. He smiled ruefully at the telly. A bloke who wasn't a lying, manipulative git would be a bit of a step up as well.

Jory and Mal came downstairs as he was bunging his plate in the dishwasher.

"You found everything all right?" Jory asked.

"Yeah. Thanks. Coffee? I'll put the kettle on."

"Thanks."

"Tea for me, please," Mal said, getting an enormous box of Corn Flakes out of the cupboard.

It was all cosily domestic, and Sam almost didn't feel like an interloper at all.

"Got any plans for today?" he asked when they were all sitting down with freshly steaming mugs.

Jory nodded. "I thought we could wander over to the castle, and I'll introduce you to Jennifer. She's, well, she's pretty much the queen of Caerdu castle. She runs the place, coordinates the volunteers and so on. Very involved with the educational side, which is how I know her. She was helping out Meena—that's your predecessor—with the exhibition, tying it in with the castle and the events they've got planned there, that sort of thing."

"Cheers. I don't want to spoil your weekend, though."

Mal flashed him a smile. "Nah, don't worry about it. I've got homework, anyhow."

"Mal's doing an Open University degree. Arts and humanities." Jory sounded so chuffed you'd have thought Mal was his kid, not his partner.

"Yeah? Good for you, mate. Must be tough doing that and the museum job. How's it going?"

"Pretty good. The studying, anyway. I've got my first-year exams in a few weeks." Mal made a face. "It's peak, man."

Sam struggled not to laugh at Mal's expression. "Good luck." Chances were he'd still be living here when they started. He made a mental note to be extra helpful around the house.

"Cheers. Keep everything crossed for me, yeah?"

"Not that you'll need luck, with all the work you've put in." Jory turned to Sam. "So if you're ready, you and I could set off in half an hour or so?"

"Sounds good."

May in Britain could mean anything, weather-wise, but it was a bright, warm morning as they set out for the castle. They were on foot, because Jory reckoned it was only half an hour's walk or so. A year ago,

Sam might have had his reservations about that *or so*, but if working at the restaurant had done nothing else for him, it'd got him more used to being on his feet. One thing he hadn't missed about academia was the tragic effect on his fitness level.

He suspected Jory wasn't taking him the most direct route, either, as they headed straight down to the coast path. Not that he was complaining. He'd forgotten already, after a year back in Luton, how much he loved being out in the countryside. The breeze blowing in off the sea was fresh and clean, and his stride was longer, more confident. He felt taller here.

The irony was, once you got out of town, Luton was surrounded by bloody countryside. He'd just been too overcome by inertia to reach it. As if his horizons had shrunk to the size of that depressing little room in the shared house.

"Does Mal know about, uh . . . why I had to leave Edinburgh?" Sam asked, and held his breath, because it wasn't *Mal's* degree of knowledge that had really been worrying him.

He'd just taken it for granted, when Jory had called him, that the bloke knew about him getting sacked and why. But ever since then, usually around 3 a.m. as he lay in bed listening to the sirens, he'd been getting these nasty little doubts. What if Jory *hadn't* heard, and had offered Sam the job thinking he was, well, still a proper academic, reputation intact?

"I . . . Yes. Sorry," Jory said, staring at his feet like *he* was the one who had anything to be embarrassed about.

"Oh. No, that's . . . that's good." Sam gave an awkward shrug, hissing as he cricked his neck. "Don't want to be here under false pretences."

Jory looked up quickly. "I wouldn't go mentioning it to anyone—I mean, it won't be an issue, but there's no point making it one."

Now Sam was worried. "It won't be a problem for you, will it? If it comes out?"

Jory's gaze darted away for a moment. "Oh, no. And I really do think you're the best man for the job."

Stupid how Jory's earnest tone affected him, had him turning his head into the wind to blink back tears, for God's sake. But it was the first time anyone had had such confidence in him for over a year.

The sea stretched out for miles in front of them, a perfect blue to match the sky. "Bloody hell, you live in a postcard. Or a holiday brochure."

Jory laughed. "It's not bad here, is it? Bit of a change from Luton, I imagine."

Gulls screamed overhead, the familiar raucous cries making Sam smile. "It's kind of like being back in Edinburgh." Especially with Jory by his side.

"Remember that time we walked up to Arthur's Seat? It was a day just like this."

Sam remembered all right. "Yeah, until we got to the top. And then it started peeing down, and I slipped on a rock and ended up with a bruise on my arse the size of Holyrood Palace."

Jory laughed. "And you caught a cold. Doug wasn't too pleased with me about that, was he?"

Sam froze for an instant before he could catch himself, and hoped Jory wouldn't notice.

No such luck. Jory's stride faltered. "Sorry. Don't suppose you want to be talking about him."

"Not a lot, no." Sam jammed his hands into his pockets and tried to lighten his tone. "Don't worry about it. All my own fault. Still, learned my lesson there."

"Bit of a harsh one."

Sam gave a jerky shrug and cast around desperately for something else to talk about. "So what's it been like for you, coming back here after Edinburgh? Good to be back nearer your kid again?"

Jory just nodded, as if words couldn't cut it, then looked awkward. "Were your family okay with you moving so far away again?"

"Yeah, well, it wasn't like I was living with them. Bit of an embarrassment, wasn't I? The promising academic, reduced to restaurant dogsbody." He said it lightly, but Christ, it still hurt. The look of disappointment on his mum's face had been harder to bear than the sacking. She'd been so proud of him for getting his PhD, seeing his name in academic journals. And then getting home to find his room rented out . . .

That wasn't fair, though. She'd said she'd give the guy notice, and Sam could sleep on the sofa until then. It'd been Sam who hadn't been able to face it. Hadn't been able to live with the constant reminder of how he'd failed his family.

"Maybe you could invite them down when the exhibition opens?" Jory suggested.

That . . . wasn't a bad idea. Sam's spirits lifted. "Yeah, maybe. Hey, is that the castle I can see?" Daft question, really. The grey stone ruins stood on a promontory, jutting out into the sea like a sentry post, and the jagged remains of walls and chimney stacks pierced the clear blue sky.

As they got closer, another building became visible, just landward of the castle. It was of modern design, with a low roof and huge plate glass windows.

"And that's where you'll be working," Jory said, as if it could be anything else.

Scaffolding was still in place, but the exhibition centre looked well on schedule to be finished in time for the planned opening in mid-July. It also looked a lot more expensive than Sam had expected. He gave a low whistle. "Sure you want to be putting someone like me in charge of all that?" He laughed to show he was joking.

He wasn't joking.

Jory didn't seem to notice. Or maybe he was just being polite. "Nice, isn't it? There are going to be heraldic pennants out front, and Kirs—a local artist is doing a sculpture of the Black Prince."

"I was expecting like a couple of ship's containers tarted up a bit," Sam confessed. "Did someone win the lottery?"

"Pretty much. Apparently getting funding for these things is an art in itself. Although a great deal of the money was put up by local businesses."

"Trying to put Porthkennack on the map?"

Jory frowned. "Well, I think it's *on the map* already, but raise its profile, yes, absolutely."

Oops. Sam should have remembered he was talking to a local lad. "Uh, yeah, I guess most of the economy round here runs on tourists?"

"That and fishing. Employment prospects are limited for young people who want to stay in Porthkennack, I'm afraid."

"So going into the family business might not be such a bad thing for your boy?"

"Yes . . . Although I do wonder if it's really right for Gawen." Jory shrugged awkwardly. "He's quite sensitive, and, well, Bran has had to make some tough decisions for commercial reasons. Decisions that haven't made him popular."

"Is that why Mal doesn't like him? Bran, I mean."

Jory sort of hunched in on himself. "Not exactly. It's to do with a friend of his. His *best* friend. He's, well, we're related, although I've only known him a couple of years. And Bran wasn't terribly welcoming when he came to find us."

Came to find them? "Uh, wrong side of the blanket job, was it?" Jory nodded.

Bloody hell. By the sound of it, having a kid on the sly was a bit of a family thing for the Roscarrocks. Sam wondered who the poor lad's dad was—Bran himself? Jory's dad? It didn't seem polite to ask. If Jory had wanted him to know, he'd have said, wouldn't he?

"But he came round in the end?" Christ, Sam hoped so. Family was family, however it was made up.

"Well . . . Oh look, here's Jennifer."

Yeah, Sam was pretty sure he wasn't imagining how glad Jory was to change the subject. A woman in late middle age, her long grey hair blowing around her face, was striding up to them across the grass with a rolling gait, as if she'd just stepped off a ship and hadn't got her land legs yet.

As they met, she stretched out her hand with a smile. "Dr. Ferreira, I presume? I'm Jennifer Solomon."

"Hi, yeah, but call me Sam."

"Jennifer, then. Not Jenny, please. Makes me feel like I date from the industrial revolution, and as I keep telling our visiting school parties, I'm not *quite* that old. Jory, how are you? And how's that boy of yours?"

"We're fine, both of us. How's your hip?"

"Buggered as ever. Excuse my French," she added to Sam with a roguish look.

"Medieval Latin, innit?" he said innocently.

She snorted. "I like a chap who knows his etymology. You know, I've wanted to do an exhibit on that for years. *The Anglo-Saxons Didn't, Actually, Have a Word for It*, or some such. The schoolkids would love it. Just can't think of how to tie it into the castle. Or get it past certain people," she added with a significant look at Jory.

Odd, because Sam couldn't remember Jory being particularly anti-swearing before. Course, he was a high school teacher now. He wouldn't want his pupils to be encouraged to go effing and blinding at him any more than they probably did already.

"Maybe we could sneak it into the Black Prince exhibition? Speculate on what all those English archers might have been shouting at the enemy on the battlefields of France? And hey, we could tie it in to that myth about the origins of the V sign."

Jennifer raised a bushy eyebrow. "'Myth'? That's controversial talk, you know."

"No, it's not. Nobody even *suggested* that's how it happened until the twentieth century—there isn't a scrap of evidence anyone actually made that gesture until then. The only contemporary account that even *mentions* fingers—"

"Hang on," Jory interrupted. "You're talking about the story about the V sign coming from English longbowmen holding up two fingers—their drawing fingers—to the French to show what they were going to kill them with? You're saying that's not true?"

"Uh, sorry, mate, but for a start, have you ever drawn a medieval longbow? A hundred pounds of pressure, that is. Two fingers aren't going to cut it. They used three—index, middle, and ring. And *that's* what's mentioned in Wavrin's contemporary account, which was basically supposed to be the English king's pep talk to his troops: *Don't get captured, lads, or they'll cut off your three middle fingers.* Not two. Three." Sam held up his own fingers in illustration.

Jory sighed. "Gawen loves that story."

"If I could remind you, *Dr.* Ferreira, that absence of evidence isn't evidence of absence?" There was something about Jennifer's stance that made Sam think of a British bulldog. Or terrier, maybe. Sam could just imagine her sinking her teeth into him and giving him a good shake to break his neck.

Thank God she had a twinkle in her eye that told him physical violence was probably off the agenda.

Jory was looking alarmed, though. "Can we save the battle reenactments for when the tourists are here?"

Jennifer smiled at him. "Oh, if ever I were tempted to make a rude gesture . . . Don't mind us, Jory. We're historians. If we ever actually agreed on anything, the universe would implode."

"Explode," Sam corrected mildly, and laughed at her mock-outraged expression.

He reckoned he was going to like it here.

CHAPTER
ELEVEN

B ran was beginning to loathe it here. He was, quite literally, sick and tired of being in hospital. He hated the indignities of illness, and hospital life with its lack of privacy and, worse, autonomy. The painkillers—which didn't so much kill the pain as blunt it very slightly—made him slow and stupid, the antibiotics upset his stomach, and the nurses insisted he stay propped up at all times, making it almost impossible to sleep deeply. He'd never imagined he'd be so desperate to lie flat. Worse, he couldn't seem to concentrate long enough to even attempt a crossword, and he constantly lost the thread of any book he tried to read.

It was as though the wretched illness had invaded his brain as well as his lungs.

Thank God he'd ended the thing with Craig. Without his phone he'd have had no way to cancel their weekly meetings, and Craig didn't react well to being stood up without notice. He didn't react well to it even *with* notice, which was one of the reasons Bran had broken with him. He couldn't abide drama.

Then again, if he stayed here much longer, he was half convinced the boredom would kill him.

Even Bea seemed too busy to visit him often. It was almost as though she were avoiding him.

Twenty-Six Years Ago

Bran was painfully aware, returning to school after an Easter break spent alone at home with a father he hardly saw, that Bea's baby was due any day now. She'd gone away to Scotland with Mother for the last few months of the pregnancy. Bran hadn't seen her since the Christmas holidays.

Childbirth was supposed to hurt horribly, wasn't it? Bran couldn't imagine it. The process seemed awful when they showed it on television, with the woman screaming and the man panicking, rushing to get her to hospital on time.

But the mothers always smiled when they saw their child.

The more Bran thought about it, the less it seemed right, to simply give away their own flesh and blood like a bundle of unwanted clothing.

Maybe Bea would change her mind, once her baby was born? Decide to keep it after all? Bran had thought he wouldn't want that, but now he wasn't so sure. Wouldn't it be something, to have a niece or a nephew? Although he wouldn't be able to call it that, of course. Mother and Father could say they'd adopted a child from abroad, so its skin colour wouldn't matter. Lots of people did that nowadays. Bea could still go to school—they'd hire a nanny—and nobody would look down on them for charity to an orphan.

He'd hated having a baby in the house when Jory was born, but it would be different this time. Bran and Bea had been children themselves then. They were older now.

Of course, if it looked too much like *that man* . . . But to be honest, after nine months Bran couldn't even remember his face particularly well, for all that the pain and humiliation were as sharp as ever.

Maybe, though, it would all come flooding back again when he saw the baby. *If* he saw the baby? They wouldn't just get rid of it without telling him, would they? No, surely they'd tell him when it was born, and he'd be able to go and see Bea. And he could suggest keeping the child, in case they hadn't thought of it. If it looked too much like . . . like *him*, then Bran could just keep quiet. Yes. That was a good plan. All he had to do was wait until one of his parents, or Bea herself, let him know she'd gone into labour and he should come and join them.

Bran waited, but no news came. In the end, when it was nearly two weeks after he'd thought she was due, he rang home.

"Yes?"

Bran swallowed. His father's sharp tones always made him forget all his carefully composed lines. "I, um, I just wondered if Bea had . . . if things had started."

Father gave an exasperated huff. "Your sister is over the worst of her illness and is recovering in Scotland with her mother."

Over her illness. So the baby had been born. And must be gone already. There was a sharp ache in Bran's chest at the thought. He hadn't had a chance to see it, to say anything at all. "But she's okay?"

"Didn't I just say so?"

"And the, uh, the—"

"You know full well what was planned. The matter is no longer of any concern to this family and will therefore not be spoken of. Do I make myself clear?"

There was an odd, painful lump in Bran's throat. He wanted to ask again about the child, but his nerve broke. "Yes."

"Good. Was there anything else?"

"N-no."

"Then you should get back to your studies. You have exams coming up. Don't you disappoint me."

The next time Bran saw Bea was when he went home from school for the summer holidays. He'd been hoping, the last couple of months, that they'd be able to put it all behind them, and go back to how things used to be. But she seemed more remote than ever.

He heard her crying in the night, sometimes, but her door was always locked so he couldn't go and comfort her. And she always denied it in the morning.

Present Day

Jory didn't come to visit him until the weekend, although he brought Gawen with him when he finally turned up, which made amends somewhat for the neglect.

"How are you doing with *Gormenghast*?" Bran asked, his room seeming suddenly brighter for the presence of one gawky teenager and his mop of blond hair.

Gawen bit his lip, glanced up at his father, then bent his head to stare at his trainers.

Jory grimaced. "Kirsty had to confiscate it at 2 a.m. the other night."

"Gawen," Bran said reprovingly. But not too sternly. "What did I tell you? Did you get it back?"

"Yes. But it wasn't *fair*. I couldn't sleep anyway because Mum and Euan were being too loud."

That was unsettling. "He stayed the night at your house?"

"No. He went home after Mum took my book. At least, I heard the front door shut and they weren't talking any more after that. Thank *God*."

"Language," Jory said.

Gawen rolled his eyes. "Everyone says it."

Bran was just relieved to find it had only been loud voices Gawen had objected to, not the noise from . . . other activities. "I hope you explained that to your mother."

"Sort of." Gawen's shoulders slumped, and he examined Bran's hospital blanket a lot more closely than it warranted.

Bran took that to mean he'd merely thrown a strop and hadn't explained it at all. Gawen could be surprisingly inarticulate when in the grips of strong emotion. Never mind. He'd have a word with Kirsty himself. "And your schoolwork? How did the French test go?"

Gawen's face turned sunny once more. "I came top!"

"That's my boy," Bran said, pleased. Jory, fetching a chair from the other side of the room, looked momentarily disgruntled.

"I still don't see why we have to learn it," Gawen went on. "I wish the French were still our enemies like when the Black Prince was fighting them. I bet nobody had to do French lessons then. If we've got to learn a language, Japanese would be much more fun. *And* more useful."

Jory scoffed. "For reading manga in the original, he means. It's the new burning ambition."

"I like manga." Gawen dug around in his school bag until he found a surprisingly pristine copy of what was clearly a comic book, with a stylised, spiky-haired character grinning manically on the cover.

"You can borrow this one, Uncle Bran. I've finished it. But please be careful not to crease the spine."

Bran opened the book, only to have it taken from him and gently replaced in his hands with the back page open. "You have to start at the back," Gawen said patiently. "And read the frames right to left."

"Thank you." Bran supposed he should be grateful the book was in English. For a given value of English, at any rate. "So where did this interest come from? Apart from Japan, obviously."

Gawen went red. "Ruby. She's new at school. She's really into manga and anime."

And quite clearly, Gawen was into *her*. Bran and Jory exchanged looks. "She seems like a nice girl," Jory offered.

Bran hoped it wouldn't end in tears. Meanwhile, that comment about the Black Prince had jogged his memory—and Bran was fairly sure Gawen would be glad if he changed the subject. He turned to Jory. "What's happening about the exhibition? *Is* anything happening about the exhibition?"

Jory startled. "Oh, no need to worry about that. I've got it all in hand. You just concentrate on getting well. You made the local paper, you know—did you see?"

"What?" Bran would definitely have preferred to be consulted about that.

"I'll see if I can dig you out a copy for next time. Although ours might have gone for recycling already. Or the bottom of the rats' cage."

"What did they write about me?" If it was anything implying he was at death's door, he'd have to jump on it firmly. The last thing he needed was potential business partners thinking he was a bad risk.

"Not a lot. *Local businessman in unprovoked attack*, I think was the headline."

"Was there anything in there about the exhibition?"

"No, but they did mention you'd been lobbying for increased CCTV coverage of the town for over a year."

That was good, at any rate. "Maybe they'll actually do something about that now."

Gawen broke in at that point. "What does 'lobbying' mean, really? I've heard it on the news, but how do you actually do it?"

Jory laughed. "It's really just persuading the people in power to do what you want."

"Yes, but *how*? Do you have to pay them?"

This time Bran laughed, and he didn't even mind the soreness in his chest it cost him. "More often than the people in power would like you to think, yes. But that sort of thing is generally frowned upon. Although on a national level, you'll often find that people and corporations who've made substantial donations to particular political parties tend to do rather well once that party comes to power."

"So how do *you* do it, Uncle Bran?"

By the time he'd finished a lengthy explanation—surely Gawen should have had a better idea of the structure of local government at his age; what on earth *was* Jory teaching him?—Bran was exhausted. Jory and Gawen left shortly afterwards.

It was only when he was lying—reclining, at any rate—in bed and trying to sleep that Bran remembered he'd never got a straight answer from Jory as to what was happening with the exhibition.

CHAPTER
TWELVE

S am's first day at work wasn't quite what he'd been expecting. Okay, so Jory had promised him there wouldn't be an interview, but he'd been prepared for a representative of the Woodstock Trust, who were funding the exhibition, to turn up and ask him some pretty searching questions under the guise of "getting to know" their new curator. He'd seen the budget for this exhibition, and it'd nearly given him a panic attack. They were seriously trusting him with a project this big? Okay, so most of the money had gone into building the exhibition centre and he wasn't in charge of anything to do with that, but still. If he fitted it out with a load of crap exhibits no one wanted to see, they'd never recoup that investment.

If it'd been *his* money, he'd have made damn sure he knew who was going to be spending it.

What actually happened was that Sam was shown to a Portakabin parked up next to the castle's visitor centre and left to get on with it.

At least his predecessor had been the methodical sort. Sam had been amazed, when he'd started postgrad work, how disorganised some historians could be. Dr. Banerjee had left files full of notes on paper, and when Sam switched on the computer, it was easy to work his way through the folders and see the progression of the plans. He'd been half-afraid the work would be seriously behind schedule, leaving him no chance to catch up before the official opening date, but actually, it looked like things were well in hand.

A number of artefacts had been begged, borrowed, or otherwise liberated from various museums or private owners. Pride of place would deservedly be going to the Black Prince's Funerary Achievements—his helm, surcoat, shield, and gauntlets—normally displayed above his tomb in Canterbury Cathedral. Sam whistled. For an untried exhibition centre, securing that loan was a serious coup—and they'd be keeping them for the whole of the summer.

At least, they would be so long as Sam did his job properly and made sure the cathedral's conservators didn't find anything to object to about the proposed display arrangement when they came to inspect the centre in . . . Sam winced. Three weeks. And they could object to all kinds of things—humidity levels, light levels, security, even the design and installation of the display case itself. Problems with any of those things could lead to the loan being reduced to as little as a day—or cancelled altogether.

Yeah, he was going to have to make sure he worked very closely with the contractor on that one. Thank God a lot of the other work had already been done. Local actors had been engaged to provide short "oral history" videos as a range of characters—medieval technology unfortunately not having run to voice recording—costumes had been sourced, and a film crew had been booked for the middle of June. There were digital mock-ups of planned displays and information boards, together with interactive exhibits for visitors of all ages. And okay, he could see straight away the text panels were going to need a bit of trimming, but that shouldn't be a major issue. There was to be a dressing-up corner, and a range with the chance to try out replica longbows, plus some more modern bows that the average visitor might actually stand a chance of drawing and shooting with. And expert replicas of the prince's armour had been commissioned, both to show the brilliant red, gold, and blue colours the prince had worn into battle—the medieval textiles having sadly faded—and to replace the originals altogether when the loan ended.

Sam frowned. Why on earth had Dr. Banerjee resigned? She'd already done most of the work.

But the more Sam saw, the more his misgivings built. There was a definite bias becoming apparent, so much so that it amounted to censorship of anything that disagreed with the general thrust. The initials BR kept showing up, vetoing anything that painted the Black Prince in a less-than-positive light. And yes, maybe Edward of Woodstock had been unfairly vilified over the centuries, with far too many people assuming the sobriquet *Black* meant he was a vicious evil bastard, but this was revisionism gone postal. The blatant cherry-picking of evidence went against all of Sam's instincts as a historian.

This wasn't an exhibition. It was a hagiography.

And Sam wasn't willing to compromise his professional integrity. He'd sworn he'd never do that again. If it came down to it he'd . . . Christ. What *would* he do? He needed this job.

Okay. Time to stop panicking and find out if those bridges actually needed crossing. Sam made his way to Jennifer's office in the castle's visitor centre, hoping she might be able to give him some hint of why this was all so one-sided.

"Found your feet, then?" she said by way of greeting.

"Yeah, I think so. The lady who was here before me—Dr. Banerjee—she was pretty good. Seems to have all the bases covered."

"Oh, she was certainly *efficient*," Jennifer said archly.

"It looks like she had some, uh, pretty strong views about Edward of Woodstock, though." He watched her closely.

Jennifer snorted. "It does seem that way, doesn't it? I should just follow your own judgement, if I were you. You seem like a young man who's able to stand up for his principles."

And didn't that hit him right in the conscience? "Okay, but reading between the lines here, am I gonna need to stand up for them? Like, is this bias actually down to Dr. Banerjee, or have the sponsors got their own agenda?" *And did she really leave due to ill health?* he wanted to ask, but he didn't want to come over all paranoid.

"I shouldn't worry about it if I were you. Sandwich?" She opened her desk drawer and took out a bulky greaseproof paper package. The sandwiches inside were made from proper baker's bread and thick-cut ham with pickle. Sam accepted one gratefully, his stomach already rumbling—he'd been too keyed up to grab lunch before he came over. He half expected her to pull out a bottle of home-made ginger beer to go with them, but apparently they weren't totally back in the 1950s. "Now, I'm particularly interested to see what you'll have on the role of common people during the many years of conflict. And I hope you'll be focussing on the experience of women. Too many curators seem to think it's all about the menfolk marching off to war, and completely forget about the women left at home to hold society together. These women were running businesses, raising families, dealing with the constant fear of widowhood—and stumping up the taxes that paid for those wars."

Taking a bite of his sandwich—it was well tasty—Sam got an uncomfortable flashback to his teens, and his mum telling him in no uncertain tones he was expected to get A-stars for all his exams. He swallowed. "Common folk, yeah, definitely. Actually, I was thinking we could get an actor in to do an oral history bit from the point of view of a French peasant? Talking about the local lords taxing them half to death to pay for the defending armies, and the English stealing or destroying all they had left. And there's going to be a section on Joan of Kent, of course."

Jennifer barked a laugh. "Of course. Nothing like a juicy scandal to whip up people's interest." She took a large bite of her own sandwich. Sam could imagine her eating up scandal with equal relish.

"Yeah, I reckoned we could have a display on the prince's gran and all. Isabella of France, I mean, obviously. Not the other one. Give a bit of background. The way the Black Prince was brought up—as a knight and a military commander from a young age—had to be related to Edward III's own upbringing. That was a seriously dysfunctional family. Both parents off having affairs with other men, and each trying to turn the kid against the other. And that's *before* mum and her new bloke had his dad killed." Sam grinned, gesturing with his sandwich. "Got to include that too. Red-hot poker up the you-know-what? Kids love that stuff."

"Yes, but let's not make it *all* about blood and guts. We need to include the feminine as well as the masculine."

"Hey, loads of girls are into blood and violence." Sam had only to think of his sisters.

"True, but a lot of them are into other subjects as well. Too many people seem to think feminism means allowing girls to have boys' things. It goes the other way as well, and there's nothing wrong with traditionally feminine preoccupations, such as relationships, family, and yes, even clothes and jewellery. Let's not throw the baby out with the bathwater."

Sam made a note to ensure the dressing-up corner was stocked with frocks as well as men's short tunics and hose, and to have none of that "boys' clothes this side" rubbish. Some of those weird women's headdresses would probably go down well with the kids. And now he thought about it, there was a bit of a gender bias in those planned videos, wasn't there? He might have to do a bit of recasting. The soldier, now, had to look male—anyone who presented as female in those days would have been told to bugger off and join the rest of the camp followers—but the armourer, they could be a woman. Plenty of widows took over their dead husband's trade in medieval times.

He scribbled down some notes on a scrap of paper and absent-mindedly picked up another sandwich from the packet. He'd taken a bite before he'd realised what he'd done. "Sh— Oops. Sorry. I'll, uh, buy you something from the shop?" There wasn't a café as such, but the shop in the visitor centre sold sandwiches, drinks, and snacks, and there were picnic tables outside for when the weather was decent.

Jennifer laughed. "I won't say no. If they've any Cornish pasties left, that'll do nicely. You should get one yourself. Put some meat on your bones. But tell you what, you stay here and I'll get them. You look like you're in the middle of a thought, and I could do with stretching my legs."

Sam grimaced. "I'm doing so well here, aren't I? First I steal your lunch, and now I've stolen your desk as well." He pulled out his wallet and handed her a tenner. It'd been lonely in there anyhow. "At least let me pay."

She waved it away. "No, no. I know what it's like when you start a new job. All the expense of moving and you have to wait a month for the first pay cheque. My treat."

"If you're sure . . ." Sam put his money away, wishing he didn't feel so relieved.

CHAPTER
THIRTEEN

B ran was halfway through Gawen's Japanese comic book for the second time when a familiar slim figure walked into the room. His suit was perfectly fitted and his hair freshly dyed blond. It was cut to flop artfully on top, as though he were only a few years out of public school and not the near decade which was actually the case. He'd brought flowers, and clearly not from a supermarket or petrol station—they were tied with twine and wrapped in paper printed with the name of a florist in Newquay.

Craig. Bran hurriedly shoved the comic book behind the dubious camouflage of his water jug. "What are you doing here?" God, he didn't want Craig to see him like this. Their roles, throughout their relationship, had been clearly defined: Craig, the younger one, eager to learn from Bran, the respected, sophisticated businessman. An updating of the classic Greek arrangement.

There was nothing remotely sophisticated or worthy of respect about lying in a hospital bed wearing a backless gown, his hair unkempt and his skin sallow with ill health. It shouldn't matter, Bran told himself. He'd ended their affair, for God's sake, so why should he care if Craig saw him in such a pitiable state?

But he did care. It was humiliating. Craig looked exactly as he had the last time Bran had seen him: fit, well-groomed, and slightly naïve. The last was a lie, as Bran well knew. That boyish, trusting air was Craig's stock-in-trade. Bran had no doubt it would take him far—but what he didn't understand was what had brought him *here*.

"What am I doing here?" Craig repeated with a puzzled frown, putting the flowers down on Bran's bedside table. Their scent was heady, washing over the dreary smell of disinfectant and the stale sweat of the sickroom. "I heard about the attack, of course. How are you? You don't look at all well. Did you really get pneumonia? I thought that was only old people."

Bran ignored the question and its unflattering implications. "How did you hear about it?"

"From the local news website, to start with. And of course it was talked about at work."

"Of course it was," Bran muttered. Craig's employers at Pennock & Hardy must have learned of Bran's indisposition with positive glee. No doubt Craig had spent a busy working day helping them prepare to rob him blind over the Constantine Bay property. Bran could hardly fault him. They'd always agreed that business and pleasure should be kept strictly separate.

"I heard you were deathly ill." Craig's low, chiding tone startled him from his musings.

"Damn it, who have you been talking to?"

"Sheryl at your solicitor's." Craig's face turned sulky. "I phoned her, since I assumed you'd rather I *not* contact your family. It wasn't pleasant, having to find out about you like that. Although you're actually looking a lot better than I was led to believe."

Given what he'd said earlier, he'd clearly expected Bran to be at death's door. Was he disappointed? Perhaps he'd expected a tearful deathbed reunion. Craig had an annoying relish for drama. "I can't imagine why you'd care about my state of health."

"Are you serious? Of course I care." Craig pulled up a chair, hitched up his trouser legs, and sat beside the bed. He reached over to grasp Bran's hand. "Look, I know you said we should stop seeing each other, but I've been thinking. Of course it wasn't working out, not the way it was. You get out of a relationship what you put into it, and there was always more putting out than putting in with us, wasn't there?" Craig's lips curved up in one of those rueful little smiles he did so well. "Why don't we start again? Properly, this time?"

God help him, Bran was tempted. He'd felt so alone, ever since the incident. He'd realised how much of his days had been filled by work—stripped of that, he was nothing. He'd thought Craig would be repulsed by his obvious weakness, but instead it seemed to have brought out a hitherto unsuspected caring side.

Bran wondered what else Craig's carefully cultivated image might hide. They'd spent so much time together—but had they really got to know one another? Bran had always desired Craig, and would presumably desire the man again, once he was no longer feeling as though a truck had hit him, but there had always been the unspoken agreement that sex, along with certain other mutual interests, was all it was, on both sides. There had been no talk of caring for one another. And now, it seemed, Craig wanted that to change. Wanted to start again. Properly.

But by *properly*, Craig meant *openly*, didn't he? Abruptly Bran's temper flared, and he snatched his hand from Craig's grasp. How *dare* he come here, when Bran wasn't himself, and try to browbeat him into coming out?

"I've told you before," he said as icily as his throat would allow. "That's not going to happen. You know my reasons—"

"Your *reasons*." Craig sent Bran a look he couldn't interpret. "A few old fuddy-duddies with one foot in the grave won't respect you anymore if they find out you like cock?"

"Keep your voice down!" It set off a paroxysm of coughing.

Craig rubbed Bran's back, which was soothing and therefore annoying in equal measure. "They probably already know. I should think everyone already knows. For God's sake, you just got gay-bashed."

"That wasn't . . ." Bran's chest was tight from coughing, and he felt hot and miserable.

Was that what it had been?

Craig was frowning. "Can you *really* not remember anything about the attack? That's what Sheryl said, but, well, office gossip. How reliable is that?"

"Please go," Bran rasped, exhausted.

"Poor you. It must have been horrible." Craig leaned over to kiss his cheek, and to his shame, Bran did nothing to stop him. "Will you think about it?" He stood up, thank God. "The more you run scared, the more people are going to attack you. Because they think they're going to win. You don't want to let them win, do you? Think about it."

He patted Bran's hand one last time and left. The flowers he'd brought lay on the bedside table, wilting, until a nurse bustled in.

"Oh, these are lush. I'll put them in water for you. Was it that nice young man who brought them? Is he another brother?"

"Please just take them away," Bran said wearily. "I don't want them."

"Sure, my lover? Well, I won't let them go to waste. Anything you need?"

Bran shook his head, and she left, taking the flowers with her.

Peace at last, thank God. Why couldn't Craig see he didn't want to come out? Didn't want a proper relationship? Love was a lie, and the only truth of it was pain. He was fine how he was.

Bran found himself missing the flowers' fragrance, even so.

The next day, Bran decided enough was enough, and insisted on being discharged from hospital. He had to sit through a stern talking-to about not letting his physio lapse this time, and getting plenty of rest—apparently he was the only one to see the contradiction in this—but eventually he was permitted to go home.

He called Bea to drive him back to Porthkennack. If he'd thought she would be pleased, he was disappointed.

Her tone was brusque. "You'll have to wait until this afternoon. I've got a . . . lunchtime meeting."

"Oh? I didn't think you liked those."

"It's important to network. Are you sure you're ready to come home?"

"Yes." Bran bit back a curse. "I'm fine."

"That's what you said last time." There was a pause. Was Bea censoring herself too? It was so hard to tell over the telephone. "I'll see you at three."

She hung up, leaving Bran uneasy and impatient to see her again. She'd been so odd in her manner, so remote, ever since . . . Ever since he'd been attacked, Bran realised.

It wasn't a comfortable drive home, what with the silent disapproval he had to endure en route. But Bea drove carefully so as not to jostle his ribs, and although the trip exhausted him, at least it didn't leave him in agony. And when they got home, she made him soup again, and sat with him while he ate.

For a while it was almost like when they'd been children.

Twenty-Nine Years Ago

"But I don't like rugby," Bran said, keeping his chin up, although his knees were showing a distressing tendency to shake. "What's the point of chasing after a stupid ball in the mud?"

They'd just got out of the car at Bran's new school. His uniform was stiff and uncomfortable, bought too large so he could grow into it, and almost all of the other boys were taller than him.

His father's frown deepened. "The point, Branok, is to toughen you up. Prepare you for life. You can't be soft in business. People will walk all over you if you are, and I'm not letting you run our family's fortunes into the ground after I'm gone. You're finished with prep school now, and you need to start learning to act like a man. Like someone who's fit to be head of the family. Stop hanging around your sister's skirts. Although I daresay she could teach you a thing or two about being tougher, come to that."

It stung. So what if Bran had spent most of the summer holidays with Bea? They'd *always* spent time together when they weren't at school. "Don't women need to be tough too?" he demanded.

"Women are tough," Father said softly, surprising him. "But it's a different sort of strength. A quiet strength. Patient and enduring."

Bran would have had to be an idiot not to know he was talking about Mother. She'd been ill for *years*. Ever since Jory had come along. At four years old now he was more annoying than ever, always wanting to be included in anything Bran and Bea did, and wearing Mother out with his whining.

Sometimes she was better for a week or two, able to leave the house and do things with them. More often, she wasn't, and only Father saw much of her then. She hadn't come with them today. Bran had had to say goodbye to her yesterday, as Father hadn't wanted her disturbed this morning before they left.

"Anyway," Father said with an air of finality. "I expect to see you in the rugby team by the end of this school year."

"What if I'm not good enough?" Bran surprised himself by asking.

"You will *be* good enough." Father's tone promised Bran would regret it if he wasn't. Then he made sure of it. "Don't you want your mother and me to be proud of you?"

Bran nodded, his gaze downcast.

Father took hold of his chin and raised it. "Then be a man."

CHAPTER
FOURTEEN

Present Day

The very next day, Bran forced himself to rise and dress. He was desperately short of energy, but more than anything, he needed to know what was going on with the exhibition. Jory's vague, *It's all in hand* response to his questions had been preying on his mind. Bran had assumed it meant Jory had done as he'd been asked and taken on the curator's role himself, but he needed to *know*.

It was impossible to find anything out from home. Jory, of course, had his phone switched off—a teacher taking calls during lessons would hardly be a good example to his pupils—and Jennifer Solomon hadn't answered Bran's emails, which rankled. Nor had she responded to the telephone messages he'd left. She might not be, strictly speaking, accountable to him, but was a modicum of courtesy too much to ask? Especially given the benefits Bran's exhibition would bring to the castle. It was time to pay a personal visit. Bran had yet to meet anyone who could ignore his physical presence. It was a cheering thought.

It was disconcerting to put on a suit and find it no longer fitted well. Bran hadn't realised how much weight he'd lost—he had to fasten his belt on the last hole, and his jacket hung off his shoulders.

His spirits took a further dip as he realised driving would be unwise. He didn't like to think what sort of strain it'd put on his ribs—turning the wheel, twisting to look over his shoulder—and in any case, he was still on painkillers. Resigned, Bran called a taxi to take him out to the castle. The driver, a weather-beaten man with fading blond dreadlocks that looked absurd coupled with his middle-aged spread, seemed to take perverse delight in hitting every pothole along the route, jarring Bran's ribs mercilessly.

"Wait here for me," he said with some reluctance once they'd reached their destination. The driver nodded wordlessly and turned up the radio.

Bran got out of the car with a curious mix of relief and nervous anticipation. The wind off the sea seemed stronger than usual, and bit through Bran's business-wear, leaving him fighting not to shiver. It seemed he was the only one feeling the cold, however. Visitors to the castle ambled by in short-sleeved shirts, some of them eating ice cream.

The castle car park was three-quarters empty, which Bran supposed wasn't surprising. It was still only May, and the children were all in school—although half-term must be coming up soon, mustn't it? Bran made a note to check the dates. He'd lost track of time lately.

It would all change once the exhibition was up and running, he told himself. Nevertheless, he'd have been happier to see more visitors there.

His first priority was to check on the construction work on the exhibition centre. Walking round to the site, Bran was relieved to see it appeared to be well on schedule. They were fitting out the interior now, and there was a wonderful sense of potential in the gleaming bare walls and empty display cases. Even the smell of the place, paint and sawdust and new carpeting, quickened his blood.

"Mr. Roscarrock?" The site foreman hailed him. "Wasn't expecting to see you back here so soon."

With anyone else, Bran might have suspected a guilty conscience. But Roarke was a good man—Bran had employed him on other projects. "All proceeding to schedule?"

Roarke nodded. "Like clockwork. Nothing to worry about here. I hear you've had some trouble down at the cannery, mind."

Bran bit back a curse. "I can't believe those idiots failed to secure their plant. You've had no break-ins here, I take it?"

"None."

"Thank God for that. The last thing we need is the cathedral panicking and deciding we won't be able to keep the prince's armour safe." But then, Roarke had never failed to provide adequate security on a site. "You'll be putting in the displays soon, then."

"Soon," Roarke said with a light emphasis that had Bran's hackles rising.

"There's a holdup? I thought Dr. Banerjee had left plans almost completed—you must have plenty to work on."

"Your new man wants us to hold off while he makes some changes."

"My—*what*?" Damn it, when would he learn not to set off a coughing fit?

Roarke waited patiently until Bran had finished hacking. "Your Dr. Ferreira."

"Ferreira, whoever he may be, isn't *my* anything." Wishing fervently for a glass of water, Bran took care to moderate his speech this time. "Who the hell is he? Where has he come from?"

Roarke rubbed his chin. "It was Dr. Solomon brought him over at the start of the week. Said he'd be running the show from now on. If I'd known you hadn't okayed it—"

"No—it's hardly your fault." *Damn* the woman. How dare she bring in her own man to curate *his* exhibition? "I'll sort this out. You carry on."

Bran reined in his steps unwillingly as he strode towards the castle. His chest was aching, and too much exertion would only set him off again.

"Where is Dr. Solomon?" he demanded of the young woman at the ticket desk.

A stranger to him, and hardly more than a girl, she visibly quailed inside her oversized tan polo shirt. "I think she was going up to the keep?"

That was one of the few mostly intact parts of the castle, with several rooms to visit and a viewing point at the very top. Dr. Solomon, Bran discovered after climbing more stone stairs than were good for him, was *not* in the keep. No doubt she was in Dr. Banerjee's office, conspiring with Ferreira.

Bran took a few, carefully controlled breaths before making his way back down the narrow spiral staircases, a stop-start affair that entailed a great deal of pressing himself to the wall to allow ascending visitors to pass.

Pushing open the door of the Portakabin, which had been left ajar, Bran got his first look at the stranger occupying Dr. Banerjee's desk. Young and brown skinned, with a shock of black hair that was tousled on top and cropped closer at the sides, he was typing two-handed with a pen sticking out of his mouth and a look of fierce concentration on his annoyingly handsome face.

The young man didn't even glance up at Bran's entry, just mumbled something completely indecipherable, which fanned the flames of Bran's annoyance. Bran walked smartly up to the desk. "Who the hell are you?" he barked.

The pen fell to the desk as the young man startled and, at last, looked up.

CHAPTER FIFTEEN

S am blinked up from his screen, still half-engrossed in the battle of Crécy, into the darkest brown eyes he'd ever seen, shaded by black brows that were lowered in fury. No—not black; they were the same bitter chocolate as the hair above them, but in this light it was as near to black as made hardly any difference. The guy scowling down at him was white, winter-pale despite the season, and in his late thirties at Sam's guess. He had well-defined cheekbones and a narrow, almost pointed, but strong jaw. Not bad looking at all, especially in what was clearly a very expensive suit—although he'd lost weight since he'd had it tailored. He showed the classic short bloke's almost military posture—ramrod straight back to make the most of every inch, and puffed-out chest like a bird seeing off a rival come mating season.

Sam had always found that sort of cute, but he was pretty sure if he mentioned it now, the guy would literally kill him.

"Well?" the man demanded.

Sam realised he'd been goggling like a fish on a slab. "Uh, I'm Sam Ferreira. And you're . . .?"

"Branok Roscarrock." He said it as though Sam should know who he was, and while Sam *did*, obviously, none of this attitude made sense.

"You're Jory's brother, right?" Sam had thought he was still ill. And bloody hell. Jory's big brother was about as unlike him as a bloke could get. His colouring was totally different—dark hair instead of blond—and where Jory was tall, and broad with it, Bran was built on a much smaller scale. A Celt instead of a Viking. Sam could understand, though, why Jory was, if not exactly scared of his brother, certainly a bit on the wary side. He had a definite air about him, Big Brother Branok did. Like he didn't need to be physically imposing.

Had Sam thought him pale? His face was darkening by the second, which probably wasn't great for an ill bloke.

"And I repeat, who are *you*?"

Sam had only just mentioned his name. "Uh, Dr. Sam Ferreira," he added, stressing the *Dr.* a bit. Maybe it was just forgetfulness—hey, the bloke had been bashed in the head, hadn't he? "I'm the new curator of the Black Prince exhibition."

A muscle tensed in Roscarrock's jaw. "Are you now? I suppose *Dr. Solomon* drafted you in, a decision, I might add, which is entirely outside her authority." He said Jennifer's name like it was a swear word. "What are your qualifications? Have you any prior experience in curating an exhibition of this importance?"

Sam was starting to see why nobody liked this bloke. "I'm qualified," he said shortly. "And it was Jory who hired me."

"Jory?" That seemed to take the guy aback, but he soon rallied. "Where did he find you?"

"We've known each other for years." And what the hell business was it of his brother's? Christ, he had a nerve. Sam would be damned if he was going to justify his existence to the bastard. Then his conscience pricked. Maybe the elder Roscarrock was just crap at making conversation, and this was his version of *How's work going?*

"And just what do you think you've been doing?"

Yeah, he really needed to work on those social skills. "What's that supposed to mean?"

"I just spoke to Roarke, and he tells me you're going against decisions that have already been made. Wasting hours of work by your predecessor. This is *not* what you're being paid to do."

What? "Excuse me, but since when are you my boss?"

"Since I started paying your wages, I should imagine."

The air practically crackled with frost as Sam stared in horrified disbelief.

"As the major investor in the exhibition centre," Roscarrock went on, clearly relishing it, "and the driving force behind the entire project."

Oh, *crap*. And Jory couldn't have mentioned this before? Sam cleared his throat. "You're the ... Woodstock Trust?"

"I'm its principal member, yes."

Big Brother Branok re-christened himself hastily in Sam's head to *Mr. Roscarrock*, although he baulked at adding a *Sir*. "Sorry," he ground out. "I didn't realise."

"Clearly. Well, then?"

Sam felt a pang of sympathy with whoever had landed Roscarrock in hospital. He had a strong urge to knock that smug expression right off the git's face.

But that'd *really* make his mum proud, wouldn't it? Sam took a deep, calming breath. "All I've been doing so far is finding out what's been done already, and working within and around that framework." Why the bloody hell hadn't Jory *warned* him?

"And yet I hear from Mr. Roarke that you've told him *not* to start installing the displays already agreed upon."

"Look, I'm not trying to reinvent the wheel. With less than two months before the exhibition's due to open, there wouldn't be time in any case. I just need to make some edits to the information panels before we get them printed up. Cut the word count down a bit. And I want to broaden the scope a little."

Roscarrock drew in a sharp breath, which seemed to pain him. His face darkened. "*Cut*— That text was agreed between me and Dr. Banerjee. I see no reason to change it. And *broaden the scope*? In what way?" He leaned over the desk.

Sam found himself sitting up straighter without even meaning to. "Just to balance the picture. Encourage visitors to look at the historical evidence from all sides."

"*From all sides*? It's the historian's job—" Roscarrock was seized with a coughing fit that almost doubled him over.

Sam stood up in alarm. "You all right, mate? Look, come and sit down, yeah? I'll get you a glass of water." He tried to offer the bloke a hand, but Roscarrock shook him off violently and coughed even worse.

Shit. He'd been working here for less than a week, and already he'd pissed off the boss and then half killed him.

"Can I call someone?" That got him an angry shake of the head. "I'll, uh, I'll get that water." Sam ran around the Portakabin to the visitor centre, dodged meandering tourists, and darted into the shop, where he grabbed a bottle of water from the fridge and yelled out, "I'll owe you," to Tim behind the counter. Then he raced back to his office.

But when he got there, panting, Roscarrock had disappeared, apparently into thin air. Like the plague doctor's ghost Mal had told Sam about the other night, that'd been seen by the swings in the park again. For a moment he almost wondered if Roscarrock's illness had been worse than they'd all thought, and the bloke was now haunting them to make sure no one screwed up his legacy.

Common sense pointed out that no self-respecting ghost would be seen dead haunting a Portakabin. Roscarrock had probably just taken the direct route back to the car park, and far from wanting to haunt him, clearly wanted nothing more than to get away from Sam.

Sam sat down heavily in his chair and twisted the top off the water bottle before taking a long, cooling drink. Christ. That had gone so bloody well, hadn't it? Jory's brother—Sam's *boss*—*hated* him.

CHAPTER
SIXTEEN

Thank God Bran had had the foresight to tell the taxi driver to wait for him. Attempting to telephone for one would have been even more humiliating than his display of infirmity in front of Ferreira had been. An iron band of pain tightening around his chest, Bran scrambled into the back seat of the car and managed to choke out his destination: Roscarrock House.

Then he closed his eyes and tried to calm his heart rate, his breathing, and the sick feeling of betrayal—by his brother, by his own body, for God's sake.

How could Jory have done this to him? Brought in this outsider to run *his* exhibition? Without even having the courtesy to inform him, let alone consult him on the appointment. Who was Sam Ferreira? Where had Jory found him? The name sounded Spanish or Portuguese, but if Bran had had to guess from looks alone, he'd have said the man was of Indian or Pakistani descent, rather than European. His accent was southern English, working class, although educated.

Sitting in the back of the taxi, the inaction allowing him no vent for his frustrations, Bran was at least able to use his phone to make a quick internet search for *Dr. Samuel Ferreira*. It brought up a small number of hits, none of them historians. Had the man just walked in off the street? Was the PhD even real? Surely no one so young, so ridiculously good-looking, could be a serious academic.

That had made his embarrassment all the more excruciating. Ferreira was absurdly handsome, with an easy, wide smile that formed laughter lines at the corners of his soft, brown eyes. The jet-black scruff that covered his jaw had given him a rakish, almost piratical air.

His thick, tousled hair had looked casually stylish, and just a little bit fluffy, as if begging to be stroked.

Bran swallowed. He did *not* need such distractions, especially at a time like this. Ferreira was his subordinate—effectively, if not legally speaking; the man was employed by the Woodstock Trust. And he'd shown worrying signs of wanting to upset the apple cart, with his *balanced picture* and his idea of encouraging the visitors to make up their own minds. The whole point of the exhibition was to tell the true story of Edward of Woodstock. To rescue him from his unfair reputation as a cold-hearted villain. Not to let the visitors go away cherishing their own ill-formed opinions as if they were worth as much or more than those of a qualified historian. Or someone who'd studied the Black Prince all his life.

Bran flinched as the dreadlocked driver hit another pothole. No, Ferreira would have to be kept on a tight rein. Bran would have to bring him round to the correct way of thinking. He was confident he could do this—once he was feeling a little better, that was.

Whatever attraction he might feel for Sam Ferreira, he certainly wasn't going to act upon it. That would only be asking for trouble.

Witness Craig's appearance at the hospital. Bran stared out of the window, wishing the journey was over. He'd have to do something about Craig too. If only he didn't feel so wretchedly exhausted at the prospect. And there was the business of his mysterious assailant. To let that go unpunished would send out entirely the wrong message. Perhaps he should get in touch with Sally Peters again. Just to see what progress had been made.

When, at length, they reached Roscarrock House, Bran paid the taxi driver his exorbitant fee, added an undeserved tip because, while he hoped he'd never see the man again, he'd be damned if he'd let the Roscarrock name become a byword for tight-fistedness, and trudged into the house. Bea wasn't home, as it was barely four o'clock, so he made himself a cup of tea and took it into his study. He felt bone-tired, and his chest was in agony.

Edward of Woodstock gazed regally down from his portrait. He'd never given up, had he? He hadn't even let his last, fatal illness stop him from campaigning. Bran would have to raise his game and follow the prince's example, that was all.

Of course, Edward of Woodstock had had a considerable number of people to aid him. Perhaps Bran should look into getting some help. Engaging a driver for a couple of weeks could hardly cost more than he'd be paying out for taxis, could it? Maybe Jory would know of some sixth-former who would be willing to take the job over half-term for a minimal wage.

Then again, being driven around by some teenager who'd only just passed his test might finish Bran off for good.

First things first, though. He needed to speak to Jory about Sam Ferreira—and make it plain he wasn't happy with the underhand way Jory had dealt with matters. He pulled out his phone and rang his brother. Jory didn't answer, of course—teaching was such a ridiculously inconvenient profession—and so Bran left a curt voice mail for him to call back *at once*, before ruining it with another coughing fit that hit him before he could end the call.

Damn it. The dregs of his now-lukewarm tea did little to soothe his throat. He made another cup, then switched on his computer. His inbox was fuller than ever, the mere sight of it exhausting him. He closed his eyes and leaned back in his chair.

If only he wasn't so tired all the time.

Fifteen Years Ago

The morning of their father's funeral, Jory slouched downstairs looking almost laughably uncomfortable in his dark-navy suit. He'd grown since Bran had bought it for him last year—what with their mother being so ill, Father had been too busy for anything like shopping—and several inches of wrist showed below his cuffs. As for the trousers, they were only saved from utter absurdity by virtue of having been bought deliberately too long. At least the boy had had the sense to wear black socks.

"He must be nearly six feet tall now," Bea murmured in Bran's ear. "Our little changeling."

Christ. That would mean Jory topped Bran by a good six inches, and he was still growing, for God's sake. "Hardly *little*. He should have told me about that suit. I could have replaced it if he'd only mentioned he'd grown out of it. Has he no concept of respect for the dead?"

"At least he's in a suit this time," Bea replied coolly. But then Bea did everything coolly, didn't she? Growing up, Bran used to wonder if they'd been born in the wrong bodies, their personalities having somehow traded places in their shared womb. She'd always been the logical one, the composed one, whereas he'd always struggled to behave as calmly as Father expected him to. Women were allowed to be emotional, but a man should be in command of himself at all times. That was what Father always said.

Had used to say.

Then again, had Father been in command of himself back when he'd . . . Bran felt a frown forming on his brow and the beginnings of a headache, just as Jory met his eye, flinched, and looked away. It didn't improve his mood.

"I made damn sure he'd be wearing a suit. After what he wore to Mother's . . ."

Bran's chest tightened. Jory had come downstairs on the morning of their mother's funeral in jeans and a sweater, protesting that those were the clothes she'd liked to see him in. Father had ordered Bran to sort it out, and he'd had to set aside his own grief to explain to a wilfully obstinate teenager that it didn't matter a damn what his mother would have liked; they were the first family in Porthkennack and standards would bloody well be maintained. He could just imagine the talk if a Roscarrock from Roscarrock House had turned up at the churchyard in *denim*.

He'd been incensed to find Jory hadn't even thought to pack a decent wardrobe for his few days home from school, the suit left hanging, useless, in the dormitory. They'd had to cobble something together from old clothes left in the attic by long-deceased uncles.

The worst of it was, if Jory had worn his own suit to Mother's funeral, Bran would have seen he'd outgrown it and replaced it by now.

"He should have told me he needed a new suit," Bran repeated. "How was I supposed to know?"

Bea shrugged. "It's not like Father's here to be offended, is it?"

No. No, it wasn't.

The vicar spoke at nauseating length about Father's importance to the local community and the weight of history behind the Roscarrock name. Bran had heard it all a million times before from the dead man himself. He clenched his fists to remain silent when the wretched clergyman lamented the "tragic accident" that'd torn Kenver Roscarrock from this world in his prime.

His father's friends—more like business acquaintances—echoed the praise of the man whose body had had to be dragged, bloated, from the sea to fill the coffin before them. Bran stumbled out a few words himself, wishing he could have left the task to Bea, who'd have done it so much better.

Nobody mentioned Father's state of mind. Nobody appeared to wonder why a man might wander the clifftops at night and in a howling summer storm.

Bran's nerves were on a knife-edge by the time they were finally allowed to leave the church and follow the coffin to the freshly dug grave on the eastern side of the churchyard.

The gravedigger had had an easy job of it; the ground had barely settled in the family plot from when they'd buried Mother a few months ago. The headstone was still with the mason. Bran entertained an idle thought that Father had planned it this way so as to be both convenient and cheaper for them, and appalled himself by actually making a choked-off sound that drew curious glances from his fellow mourners. He looked down. Let them think it a sob.

Bea's hand crept around his arm, and Bran allowed himself to be comforted. Christ. What would he have done without her, all these years with Mother ill and Father . . . unhappy?

Should he tell her what Father had done?

No. Father hadn't wanted her to know, had he? Or his final letter would have been addressed to both of them. Bran couldn't go against that—certainly not today, of all days, with his father's body only just lowered into the ground.

It was Bran's burden alone.

CHAPTER
SEVENTEEN

Present Day

S am's concentration was shot to hell for the rest of the day. The disastrous conversation with Branok Roscarrock kept running through his brain, along with a sneering voice inside him helpfully pointing out exactly why antagonising his boss was such a crap idea. As if he were likely to forget he was in debt up to his ears and practically unemployable to boot.

At five o'clock sharp, he gave up, shut down his computer, and drove out to the cliffs on the northern side of the headland in an attempt to clear his mind before going back to Jory's. The fresh sea air was calming, and he was able to stretch out muscles cramped from sitting hunched over his computer. Staring out over the sea, far-off gulls screaming as they flitted about like gnats, somehow put things into perspective. So what if Branok Roscarrock didn't like him? Sam didn't like *him*, either. Shrewd, dark eyes and that compelling air of self-assurance notwithstanding. And the bloke wasn't going to be hanging around all the time. He had his own business to run, didn't he? The business Jory's son was supposed to be taking over when he grew up. Some property empire or something.

Christ, Roscarrock must be *loaded*. The thought left a bitter taste. Big Brother Branok could have a flutter on the horses—footie or the dogs would be too lower-class for him, wouldn't they?—anytime he wanted, and not even care if he won or lost. He'd probably never had to worry about money in his life, with his public school accent and his air of bloody entitlement.

No wonder he expected any arguments over the exhibition to go his way. Everything else in his life of luxury and privilege obviously always had done and always would.

Sod it. Forget Branok Roscarrock for a while. Sam rambled along the cliff path, and was rewarded with the sight of the lighthouse, shining a warm, optimistic white in the late-afternoon sun. That place probably had some stories to tell. Maybe he should pay it a visit? Yeah, that was what he needed to do. Get out and about while he was here. See the sights. Get some exercise and fill his lungs with fresh, salty air.

Stay away from that bloody betting site. He should never have let himself get sucked in, but after Doug—a lot of crap had happened in his life after Doug. Sam had deleted the app before he'd moved down here, intending to make a fresh start, but reinstalling it would only take seconds, and the website was just a few clicks away in his browser. The knowledge tugged at him every time he switched on his phone, although he'd managed to stay off since he'd come to Cornwall. It was just . . . while he was on there, everything else went away for a while. There was nothing but the thrill of the gamble. The sheer buzz of winning.

Yeah, and the crushing depression of realising he'd just blown another few hundred quid in minutes. Sam needed to remember that. Needed to get his head sorted out, save his money, and pay off those debts.

With a bit of luck, Jory wouldn't have the nerve to ask him to find his own place for a couple of months once Sam confronted him about his bloody big brother.

Right. Apparently forgetting about Branok Roscarrock wasn't going to be an option. Might as well head home.

Half an hour later, Sam parked his Mini in front of Jory's house and pulled the handbrake on with a vicious jerk. Then he felt bad about it and gave the steering wheel a pat. "Sorry, babe. Not your fault."

When he went inside, there was no one in the living room, but he could hear sounds coming from the kitchen. "Hello?" he called.

"Anyone home, or is that the burglar? Don't bother with the small bedroom, there's nothing worth nicking in there."

"It's me," Jory called. "I'm making a start on dinner."

Sam kicked off his shoes—a bit late, but it was the thought that counted—and padded into the kitchen.

Jory looked up, red-eyed from the onion he was chopping. "I'm making curry. Is that all right? It's only us tonight. Mal's got college until nine, so he's eating there."

"Yeah, curry's fine." Sam leaned against the counter where Jory couldn't fail to see him, and folded his arms. "I met your big brother today. Or, as I call him, *my boss.*"

Jory blinked, and mopped at his eyes with a sheet of kitchen roll. Probably for a bit longer than they needed. "Oh—Bran's out of hospital?"

Sam snorted. "Yeah, he's out of hospital. He turned up at the castle, and guess how happy he was to see me?"

"Uh . . ."

"That's right. He wasn't, seeing as how he didn't even know I'd be there. Mate, why didn't you tell him about me?"

"I was going to." Jory's face had gone bright red to match his eyes. "I just wanted to give you time to get properly established first. If I'd known he was on his way—"

"Yeah, and how come you didn't tell *me* about *him*? It's not like the subject never came up. All those times I asked you about the Woodstock Trust, all those times your brother's name came up in conversation—it didn't occur to you to let me in on the secret that they're the same thing?"

"Bran's only one member of the Woodstock Trust." Jory looked shifty. He even *sounded* shifty. If he'd been any bloody shiftier, he'd have been in the next room by now.

"Not the way he tells it. According to him, the whole flippin' project is his baby and he doesn't like to share. I *thought* I'd been left to myself a bit much. Should've known there was a reason for it. What is all this anyway? Some sibling-rivalry thing?"

"No, of course not. I just wanted what's best for the exhibition." Jory took a deep breath. "Look, Dr. Banerjee told me before she left that Bran had been putting pressure on her from day one to . . .

present a certain view of the prince. To leave out anything that showed Edward in a bad light. I don't think he realises . . . Anyway, I thought if you had time to establish yourself, you wouldn't be so susceptible, that's all. I didn't want you thinking you had to toe the party line just because he's my brother."

"Funny. Cos from what he said today, that's *exactly* what your brother's expecting me to do." Sam shook his head. "I can't believe he hasn't been in touch with you himself. He was in a foul mood with me."

Jory glanced guiltily over to where his phone sat charging by the kettle. "I, er, might have got a voice mail from him. I haven't got around to listening to it yet."

Yeah, Sam could sympathise with that. He'd had a few messages that he hadn't wanted to face on an empty stomach.

"I'm sorry," Jory said. "I shouldn't have dumped you into this situation without warning you. I honestly didn't think Bran would be out of hospital yet." He paused. "How was he? I mean, as far as you could tell."

"You mean, apart from terminally pissed off? Nasty cough. And I think his ribs were still hurting, from the way he moved."

Jory winced. "Did he stay long?"

Sam shook his head. "Long enough to have a rant and hack up half a lung, that's all. Maybe you should go visit him?" *And get him off my back*, he thought, then felt bad about it. He didn't have the right to be too pissed off with Jory—the bloke had still got him the job, even if he hadn't given him the full picture about it.

Jory nodded. "I will. After we've eaten."

CHAPTER EIGHTEEN

B ran startled awake, disorientated. He'd fallen asleep in his chair by the fire, and now his neck ached in tandem with his ribs. He needed to eat something so he could take some more painkillers.

"Bran?" Bea's voice sounded from the hallway.

"In the study," he called, his voice croaky. It must have been her return that had woken him. He took a sip of stone-cold tea and grimaced. What time was it? Christ, almost seven o'clock.

"You don't sound too good." Bea appeared in the doorway, her mouth downturned.

"I'm fine."

"Have you eaten?"

"Not yet."

Bea's expression hardened. "I'll heat something up."

"I can do it myself." He wasn't an invalid. He started to heave himself out of his chair.

She strode off, ignoring him, and he sank back into the cushions. It wasn't worth fighting about. Let her fuss over him if she wanted to; she'd tire of it soon enough. Although it was odd how she seemed more angry than solicitous. Bran gave a minute shake of his head and pulled out his phone. Jory still hadn't called him back. He debated calling again, but decided silence would better convey his disapproval.

He ate the soup Bea provided, and then turned, reluctantly, to his emails. Did all these issues *really* need his personal attention? What was the point in building up the business if it all went to hell the minute he took his eye off things?

Jory appeared around eight o'clock, just as Bran was wondering if it was too ridiculously early to go to bed and whether he really cared if it was. Despite his unplanned nap earlier, he was exhausted.

At least Jory's arrival gave him the energy of annoyance. "I take it you've finally come to let me know about my new employee."

"Sam's employed by the trust," Jory said. "And yes. I don't know what you're so up in arms about. You asked me to get a new curator, and I did."

"I asked you to *be* the new curator."

"And I told you I couldn't do it. Sam's a good man, and he knows a great deal about the Black Prince."

"And you didn't think I might like some say in who's spending my money?"

"Oh, for— You were in hospital! *Again.* I wasn't going to worry you over something that was perfectly well in hand." Jory narrowed his eyes. "*You* didn't bother telling me you were out of hospital, for that matter. I was planning to bring Gawen to see you after school tomorrow."

"Bea didn't—"

"No. She didn't." Jory folded his arms.

Bran sank back in his chair, wearier than ever. "You'll bring him here instead?" He hated how plaintive his voice sounded.

At least it seemed to calm Jory's belligerence. "Yes. Of course. He's been looking forward to seeing you. Look, about Sam—it wasn't like it was some big secret. If I'd known you'd be going over there today, obviously I'd have told you all about him sooner. We're lucky to have him, you know. Especially at such short notice."

The man's ready availability was suspicious in itself, in Bran's considered opinion, but he couldn't muster the energy to carry on the fight. "He said he was an old friend. You think he's the best man for the job?" he asked instead.

"Oh, absolutely. He's worked at the National Museum of Scotland."

"So he *is* qualified, at least?" That was . . . better than expected.

"Oh yes. I'm sure you'll like him when you get to know him." Jory's tone called him a liar, and his face was equally dubious. "Could you try to get on with him, at least? Trust him to do a good job? It can't be good for your health, getting so stressed about everything."

And that was why Bran *hated* his physical weakness so much. People took advantage of the weak, rode roughshod over their wishes. Oh, they might dress it up as concern, but the end result was a loss of control. Of independence.

Bran would be damned if he'd lose control over his own life. "You should have consulted me over his appointment. I expect to see a copy of his CV by the end of the week." Another coughing fit took him, and Jory fussed about offering drinks and calling Bea.

It was only after Jory had gone that Bran realised he'd never had an answer about Ferreira's CV.

Thirteen Years Ago

"He has dark hair," was all Bran could think of to say on seeing his nephew—Jory's son—for the first time, wrapped in a hospital blanket and cradled in Bran's sister-in-law's arms. Kirsty's pale hair was lank and she looked older than her twenty-two years today, but happy. Jory, hovering awkwardly by her bed, might have been an unusually tall fifteen-year-old rather than only three years her junior. Anyone looking at their little group likely thought Bran was the baby's father.

"For now, anyway," Kirsty said. "I had dark hair when I was born, Mum told me, but it all fell out by the time I was six weeks old and grew back blond. You can tell he's Jory's kid, though, can't you?"

Was she trying to convince them? Bran made a mental note to look into DNA testing. But the child did seem to resemble Jory, in his eyes, the shape of his forehead.

Jory squared his shoulders. "His name's Gawen. I wanted him to have a Cornish name."

At least he'd had some regard for family tradition.

"And he's healthy?" Bran asked.

"Perfect scores all round," Kirsty said, smiling at her son. "Do you want to hold him?"

"I— Yes, all right." Bran took the bundle she held out to him. It seemed absurdly light for a person. For the Roscarrock heir. The baby, barely visible in his swaddling, was warm and smelled faintly of milk. *Gawen*, Bran reminded himself. As he gazed down at his nephew, deep-blue eyes blinked open for a moment and the tiny, toothless mouth made a perfect O of a yawn. Then, with a twitch of limbs and a snuffle of the snub little nose, Gawen settled back into sleep in Bran's arms.

For an instant, Bran saw himself as a teenager, in a past that had never happened. Holding another new-born nephew. Had that child's eyes been so blue? Gawen's were as deep as the high-tide seas that crashed against the cliffs far below Roscarrock House.

"He likes you," Kirsty said softly.

His chest tight, Bran banished all thoughts of Bea's son. Whoever that child was now, he wasn't part of their family. *This* boy, this tiny scrap of humanity, was their future. Damn the bloody DNA tests. This was Bran's nephew, a Roscarrock by name as well as by blood, and Bran was going to see to it that Gawen lacked for nothing.

CHAPTER NINETEEN

Present Day

Jory had come back from his big brother's house with assurances that everything had been smoothed over. Mal, who was home from college by then, sent Sam a look that said no, he didn't believe it either.

Sam half expected Bran Roscarrock to be waiting for him when he got to work the next day, but there wasn't so much as a stern email from the bloke. Sam shrugged and got on with his work, and tried not to wait for the other shoe to drop.

It didn't happen until Friday, when Jennifer poked her head around his door. "Sorry to be the bearer of ill tidings, but you've been summoned."

"Uh, what? Who by?" Although Sam had his suspicions.

"Your lord and master. I had the misfortune to bump into him as he arrived. He awaits you yonder, in the place of execution. Sorry, I mean *exhibition*. Slip of the tongue."

Sam gave her a sardonic look. "'Slip of the tongue'? My ar . . . mpit."

Jennifer burst out laughing. "Censoring your language? It's been a while since anyone worried about offending my delicate, maidenly ears, I can tell you."

Embarrassed, Sam rubbed the back of his neck. "Too many memories of getting my wrists slapped by one of my sisters for swearing. S'pose I'd better get over there before I offend his delicate, maidenly self." He snorted at the thought of either description applied to Bran Roscarrock.

Then he felt bad because the bloke was ill, after all. He was probably a lot more delicate than he looked right now. Actually, come to think of it, *maidenly* might not be too far off either, because seriously, even with those dark good looks, who'd want to go out with an arrogant, obnoxious prat like Bran? Sam amused himself trying to picture the man's hypothetical significant other. Some mousy woman who thought he was the dog's bollocks, probably. Either that or he went completely in the other direction and could only get it up for a dominatrix.

Sam found Bran in the reception area of the exhibition centre, talking with one of the workmen. Their voices were low and even, and on catching sight of Sam, the workman gave Bran a respectful nod and got back to his task.

Apparently Bran didn't spread fire and brimstone *everywhere* he went. Only where Sam was treading. As Sam approached, Bran took a few stiff steps to meet him. Bran was wearing another dark suit today, this one with a subtle stripe, and what could only be an old school or college tie. Battle armour? Sam squared his shoulders and prepared to give as good as he got.

Bran gave him a brief nod. "I thought we should have a proper talk. Now there are no more misunderstandings."

His tone was empty of aggression, and Sam relaxed a little. "Yeah, that'd be a good idea. We didn't exactly start off on the right foot." Shit, was he supposed to apologise? But what for, exactly?

"I don't suppose either of us was left with a good first impression of the other," Bran went on.

That was a polite way of saying he'd hated Sam on sight. "No," Sam agreed shortly.

"My brother has assured me you have the qualifications for the role you now find yourself in."

Find yourself in. Like he'd just wandered in off the street and stumbled into the job. "I do."

"He said you used to work in the Scottish National Museum." Bran's voice turned curt, as if Sam's monosyllabic answers were getting to him.

Best make more of an effort. Particularly as he wasn't on steady ground here—yeah, he'd worked there, but it'd been a brief internship, not a permanent job. "That's right. So I know what curating an exhibition involves."

"You've done it before, then? A major exhibition like this?" Bran leaned forward, his eyes brighter.

"Not exactly, but don't forget, I'm simply carrying on with work that's already begun. It's not like I'm designing the whole thing from scratch. Dr. Banerjee's laid some sturdy foundations for me to build on." Sam hesitated, then plunged on. "I really appreciate the chance to work on this exhibition. The Hundred Years War was my specialism at PhD level, so this is pretty much my dream job."

It probably sounded like he was brown-nosing, but sod it, it was all true, so why not say it?

And Bran was definitely looking happier. "What sparked your interest?"

Safer ground, thank God. "I think it was the whole idea of parts of France belonging to England. These days, a lot of us like to think of Britain as an island apart from Europe, and forget that that wasn't always the case. Considering how much more hazardous the crossing was in those days, there was an awful lot of popping back and forth across the channel in medieval times. And with all the intermarriages between the noble families, the distinctions really were blurred. Especially since Norman French was the language of the king and his court up to the end of the fourteenth century. And the Hundred Years War was what changed all that. What gave us, in effect, an English national identity." Sam realised he'd let himself get carried away, but hey, the bloke had asked.

Bran nodded, so at least they agreed on some things. "And your views on the Black Prince himself?"

Sam wasn't much into sci-fi, but a mate had once made him sit through as many episodes of *Lost in Space* as they could fit into one beer-soaked weekend, which was probably why he had *Danger, Will Robinson* blaring through his brain right now. "Well, there's no question he was a brilliant military campaigner from an early age."

"Some might call his treatment of the French brutal." Bran said it so mildly it *had* to be a front.

And yeah, okay, the klaxons were going off and the red lights were flashing, but Sam couldn't let this one go. "*Some*? Mate, he burned their towns and villages to the ground. Got the job done, yeah, but a hell of a lot of peasants starved to death on his account."

"What would you have had him do? Leave provisions for his opponent's army? This was *war*." Bran's expression hardened, and Sam got a weird flash of him in a different sort of armour, leading his troops into battle and giving no quarter.

"I'm just saying, you can't forget the human cost." Sam folded his arms. Historical debate? He could do this all day.

"And I suppose *you'll* want to focus on that to the detriment of all else? Are these the changes you've been making?" Bran's sharp features were stonier than the castle walls and a lot less likely to crumble.

"Now you're putting words in my mouth. I just want to present a balanced picture, that's all. Bring in more of the female viewpoint—"

"That was already represented. Are you accusing me of misogyny?"

"What? Of course not. I'm not accusing you of anything." For a start, Sam couldn't afford to get sued for slander. "Just, it was a bit . . . token, that's all."

"*Token*?" Bran drew in a breath, and Sam braced himself.

"Mr. Roscarrock?" It was Roarke, the site foreman. "Sorry to interrupt, but there's something I need to go over with you, and it can't wait."

Couldn't it? Sam didn't fool himself this meant Roarke's loyalty was to him, rather than Bran. Most likely the bloke just liked to keep the peace in his workplace. "I'll, uh, leave you to it," he said. "I'll be in my office if you need me for anything more."

Bran nodded to him. "This isn't over."

No, that wasn't ominous at *all*.

Sam spent the rest of the day mustering a coherent defence of his position, only to feel keenly disappointed when Bran didn't show for the fight. Maybe he was trying to lull Sam into a false sense of security. Or busy finding a replacement curator. Bloody hell, why couldn't the man just get on with it? Even if Sam got fired, at least a decent shouting match would clear the tension yoking his shoulders and giving him a headache.

Then again, Sam's CV wasn't looking too hot already. If he got sacked from this job in his first week, he might as well give up on being employed at above minimum wage ever again. Maybe a delay was all to the good—it'd give Bran a chance to cool down. Realise today's public distrusted anything other than a balanced picture.

Yeah, right.

Mal was in on his own when Sam got back to the house. He was playing with his rats, which Sam had been making an effort to get used to. And mostly failing.

"All right, mate?" Mal called out from his seat on the floor, where he was being crawled all over by at least two well-fed rodents Sam would *not* have liked to meet in a dark alley. "What's a rat's favourite game?"

"You tell me."

"Hide and squeak!" Mal cackled.

"Yeah, good luck with that career writing cracker jokes." Sam turned towards the kitchen.

"Hold on, I've got another. What do you call a bloke with a rat on his head?"

Sam gave him a blank stare, tried not to cringe on seeing that yes, Mal *did* have a rat on his head now, and waited.

Mal grinned. "Someone who's really hoping the housetraining took. Wanna hold one? This is Neville, he's really friendly." He held up the black-and-white rat that'd been nibbling at the hem of his T-shirt. To Sam's eyes, it looked identical to Myrtle, but presumably Mal had some way of telling them apart.

"Thanks, but I'll pass. Cup of tea?"

"Cheers, mate."

"Anything for Neville?"

"Nah, he's trying to cut down the caffeine. But you could grab him a strawberry out of the fridge. And one for Pansy."

When Sam found himself carefully comparing the strawberries in the punnet to make sure he selected two of equal size and ripeness so neither rat would feel hard done by, he knew he'd lost it.

Carrying the mugs in one hand and the strawberries in the other, he made his way back to the living room.

"Ah, cheers, mate." Mal took the berries, and Sam put his tea down on the floor near him. "You're the best."

"No problem. How's it going at the museum?"

"Not bad. Think we're all ready for half-term next week—got some living crafts people in to do demos and let the kids have a go at stuff. We've even got some ship's biscuits baked up for them to try, but they wouldn't let me add any weevils to the mix. It's health and safety gone mad, I tell you." Noses twitched at the strawberries, and Pansy ran down Mal's arm to get her treat. Neville already had his.

Okay, they *were* kind of cute holding the berries in their little pink hands and nibbling. "Shame. It's just not going to be an authentic experience."

"That's what I said! *And* they keep insisting no one gets a tot of rum without two kinds of ID and a note from their mum. Where would we have been, I ask you, if all them cabin boys and powder monkeys back in the day hadn't got their tots of rum? They'd have mutinied straight off. I would've." Mal's eyes were wide and earnest.

Sam had to laugh. "S'pose the live floggings are out too, are they?"

"Well, if you're volunteering to be the whipping boy, I might be able to swing it last minute."

"Cheers, but I wouldn't want to get you in trouble." They grinned at each other.

Jory was a lucky bastard. And Sam seriously needed to find himself a bloke. He missed this—being with someone he could have a laugh with at the end of the day. Okay, him and Mal were doing that right now, but it wasn't the same. Mal was Jory's.

Sam could hardly remember the last time he'd had someone who was all his. He'd thought Doug had been his, or at any rate had been *going* to be his—but he'd been wrong. So badly wrong. He shivered.

"Someone walk over your grave?" Mal frowned. "Huh, weird idea that, innit? Think you still get that feeling if you're gonna be cremated?"

Sam shrugged. "You're asking the wrong bloke. I come from a long line of Goan Catholics. My mum's pretty open-minded about most things, but she's a hard-line traditionalist on funeral rites. If I got cremated instead of buried, she'd kill me. Hey, I wanted to ask you something . . ." Sam hesitated, not sure how to put it. "Did they ask you to take over the exhibition?"

Mal stared. "Do what now?"

"Uh, well, you work at a museum. And Bran knows you, obviously, so I thought maybe—"

"Mate, seriously. Bran ask *me* to look after his pet project? Not if I was the last person on earth. Bury me under the foundations as a sacrifice to the gods—yeah, I could see him doing that."

Okay, that sounded a little extreme. "What's he got against you?"

"What hasn't he?" Mal ran a hand through his hair—not, so far as Sam could tell, dislodging any evidence that Pansy had disgraced herself, thank God—then gave a sheepish grin. "Nah, that ain't fair. I mean, it don't all come from his side. I'm mad at him cos he was a git to my mate Dev, and he hates me cos I was the reason Jory finally got a divorce from Kirsty. Like he thought they were actually going to get back together, and by 'back together' I mean *actually* together for the first time. See, Bran, he's got, like, these Bran-colour specs on, you know?"

Sam couldn't help laughing. "'Bran-colour'? What's that? Sort of dark brown?" Like his eyes, and his hair.

"Probably, but that ain't what I meant. If you wear rose-colour specs, you see everything all happy-smiley, right? Bran-colour specs make that git see things the way he thinks they are. Or how he thinks they ought to be, whatever."

"Yeah, I can buy that. So, uh, it's not cos you're a bloke?"

"Could be a bit of that and all. Who knows?" Mal stretched expansively and grinned again. "Who cares?"

"Us poor sods who have to work for him?"

"Rather you than me, mate. Right, Jory's round at Kirsty's for his dinner, so it's you and me cooking tonight. And to be honest, mate? I can't be arsed. So, chippy?"

Sam nodded. Yeah, cheap as chips would do him for tonight.

CHAPTER TWENTY

Bran spent the next few days marshalling his forces, metaphorically speaking. Thank God he'd taken a couple of days to rest after first encountering Ferreira. He felt . . . not *well*, precisely, but better. His head was clearer, and the horrid feeling of being overwhelmed by everything had dissipated. The Black Prince exhibition was going to need his close attention while under Ferreira's oversight. The man was both passionate in his opinions and articulate in his arguments—a significantly greater challenge than Dr. Banerjee had been. And Bran was not one to back down from a challenge.

He could, he supposed, simply fire the man, and after their first meeting he'd had every mind to. Quieter reflection had convinced him this would be a mistake, however. Finding a replacement would be difficult at this stage. Jory would be unlikely to offer any assistance, for one thing. For another, it would sour the tentative reconciliation which had begun between Bran and Jory over the last year, which shouldn't have been a serious deterrent—after all, this was a business decision—but undeniably *was*. In any case, it would be more satisfying to persuade Sam to Bran's point of view. He was an intelligent man who knew his subject well—victory over him would be a worthy conquest indeed.

Accordingly, Bran dedicated himself to freeing up his workload. Eileen McGregor, who'd caught his attention when he'd had dealings with her property management company in the past, proved amenable to taking on a number of his interests—in particular, the Constantine Bay property, which had been causing him far more trouble than it was worth. He was able to pass fully half of his unanswered emails over to her, making the remainder far more manageable.

A welcome side effect was that it would prevent any awkward meetings with Craig in a business context. Yes, he should have taken this step long ago. Furthermore, the timing was excellent—this was half-term week, and Bran would have more leisure to spend with Gawen.

On Sunday, he and Bea had Sunday lunch at the golf club. "You've seemed more cheerful, the last couple of days," Bea said coolly as they ate. "Have the police tracked down that missing equipment for the cannery contractor?"

"Not that I've heard." Bran frowned. "I shan't be employing that firm again. I'll have to let Eileen know about their lack of adequate security too."

Bea took a sip of water. As usual, she didn't seem particularly interested in her food. Bran considered telling her she had no need to watch her weight, then decided against it. If he called attention to her lack of appetite, she might stop eating altogether. "I wouldn't interfere too much if I were you. What's the point of employing her and then micromanaging anyway?"

Bran gave her a sharp look. "You're not annoyed that I've handed over management of some of our properties to her, are you?"

"Of course not." She neatly filleted her fish, but didn't take a bite. "You've always worked too hard."

"One could say the same about you." Her whole life appeared to revolve around her career as a financial advisor.

"I enjoy what I do." Bea said it quickly—too quickly?

"I should hope so, as you chose it." Bran meant that sincerely. She'd excelled at school, even more than he had. She could have done anything she wanted to.

"Do you resent me for that? When Father never gave you a choice?"

Why did she sound so defensive? "Of course I don't resent you. Don't be absurd. You've every right to choose your own path, and I'm quite happy with my life."

"Oh? Then I'm glad." Bea took a minuscule bite of fish.

Was he happy with his life? Bran had never really questioned it before—but it was undeniable how much lighter he felt having farmed out half his workload. And it was true that the life had chosen him, and not the other way around. He'd never chafed at the yoke, though. He'd seen it as a duty, perhaps—but not an unwelcome one. It was an honour, to look after the family's interests so they could be passed on to the next generation with pride.

To Gawen. Although . . . perhaps expecting him to manage the family's interests personally was blinkered thinking? Bran frowned at his excellent roast lamb. He should have a talk with the boy. Possibly with Kirsty as well, although she could be surprisingly resistant to the idea of planning for the future.

Well. Perhaps it wasn't all that surprising. She'd always had something of a *que sera, sera* approach to life.

Bea laid her knife and fork neatly together, and Bran turned his attention back to his food, finishing it a little more quickly than he might have liked.

The waitress—clearly new here—approached the table and gave Bea's still-laden plate a concerned frown. "Was everything all right?"

"Perfectly, thank you. You can take it away now. And I'll have a black coffee." Bea took out her phone.

"The lamb was superb, thank you," Bran said to reassure the girl, and ordered dessert.

They spoke of impersonal things while they waited, which was something of a relief. Bea had a disconcerting way of making him *think*.

She proved it once again not long after their order had arrived. "Have you heard from the police about your attack?" Bea asked, her bone china coffee cup seeming larger and rougher in her delicate hands.

"No." Bran's Eton Mess no longer tasted quite so sweet. "I suppose I should get in touch with Constable Peters." He'd meant to do that earlier, it was true, but other considerations had taken precedence.

"You don't sound very keen. I'd have thought you'd be determined to make whoever attacked you pay."

He had been, hadn't he? But then he'd got ill, and since then, he'd had Ferreira to contend with. *That* was a fight he could relish. Dealing with someone who used physical violence as an argument was an entirely different matter. Bran wished, for one shameful moment, that he could simply forget about the attack. Pretend it hadn't happened.

But that would be the act of a coward, wouldn't it? Besides, his ribs were unlikely to let him forget so soon.

"I'll speak to her," Bea said.

Bran flushed. "No, that won't be necessary. I'll do it."

"*Someone* needs to make sure nothing is let slide."

"I said I'll do it." Bran couldn't keep the irritation out of his tone.

Bea's face hardened. "Fine, then. But I thought you wanted to cut down on stress."

Bran had the uncharitable thought that maybe he should stop lunching with his sister, in that case. He didn't voice it.

Craig called again that evening. He'd left several messages over the course of the last few days. Bran had been too busy to call him back, and doubted it would be advisable in any case. It would only encourage him.

Now that Bran wasn't dealing personally with the Constantine Bay property dispute, there was really no reason for them to see each other anymore.

Monday morning, Bran was up early and in Ferreira's office before the man himself turned up for the day. He tried not to look too pleased at Ferreira's obvious discomfort on finding him there, sitting at the desk and flicking through files.

"Uh, would you like a coffee?" Ferreira offered. He was casually dressed again, in a long-sleeved T-shirt with the sleeves pushed up over his strong brown forearms.

"I've already had one, thank you. But do go ahead, if you want to get yourself a cup."

Ferreira sidled off, an uneasy look on his face.

Bran smiled to himself. People were often so much easier to deal with if you caught them before they'd had their morning fix of caffeine.

When Ferreira returned, after a longer-than-expected gap, he was carrying a heavy wooden chair, hefting the weight with one hand as though it were made of matchsticks. By the look of it, it'd come from the public rooms of the castle, and one of the volunteers was going to be cursing him later when they had nowhere to sit for hours on end.

Sam—rather pointedly—pulled the chair up to the other side of the desk.

"Thank you," Bran said, annoyed. He'd been perfectly prepared to give the man his seat back. For one thing, it would have given him the height advantage to be leaning over Ferreira's shoulder.

Ferreira nodded and left again.

Surrendering to the inevitable, Bran had moved around by the time Ferreira returned with his mug of coffee. Ferreira actually raised an eyebrow, as if he hadn't expected Bran to cede territory.

Bran waited for him to sit down before he pounced. "Now then, Dr. Ferreira, I think we should discuss this broadening of the exhibition you've been planning."

Ferreira visibly squared his shoulders and met Bran's gaze head on. "Sam. You should call me Sam, if we're going to be working together."

Bran nodded. "Sam, then. And I'm Bran, of course." He smiled.

Ferreira—Sam—tensed as though fighting the urge to recoil. Good. It hadn't been intended as a *reassuring* smile.

"Perhaps you could explain to me your rationale for changing exhibits that have already been approved?"

Sam took a drink from his mug before he answered. Typical delaying tactic. "I just think we need to make sure we're really getting under the skin of fourteenth-century people. Visitors need to be able to relate to the characters we're telling them about—that's what fires up the imagination, gets people really interested. And not everyone relates to military strategists."

Bran frowned. "Not everyone has the ability to think strategically, it's true. But chivalry, bravery in battle—that's what captures people's imaginations about the Middle Ages. Tales of knights and their adventures have been popular for centuries. Look at any medium you care to mention—the written word, television, film, even song."

"Knights are part of it, but they're not the only thing worth knowing about. It's fascinating to learn how ordinary people lived in those times, with no technology, nothing but the most rudimentary health care—how did they survive? What did they eat? What did they do for entertainment? That's all part of the story." Sam gestured as he spoke, as if his passion for his subject couldn't be contained in mere words.

Bran felt a moment's kinship with the man, which he struggled to suppress. They were adversaries, not allies, and fellow feeling wouldn't help him win his point. "Hardly the most important part." Who would ever make a movie about King Arthur's *cooks* of the round table, for God's sake?

"Don't just assume that if *you're* not interested in ordinary people, nobody is."

Bran's jaw tightened. Sam was entirely—and no doubt wilfully—missing the point. "This isn't *about* ordinary people. It's the Black Prince exhibition, not the museum of medieval life."

"And you can't get a clear picture of a man without knowing the context he lived in. Those battles he won—it was ordinary people who did most of the fighting. The whole Hundred Years War was a victory for the English archer, and they all came from peasant stock. Those ordinary people you don't think are worth knowing about."

Lulled by Sam's warm, persuasive voice as he was, Bran heartily disliked the tone of the last part. "Are you accusing me of snobbery?"

Sam visibly battled to control himself. "I'm just saying, we need to see the bigger picture."

"Without Edward of Woodstock there would *be* no picture!"

"Come off it. British people would have still lived and died pretty much the same as they always did."

"And as I said before, this is *not* a museum of medieval life. The whole impetus for the exhibition—the whole reason visitors will come to the place—is Edward of Woodstock. The Black Prince. Possibly our greatest-ever military strategist, yet he's a historical figure of whom everyone's heard but nobody knows anything about. It's a crime that people in this country grow up ignorant of his many triumphs—for God's sake, if you asked the man in the street who the Black Prince was, you'd either get a vague, *Oh, was he the prince Robin Hood didn't like?* or a reference to Monty Python! And this, about one of the greatest-ever warriors of our warrior nation."

"Yeah, and that's where you'll find not everyone agrees with you. You may not have noticed, but invading other people's countries gets a bit of a bad press these days."

"You're— You know as well as I do that Edward III had a legitimate claim to the French throne. This is nothing to do with empire and conquest. This is about a king fighting against the regime that disinherited his mother and harried his lands from the sea."

"And again, not everyone agrees with that view. Look, obviously it wasn't right that women were excluded from the French succession, but the Salic Law wasn't something they made up just for Edward's mum. And you can't blame the French for wanting a king who was actually from France, and had their country's best interests at heart."

Bran found himself on his feet, fists clenched. "Neither can you blame a man for fighting for his family's rights and his own country's welfare. You're just espousing revisionism for the sake of it, as if iconoclasm were a worthy aim in its own right."

"Me? You're accusing *me* of trying to overturn accepted thinking? Mate, this is the twenty-first century—for most of us, at any rate. And *you're* the one who's set up a whole bloody exhibition to change how people think about our history."

"Because they're wrong!"

"What, because they don't agree with everything you say? You've got your own little version of history, haven't you? And anyone who disagrees can go screw themselves."

Bran took a convulsive step forward, one fist rising—then caught himself, appalled. He stepped back again, managing not to fall into his chair.

"I need to talk to Roarke. We'll continue this discussion later." Bran strode out of the Portakabin, knowing his retreat to be shameful but desperate for an end to the confrontation before he said—or did—something unforgiveable.

CHAPTER
TWENTY-ONE

S am collapsed into his chair and leaned back, his eyes closed as if he could somehow shut out reality. Christ, what had he been *thinking*? He might as well pack up his stuff now and crawl home to Luton to beg for his old job back. He'd completely lost it with Bran—his *boss*. Had accused him of snobbery and egocentrism and living in the past.

And yeah, it might very well all be true, but Jesus, Ferreira, would a little tact have killed you?

He'd been preparing all weekend to persuade Roscarrock that going along with Sam's plans would be in his own best interests, and more particularly those of the exhibition. He'd had a shedload of reasoned arguments at his fingertips, for God's sake—and they'd all gone straight out of the castle window the minute Bran started in on him. No, earlier—the minute he saw that smug git sitting in his chair.

What was it about Bran bloody Roscarrock that pushed all of Sam's buttons? Did the bastard do that to everyone? Maybe he was just naturally talented at being a dick.

Christ. Sam was going to have to apologise. Bran would just *love* that, wouldn't he? But if it was that or lose his job . . . Sam couldn't afford to lose his job.

Sod it. He needed to go and find the bloke before any irrevocable decisions were made. He ran his hands briskly through his hair, took a gulp of coffee from his neglected mug, and grimaced at the lukewarm temperature. Then he headed out of his Portakabin to do some damage limitation.

He bumped into Jennifer almost literally, not three feet from his door. "I hear—and *hear* would be the operative word; your walls are more than a little on the thin side—that you and Bran are getting along like a house on fire."

Sam scowled. "Yeah, yeah. Rampant destruction, people shouting, imminent death. I get it."

"Rampant, was he?" Jennifer's eyes sparkled with humour, and unwillingly, Sam felt his mood lift.

"If he'd been a unicorn, I'd have been gored to death, believe me. Is he still here? I need to go and tug a forelock or something."

"And now you're just *asking* for the innuendo. I'll spare you this time; it'd be like shooting fish in a barrel. He's in the exhibition centre, or at least that was the view from my window two minutes ago."

"Thanks. You're a lifesaver. Or at least a jobsaver. Any tips for getting on the git's good side?"

"Well, you'll have to locate it first. I gave up trying long ago. But I wouldn't do anything to challenge his authority in front of Mr. Roarke and his chaps, if I were you."

"Got it. No making him look bad in front of the minions."

"I meant, you'd be making yourself rather unpopular. God knows I can't stand the man, but Bran Roscarrock has a long and successful working relationship with Roarke's firm, and he's known to be a good man to work for. Doesn't stand for cutting corners with employees' safety, for instance, and no quibbling about overtime when it's due."

Huh. That didn't exactly fit with the image Sam had formed of Bran as a petty dictator. *Or* what she'd said a moment ago. "Right. I'd better go and catch him," he said, and left.

He found Bran in the exhibition centre just like she'd said. He and the foreman stood together, poring over plans spread over the reception desk. Sam watched them for a moment. From a distance, they could almost have been father and son, with Roarke's grizzled head bent low beside Bran's darker one. Bran used sharp, decisive gestures that were oddly graceful, his face animated, and somehow dominated the scene despite his smaller stature—even when he stopped talking and listened to what Roarke had to say.

Bran was obviously *capable* of having a rational exchange of views. Just not with Sam, apparently. Should he leave them to it? Interrupting now might just get Bran's back up all over again. But then Roarke nodded and rolled up the plans, and Bran took a step away from the desk.

Right. Now or never.

Bran looked surprised to see Sam walking hesitantly over to him. He also looked a lot calmer already, which was a relief, although the animation in his eyes had been replaced by wariness. Sam found himself missing it.

"Mr. Roscarrock." Sam reckoned a bit of formality couldn't hurt. "Might I have a word?"

Bran glanced at Roarke, who was lingering nearby. "Thank you, Mr. Roarke. You can carry on."

He led Sam over to a corner far from any of the workmen.

"I want to apologise," Sam said before Bran could utter a word. "I was out of line."

That, of all things, seemed to throw Bran off-balance. After a moment, the tension seemed to leave his body. Odd, how much younger it made him look. How old must he be, anyway, from what Jory had said? Forty-one? Forty-two? Right now you could knock ten years off that. He'd probably always looked young for his age, and with his relatively short stature, Sam guessed that had been more of a burden than a blessing.

Bran rocked forward on his feet. "I think tempers were high on both sides."

"Yeah. Look, you, uh, surprised me this morning. I didn't express myself well. I really do think broadening the scope of the displays is for the best, if we want the exhibition to be a success. Which I know I do, and I'm sure you do too. And I think you've got the wrong end of the stick about how major the changes I've got in mind will be." Sam paused for breath. "The information boards, for instance. I've got no issues with the text, but it's a bit . . . wordy. We need to get it down to, say, around six hundred words per panel. For most of them that just means cutting it by half."

Bran frowned. "Six hundred words? Cutting it in *half*? How the hell do you expect to explain the Crécy campaign in six hundred words? And why, for God's sake?"

Christ, this was supposed to be the *easy* bit. "Because there's no point having a detailed analysis of the political background and military strategy if ninety percent of your visitors look at it, think 'Too long; don't read,' and walk away. Trust me—it's the first thing I learned at the Museum of Scotland."

"So you're suggesting we throw away all Dr. Banerjee's work." Bran looked as though Sam had just forced him to swallow a rotten oyster.

Sam actually had some sympathy. It'd been a hard lesson for him to learn too, that not everyone was as interested in history as he was. But he wasn't going to back down on this. "We can put the fuller version in a booklet and let people read it at their leisure. So they'll still be taking away something of value, educationally speaking. Look, all the major museums work on this principle."

Bran folded his arms. "What about the other changes you were planning?"

Yeah, Sam hadn't missed the way Bran had failed to actually agree to Sam's proposals. And he had a strong feeling the next bit was going to be even less popular. "Okay, well, it's essential, when seeking to inform the public, that we present a balanced picture," Sam began.

Bran's frown deepened. "It's essential that we present the truth."

"And the truth is a matter of interpretation. You must know that."

"Which is why it's so important that the *correct* interpretation is given."

"There can be more than one valid interpretation—"

"There is, however, only one *truth.*"

It was like banging his head against a brick wall. Sam grabbed at his hair, frustrated beyond belief. "You can't spoon-feed people your version of history and expect them not to spit it right back up again. People don't work like that. If you want someone—*anyone*—to come round to your point of view, you've got to reason with them. Show them the evidence and let them make up their own mind. Otherwise, yeah, people might go away thinking you're right—if they think about it at all, that is, because failing to engage with people's brains makes you and your subject about as memorable as last year's *X Factor* winner— but the first time they come across any conflicting evidence, they're going to think *that's* the gospel truth and your whole argument's a load of bollocks."

He was breathing hard by the time he finished. Didn't Bran see that what he was trying to do would set the exhibition up for failure? For all those journalists they'd invited to the grand opening to give them the worst possible reviews? Did he *want* the place to look like a vanity project?

Bran's face had darkened. "You talk about the visitors as if they're reasonable, intelligent men and women. If history teaches us anything, it's that most people *aren't*. How do we know they're even capable of reasoning to a conclusion? What if they get it wrong?"

By which he meant, come to a different conclusion than Bran clearly had. "Then they get it wrong. What does it matter? Seriously. *What does it matter?*"

"Have you any idea the harm that can be caused by what people think? 'Give a dog a bad name and hang him.' I'm sure you've heard the saying. A man's reputation doesn't just govern how people think about him; it governs how they treat him as well. Or does the phrase *witch hunts* mean nothing to you?"

"Oh, believe me, I know *plenty* about all that." Shit, was that giving too much away? "Growing up brown *and* gay in Luton wasn't always easy. And when the hell did you ever have to worry about anyone treating you bad because of what they thought about you, Mr. White Privilege Poster Boy?"

Bran looked close to apoplexy. "When I was beaten in the street in my own town!"

Oh. Oh crap. How the hell had Sam forgotten about that? And while half of him wanted to snap out *No, that was just what you get for being a total git*, that would have been going too far. "I'm sorry," he said stiffly. "But you have to understand—"

"*You're* the one who doesn't understand. Have you any idea what it's like to be born into a position of responsibility, of duty, and to have to make hard decisions for the good of those who depend on you, only to hear yourself described as brutal, ruthless, and uncaring?"

Were they even talking about the Black Prince anymore?

"When have I ever described you as . . . as all that stuff?" Sam was losing his words. This was *not* a good sign. But Christ, was that really how Bran thought people saw him? Was he right? Sam couldn't imagine living like that.

Except... Sam knew *exactly* what it felt like to be a disappointment to the people around him. It felt like crap. Was this why Bran was so bloody prickly and defensive all the time? Because he was used to people thinking the worst of him?

"You seemed perfectly willing to ascribe any number of other vices to me, so I'm sure it's simply a matter of time." Bran drew in a deep breath, and now that Sam was looking for it, he could see the hurt in those dark eyes. He wasn't sure it made him *like* the git any better, but he couldn't help feeling sympathy for him. No wonder the bloke idolised a much-maligned military hero.

Bran turned his face away from Sam's scrutiny. "This discussion is going nowhere."

"*Finally* something we agree on." Oh Jesus. Sam made a superhuman effort to get himself under control. "Look, why don't I prepare a detailed list of the changes I'm suggesting, and you can go through them and see if there's any you'd actually be happy with?"

Maybe he'd see the issues more clearly once they were set out in black and white, although Sam wasn't going to hold his breath.

Bran gave him a long look, then nodded curtly.

"Right. I'll get onto that." Sam hesitated a moment—why, he wasn't sure—then turned on his heel and strode back towards the castle.

By five o'clock, Sam had something more-or-less fit to send to Bran: all his proposed changes detailed, together with his best arguments in their favour. The ones that increased inclusion and diversity, he was fairly confident about. The ones that simply sought to show a more balanced picture of Edward of Woodstock . . . well, he'd just have to see how those went down, wouldn't he? There were only so many times he could repeat the same line of reasoning.

Sam composed the email, attached the document . . . then decided to sleep on it. He doubted Bran would be expecting his report so soon, and if he didn't send it until tomorrow, that'd at least hold off another early-morning ambush. Trust Bran to make sure he had keys to the Portakabin so he could poke his nose in whenever he wanted.

Sam hoped coming out to Bran hadn't been a bad idea. He'd panicked, worried that admitting to being the target of a witch hunt might've led Bran to do a bit of digging and maybe find out about the Edinburgh fiasco. Being gay had been the quickest alternative explanation he'd been able to come up with on the fly—but would it just make Bran even less likely to listen to him? After what Mal had said about the bloke . . .

Sod it. What was done was done. And Sam wasn't planning to live in a closet, so Bran would've found out sooner or later anyhow.

Needing some air after all that, instead of heading for the car park when he left the castle, Sam took the clifftop footpath that skirted the castle walls. He followed the jagged coastline around the headland. Presumably it kept going, and would eventually meet up with the path he'd taken in the opposite direction on his first day. It had been a cloudy day, but dry, and now the skies were clearing to show ever-expanding patches of blue. Sam could follow the shadows of the clouds with his gaze as they swept across the endless sea, changing its colour from brilliant blue to smoky aqua and back again. In a few hours the colours would be even more striking. Sam had always loved early evening walks in Edinburgh, the warming light turning greenery to emerald and beige stone to gold.

For a moment he missed the place fiercely, savagely—far more than he ever had during those numb days back in Luton. But what had he left there, really? A university embarrassed by him, and a lover who'd abandoned him to the wolves.

No. It was good that he'd come to Porthkennack. Here, he could make a fresh start. Be a new man.

The breeze ruffled Sam's hair, as though a giant hand were combing through it, and he stood facing the wind for a moment, letting it buffet his body. An elderly couple in precautionary pac-a-macs ambled towards him. "This'll blow the cobwebs away," the lady said cheerfully as they passed.

Yeah. Maybe it would, at that. Sam smiled and walked on. As he rounded the headland, the lighthouse came into view, reminding him he'd planned to pay it a visit. It didn't look too far away. Maybe he should seize the moment?

As he hesitated, his phone chirped. He thumbed it on to check the notifications, and wished he hadn't. Another text from the debt collectors. His stomach lurched, and he deleted it with a curse. He was going to pay the money he owed. It was just going to take time, that was all. Why couldn't they leave him alone for now?

His walk soured, Sam turned and headed back to his car.

Sam wasn't sure who to expect at home when he got back to Jory's house. It was half-term holidays this week, so Jory wasn't working, but he'd been planning to spend the day with Gawen. They could be anywhere and Mal might be with them, or might not. Half-term was a busy week for him, so he could even have stayed late at the museum.

Turned out, though, that they were all at Jory's. When Sam walked in, he found Gawen sitting on the floor feeding a cut-up apple to Pansy, or possibly Millie—Sam had no idea how Mal told those two apart; like Neville and Myrtle, their black and white markings were so identical they could have been photocopies—while Mal, also on the floor, told him some story that involved extravagant gestures. Some of them were hampered by Neville, who was using Mal as a climbing frame again. Unless it was Myrtle this time.

Jory was on the sofa with a large stack of exercise books, which he was ignoring in favour of a battered paperback that was thicker than the average brick.

"Good book?" Sam asked.

"Not bad," Jory said, with a glance at his son. "It's Gawen's. *The Gormenghast Trilogy.*"

Gawen looked up with owlish enthusiasm. "It's really good. Uncle Bran gave it to me. I'm onto the second book now. I like Steerpike the best. Have you read it?"

Sam felt obscurely bad about letting the kid down. "Uh, no, sorry. Think I saw a bit of it on TV years ago."

"It's been on TV? Can I watch it, Dad?"

Jory smiled. "What do I always say?"

"*Read the book first.*" Gawen gave a classic teenage eye roll. "But after I've finished it, can I watch it?"

"If we can find it. You might be disappointed, though. I'm pretty sure the TV adaptation is older than you are, and some of these things date badly."

"Hey, I remember that," Mal threw in. "That's the one with the weird twins in, right? Maybe that's why your uncle likes it so much." He raised an eyebrow at Sam.

Jory frowned at him.

Gawen nodded, oblivious. "Cora and Clarice. They're silly. They don't really do much."

"It's all about power, really." Jory got up and stretched. "Now, who's hungry?"

"Depends." Sam flopped down on the sofa. "If I say I am, do I get volunteered to cook?"

"Nope." Mal grinned. "JJ's cooking, aren't you, mate?"

Gawen scrambled to his feet. "We're having pizza! Come on, Dad." He grabbed Jory by the arm and dragged him in the direction of the kitchen.

"Pizza's great," Sam called after them. "But for the love of God, put the rat down and wash your hands before you start handling food!"

Kirsty picked Gawen up around nine o'clock. Sam felt bad on realising that if he hadn't been monopolising the spare room, Gawen might well have stayed over. Maybe he should think about finding his own place after all.

He was surprised when, after flinging his arms around Jory and Mal in turn, Gawen gave Sam a goodbye hug too.

"He's a good kid," he found himself saying after they'd waved him off.

Jory smiled. "He's the best. Kirsty's done a great job with him."

"Are you seeing him tomorrow?"

"No, actually Bran's taking him out for the day. To the Eden project. He's been before, of course, but he likes going again. I thought Bran would want to cancel, what with everything, but he's insisting on carrying on as normal."

Sam felt a heady rush of relief. A whole day, Bran-free. He'd actually be able to get some work done tomorrow. "That's that biodome thing, right? With the different environments and that? Is it worth a visit, then?"

Jory shrugged and looked sheepish. "I've never actually been. It's always Bran who takes him."

"Likes his educational visits, Bran does," Mal put in. "He's taken him to the space centre too—long trip, that, from here."

"So he's quite involved, as an uncle, is he?" Sam asked, intrigued by the thought of Bran interacting with kids. Did he wear a suit when they went on day trips? Sam couldn't imagine him in anything less formal.

Mal rolled his eyes. "JJ's his *heir*, ain't he? Course he's involved. Wants to make sure he turns out all right before he hands over the family fortune."

Maybe, but Sam was pretty sure expensive—and lengthy—trips to places that caught Gawen's interest didn't have to be part of that. It was starting to sound like Kirsty wasn't the only one who'd done a good job with Gawen.

While they were on the subject of Bran . . . Sam coughed. "Just to warn you, Bran and I locked horns a couple of times today."

"Okay, now that's gonna haunt me." Mal cackled. "Good, was it? You, getting horny with Bran?"

Jory winced.

"In a word . . ." Sam closed his eyes. "There are no words. No polite ones, anyhow. But we finished up more or less civil to each other," he added, seeing Jory's worried frown.

"Is this just what Jennifer was saying about historians always arguing, or is it more serious than that?"

Sam hesitated. "Uh . . . there might be something of a personality clash going on too. But I'm working on it."

"Are you sure it's okay? I don't like to think I've landed you in a toxic working environment."

"It's fine. We'll be fine."

CHAPTER
TWENTY-TWO

"It's not good, I'm afraid." Constable Peters gave Bran a sympathetic look. "Without CCTV, or any witnesses, we haven't been able to make any progress. I can tell you there haven't been any similar attacks in Porthkennack since then."

He'd arranged to meet her for a coffee in town on Wednesday, directly after his appointment with his doctor, who had reluctantly agreed that Bran's ribs appeared to be healing well, listened to his lungs, and told him to keep up the physio with an air of not believing he'd been doing any in the first place. It was entirely uncalled for. Bran had been doing his breathing exercises religiously—this time.

They were sitting inside the Seven Stars tea room, the constable nursing a mint tea and Bran a thick, sweet Turkish coffee. Normally he'd have kept things more formal and arranged a meeting at the police station, but it didn't seem necessary with Sally Peters. Besides, he'd always enjoyed coming to the tea room, with its intricately patterned tiled walls, cosmopolitan atmosphere, and reassuringly high prices. And their pistachio baklava was excellent.

Bran sipped his coffee and returned his thoughts to the matter at hand. "You mean there have been no street thefts where a similar level of violence was used?" He disliked describing the attack as a "mugging" for reasons he didn't care to examine.

She nodded.

"So it was definitely personal." Bran took a bite of baklava, hoping it would ease the hollow feeling inside him.

"Not necessarily—your attacker may be keeping his head down, or he may only have been passing through. And although your injuries were consistent with a grudge being involved, if you refused to hand over your wallet when threatened, that might have been enough to anger an already keyed-up, possibly intoxicated assailant." She met his gaze. "Do you think it's likely you would have done that?"

Bran couldn't imagine anything *less* likely. The loss of a wallet, weighed against the chance of serious injury? There was no contest. He'd have expended his effort on memorising the mugger's appearance for the later use of the authorities, not on futile resistance that might get him killed. Much as he disliked admitting it, there were few men who didn't have a height and weight advantage on him. "No. It's most unlikely."

"Hm. Please don't take this as implying you were to blame for the attack, because it's not, but do you think you might have said something to anger your attacker?"

Bran narrowed his eyes. "Such as?"

"Well, it would be natural to be indignant at someone demanding cash you'd worked hard for. A lot of people might be tempted to say something like, 'Go get a job instead of stealing from decent people.'"

"I might have thought it, but I doubt I'd be such an idiot as to antagonise someone who was already threatening me with violence. Why?"

"Some of the people I've spoken to about the case seem to think you can be . . . They seemed pretty certain you're not one to take any infringement of your rights lying down."

Which had, in fact, been what he'd done. Literally. Bran wondered just who these people had been—Jago Andrewartha? Gerren Ede's nearest and dearest?—and what had been the description of him she'd shied away from repeating. Abrasive? Abusive? Egomaniac? He swallowed. "I've never believed in weakness being a virtue. But in any case, this is academic. As I've told you, I have no recollection of the attack, so I can't tell you how I behaved." It was still a black hole in his memory—not even that, in fact. Simply an absence of time.

She sighed. "In a case like this, there's really not a lot we can do without either hard evidence or anyone willing to talk to us."

"I realise you're doing your best."

Sally cocked her head. "You know, when I first met you, I was sure you were going to be the sort that's all 'This isn't good enough, what do I pay my taxes for?' and 'I shall be speaking to your superior.' Funny how first impressions can deceive." She finished her baklava and licked her fingers, then sent him a mock-challenging look. "I know, terrible manners. Where's a moist lemon-scented towelette when you need one?"

Bran smiled despite himself. "They are rather sticky, aren't they?"

"Good, though. I can't believe I've never been to this place before." Her smile faded. "Did you have any further ideas about who might have attacked you?"

"No. Nothing I haven't already told you." He stared at his plate, which was regrettably empty.

"Don't forget there are resources to help you get through this."

Bran knew that, of course. Various schemes and services, all with the word *Victim* prominent in their titles. He'd taken one look at the government website she'd directed him to and vowed never to seek it out again. "Thank you," he said, because she meant well.

Sam's report on his proposed changes to the exhibition had come through while Bran was out with Sally Peters. Bran ate a quick lunch, then downloaded the document and went through it carefully.

It turned out to be less problematic than he'd expected. Sam had laid out his reasons for each of the changes or additions he'd planned, supporting them with statistics wherever he could. He'd even included links to his source material. It was sobering to realise how much Bran's own unconscious biases had influenced his view of, for example, the diversity included in the exhibition. Had the representation of women really been as low as Sam claimed? Yes, it had—the figures Sam quoted couldn't be argued with.

Bran recalled, on a number of occasions, telling Dr. Banerjee in no uncertain terms not to bother with "unimportant" aspects of history. She'd fought him on some points and caved on others, but he'd always won in the end. He hadn't realised it had resulted in the exhibition becoming so . . . male-centric.

Had Dr. Banerjee ever mentioned it? She'd certainly never set things out in black and white like this. Never explained things. And when they'd clashed, she'd always dragged in Jennifer Solomon to back her up, which had had Bran closing his ears to her arguments before they'd even started. He was quite aware Dr. Solomon both disliked him personally and despised him as a dilettante in her chosen field—which was totally unfair; he might not have a PhD in history, but he'd read extensively about the Black Prince over the years.

Bran swallowed. He'd allowed personal feelings to overcome his judgement—again. He could hear Father's voice in his head, berating him and repeating that business should *never* be tainted by emotion. But this exhibition wasn't simply a business matter.

This was *important*.

Increasing the representation of women necessarily involved including the lives of ordinary, noncombatant people, which was the only reason Bran had opposed it. At least, he hoped it was. He was starting to second-guess himself now, and horrified to think that feeling ganged up on by the two women had made him not only defensive but also petty.

He was starting to think he owed Dr. Banerjee an apology. Possibly Dr. Solomon as well, although in her case the words would probably choke him.

Sam, instead of trying to browbeat him as Bran had expected, had set out a reasoned argument. Bran's accusations turned out to have been embarrassingly unfounded: Sam wasn't proposing changes for the sake of it. He'd tied everything in to the military campaigns—not just showing how higher taxation to pay for war affected the poor, but also how that in turn affected support for King Edward and his son the Black Prince. No wonder Sam had had the courage of his convictions to stand up to Bran. He'd behaved professionally throughout—until Bran had managed to insult him beyond bearing.

Bran was left with the shamed realisation that he'd flown off the handle for no reason at all, and not only alienated his curator but also given him a lot of unnecessary extra work to do.

He'd been trying not to think about Sam's casual admission that he was gay. Should Bran have known? There was nothing camp about him, which had been Father's preferred way of telling if someone were gay. Bran snorted. He'd never found it to be a particularly reliable indicator. One of the campest men of his acquaintance was currently divorcing his wife so he could marry his mistress—again.

Bran wondered if Sam was seeing someone. He seemed far too good-looking, with his merry eyes and full, sensual lips, not to mention intelligent and engaging, to be single. Would Bran be forced to make small talk when some long-distance boyfriend—probably equally highly educated, with more letters after his name than were in it—arrived for a visit? Or did Sam prefer to keep things casual, choosing hookups over relationships?

But it was none of Bran's business what Sam did in his spare time, and it didn't change anything—why should it? Just because they shared a preference for men didn't mean Sam and he were about to become best friends. Still, Bran regretted his outburst.

Until, that was, he reached the section on the Siege of Limoges.

CHAPTER
TWENTY-THREE

S am half expected to be collared by Bran first thing Wednesday morning, demanding to know why he hadn't received Sam's . . . report, defence of his position, whatever, yet. He'd chickened out of emailing it Tuesday afternoon, telling himself the bloke would've had a long day, traipsing around the biodomes with a kid, so he was really doing Bran a favour by not giving him any reason to spend the evening on work.

The fact that not sending it until Wednesday morning would stave off any blowups at least until Sam had had his morning coffee was just an added bonus, that was all.

Yeah, right.

In fact, Bran didn't seem to be at the castle at all. Well, it wasn't like the exhibition was *his* full-time job. Sam supposed Bran must be off . . . doing whatever he did to make shedloads of money turn into bigger shedloads of money. Warehouse-loads, maybe. Aircraft hangars full. Well, he wasn't going to look that gift horse in the mouth. Sam clicked Send on the report and then got on with his work, sorting out some correspondence and talking to the caterers for the grand opening.

Late in the afternoon, Sam was walking past the castle's visitor centre, on his way back to his Portakabin with a cup of tea, when Bran appeared. Sam gave him an automatic smile of greeting, but it was met with the darkest look Sam had ever received.

Bran's voice was icy cold. "I have to question why you think yourself suitable to curate this exhibition. As I find you subscribe to the view that Edward of Woodstock was a mass murderer."

Christ. So they were back to daggers drawn, were they? It was *on*. "Excuse me, where in that report I sent you does it say anything like that?"

"Does the Siege of Limoges ring any bells?"

Yeah, he'd had a bad feeling about that bit. Not that he'd change a word of it. "*Nowhere* do I say he was guilty of massacre." Sam tamped down his temper. "If we're going to have this discussion, we're going inside."

"Don't split hairs." Bran followed him into the Portakabin and shut the door with a slam that shook the whole structure. "Your proposed display repeats the slander that he was a mass murderer—and you even link it to him becoming known as the Black Prince."

Sam managed not to slop his tea as he put it down on his desk. "I'm not slandering anyone! I said it's been *suggested* that's why he was called the Black Prince, that's all. I simply present the conflicting historical records. Froissart said he killed the entire population of Limoges after the siege; Edward himself said he didn't. It's not cut-and-dried. We have these reports passed down to us—we can't just ignore them. It's important for context, for the complete picture—"

"'Complete picture'? Complete fabrication, more like." Bran made a wild, angry gesture, his dark eyes flashing. "You call Froissart a reliable source? And massacring the entire population of a city wouldn't even make *sense*. It wouldn't be a stamp of his authority on the citizens of Limoges—it would have been seen as an admission that he *had* no authority over them."

"Oh, and people never do stuff for daft reasons, do they? Edward of Woodstock was ill. His mum had just died, and the Bishop of Limoges—one of his best mates—gave the place up to the French without a fight. You're telling me it's beyond the bounds of possibility that he lost it and lashed out? Seriously?" Sam's fists clenched so tightly they ached, but it was better than what they really wanted to do—grab hold of Bran and shake some sense into him.

The worst of it was, they ought to be on the same side. Sam didn't even *believe* the Black Prince had killed all those civilians, but Bran's refusal to allow any other point of view made him see red. Couldn't he see there was a place for sticking rigidly to your guns, and historical debate wasn't it? "We can't just ignore all the people throughout history who've assumed that's why he's called the Black Prince. Do I like people equating *black* with *bad*? Fuck, no. But it happens a hell of a lot, even now. Six hundred years ago? How many people do you think even thought to question it?"

"And yet you're happy to perpetuate it?"

"Oh, for— What the hell am I supposed to do? Pretend it never happened? It's part of history. *Black heart, black magic, the devil's not as black as he's painted*—people say all kinds of crap linking black and bad even in this day and age. You can't tackle an issue if you refuse to admit it exists."

"We don't have to admit it—the whole point is that it's what people already assume."

"So we tackle it head-on. Denial doesn't solve anything, and it never has. You're like one of those bastards who go around spouting homophobic bollocks who turn out to be so far in the closet they're covered in bloody mothballs!"

Bran took a step back, looking like Sam had punched him in the gut.

Sam stared, his anger draining away. "Seriously?"

"That has *nothing* to do with the subject under discussion." Bran's voice was ragged, and he'd gone so bloody pale he was almost grey.

Sam couldn't bring himself to twist the knife further, even if the bloke was a total dick. He tried to make his tone conciliatory. "Look, what I think about the Black Prince has nothing to do with him being called *black*. It's about what he did."

Bran swallowed, and when he spoke again, his voice was stronger. "Waged successful campaigns to protect English interests from the age of sixteen? I fail to see what's so despicable about that."

No, because you've got your head so far up your own arse you could lick your tonsils. Sam didn't say it, because he didn't kick a bloke when he was down. "You can't ignore the human cost. The Black Prince rampaged through France, pillaging what he could take and burning the rest. Thousands must have starved as a direct result. Chivalry, my arse. It just meant they treated anyone with a title like they were all mates and this was just a friendly game of cricket, and the common peasants—the mums and dads and brothers and sisters of those very bowmen who won the battles of Crécy and Agincourt for England—got shafted. Why do you think the peasants eventually revolted under Richard II? When people react with violence, it's usually for a reason. You can only kick a dog for so long before it turns and bites you."

Bran's face darkened again, as if he was a hair's breadth from reacting with violence himself, and oh *crap*. Had Sam just implied it was Bran's own fault he'd got mugged? "Are you suggesting—"

"Have you two murdered each other yet?" Jennifer Solomon's dry tones cleaved the atmosphere like a broadsword slicing through armour.

Sam whirled.

"You do realise you're scaring the staff, don't you?" Jennifer continued. "We'll have no volunteers left come summer if you two don't kiss and make up." Bran startled, and her eyes narrowed. "Figuratively speaking, of course," she added with unnecessary archness.

"This is ridiculous," Bran snapped, and strode away from them both, his footsteps echoing on the stone floor.

There was a silence.

"That didn't go very well," Jennifer said at last.

"No." Sam cleared his throat. Had she heard what he'd said to Bran? Selfishly, he hoped she hadn't. "No, it didn't."

She sighed. "I'm asking you, Sam, as the reasonable one, to make an effort. If you can't manage a peace treaty, then a cease-fire would be acceptable. Nobody likes working in a war zone."

"I'll try. He just..." Sam threw up his hands in frustration. "It's like he's a keg of gunpowder, and I'm a spark. Or the other way around."

"Or he's a festering boil, and you're the doctor's scalpel?"

"Yeah, thanks for that image. Really, thanks. Christ, what a shit-storm." Sam grimaced.

"I wouldn't mind, but the man's not even a historian. He's just read a few books and now thinks he knows all there is to know about the subject."

Okay, that seemed a little unfair. Bran might be pigheaded on interpretation, but from what Sam had seen, he knew his facts inside out. "He was okay with some of the changes, though. He didn't say a word against the ones intended to balance out the gender ratio."

She snorted. "And if *that's* not bloody typical, I don't know what is."

"I thought you'd be pleased."

"Oh, I am. Just frustrated to find it apparently takes a *man* to get through to him."

Sam winced. "Sorry?"

"Don't worry about it. *You* can't help it, after all." She left, then, leaving Sam in an office that seemed too quiet, even with the echoes of the argument still bouncing around the walls.

Was Jennifer right? Had Bran listened to him, and not her and Dr. Banerjee, because Sam was a guy? Sam found he didn't want to think it was true. Bran was . . . Okay, he was a dick about some issues connected with the Black Prince, but that was because he cared so much. He'd been pretty reasonable about other things, once they were explained to him. Of course, the trick was getting the bloke to climb off his high horse and hear the explanation in the first place.

And what about that lucky guess he'd made earlier about Bran being a closet case? From Bran's reaction, Sam had hit the nail right on the head. If that was true, if Bran was gay, did it change anything? Being gay didn't make him any less of a git, but Sam couldn't help feeling some kind of kinship with the bloke.

Whether Bran would see it the same way, though, was a whole other matter. Sam had yet to see one single sign that the bloke actually liked him.

Sam laughed out loud as a ridiculous thought hit him. Did Bran maybe *like* like him? Was all this business of getting on Sam's case about the exhibition just a grown-up version of pigtail-pulling? Okay, not *that* grown-up. But he'd jumped a mile when Jennifer told them to kiss and make up . . . Sam shook his head ruefully. All these arguments must really be getting to him. The options were (a) Bran was a dick and (b) Bran fancied him.

No sane person was going to pick (b).

CHAPTER
TWENTY-FOUR

Oh God. Bran had had to get away.
You can only kick a dog for so long . . .
Was that why Bran had been attacked? He'd known certain of his business practices had made him less than popular with tenants, but he'd always prided himself upon sticking to his guns and never letting anyone take advantage of him. If he hadn't managed his business with an iron hand, he wouldn't have been able to invest in the Black Prince exhibition centre, which would benefit tourism, bring more jobs to the area . . .
You can't ignore the human cost.
The Edes had acted like he was some kind of monster, accusing him of turning them out of their home before its official tenant was cold in his grave. But Bran had thought his actions, at the time, entirely reasonable. He'd needed to get the house up to scratch for the next tenant, and the contractor had been adamant they had to start work straight away. And it was *his* house, damn it.
But then, that was only because of an accident of birth, wasn't it? The same kind of accident that made some men kings and some commoners. Oh, he'd added plenty to the family fortunes over the years—but it wasn't like he'd had to start from scratch. Perhaps he could have behaved with more compassion. The Edes had just lost a family member who, by all accounts, had been well loved.
His hand ghosted over his still-painful ribs. Was that what the attack had been? Retribution for perceived oppression? It wasn't a new thought, of course. He'd wondered from the start if the Edes, so vocal in their righteous outrage at his actions, had something to do with the attack. But for the first time he found himself wondering: had he deserved it?

No. No, that was absurd. He was in the right, legally speaking, and they were in the wrong. Completely.

And yet . . .

Bran swallowed. He'd found it almost physically painful to listen to Sam's passionate tirade on why Edward of Woodstock was not, in his view, wholly admirable. Could he bear it if that fierce judgement were to be turned on him, Branok Roscarrock? Could he stand to listen to his own failings, listed in that voice, coming from those lips? From that man? It would be a damning list, he knew.

Father would have been so disappointed in him.

Bran wished he'd never met Sam Ferreira. What gave Sam such power over him? Was it that he saw in Sam what he'd struggled so hard to deal with in himself?

So far in the closet you're covered in mothballs?

Shame tightened his chest, and he *hated* Sam, Jory, and all the rest of them for not feeling like he did. How could they be so easy in their skin, be out and proud? All his life, Bran had lived swamped by the certainty of how bitterly disappointed Father would have been to know his eldest son was a homosexual. He'd told himself it didn't matter, so long as nobody knew. And now Sam had guessed his secret on a few days' acquaintance, and tossed it out as casually as he might a used tissue. It only made it worse that Sam was so bloody good-looking, with his *hair* and his *smile* and those strong arms . . . Bran had tried not to notice, had tried to ignore his attraction to the man. He'd told himself it was merely physical, a bodily urge he could easily overcome. But it wasn't just that. Sam was confident in himself, passionate, and principled. And he quite clearly thought Bran no better than some oppressive tyrant who'd deserved all he'd got at the hands of his attacker.

Bran couldn't bear it. God help him, he wanted Sam to think well of him.

Bran didn't go near the castle for the rest of the week. With his now-reduced workload, he found himself with too much time on his hands. Time to think about what a mess he'd made of things.

He even found himself considering responding to Craig's calls. What harm could it do now? Apparently it was obvious to anyone with half a brain that Bran was as queer as they came, so why not give in to what Craig wanted? Live openly in a relationship with a man? Craig was good-looking enough, intelligent enough, good enough company.

Bran wasn't sure he wanted *enough*. But he was clearly never going to get what he suspected he *did* want, so why not make the best of a bad job? At least . . . at least Craig wanted him. And they'd had some good times together. Mostly in bed, it was true, but there had also been quiet dinners together. Nights at the theatre. Bran had been content with his life, back then, hadn't he?

He missed that feeling with an ache in his chest wholly unlike the pains his ribs were causing him. What was the point in suffering, when . . . if not happiness, then perhaps contentment, was there for the taking? Who knew how long he would have left in this world?

But how would Bea react to him living openly as a gay man? He shied away from the thought of asking her, fearing he knew all too well what she'd say. After all, she'd been brought up with their father's principles as much as he had, and she certainly wasn't on good terms with her other gay brother. Bran's resolve faltered at the thought of becoming estranged from her—but then again, things had been strained between them lately in any case, although he wasn't sure why. Perhaps she'd be pleased if he consulted her beforehand?

Equally possibly, though, she might be appalled. No, best to present her with a fait accompli. She would be practical, then. Would work out a way to counter any disadvantage to the family interests.

Bran's phone had crept into his hand without his conscious awareness. It would be so easy to bring up Craig's number and dial—

The phone rang, startling him so much he almost dropped it. He got a grip on himself, and frowned at the display before accepting the call.

"Kirsty? Is everything all right?"

"Everything's fine. I was just calling to ask a favour. You know I wouldn't normally, but you said you had more time to yourself now, so . . ." He heard her intake of breath. "Could you have Gawen on

Friday? It's just, Euan and I were hoping to, um, crack on with the sculpture, and it turns out Jory's already made other arrangements."

Apparently the thing with Euan was serious. Bran didn't believe for one moment this was about the sculpture. Reading between the lines, a week during school holidays with Kirsty's child by another man was becoming a little too much for Euan. Although possibly Bran was being uncharitable. "I'd love to have him. He was talking on Tuesday about the Lobster Hatchery in Padstow—apparently one of his friends went a while back—so I could take him there."

"Thanks, Bran. You're the best."

"I'll pick him up at nine." Bran decided to dig a little. "Euan's job has flexible hours, does it?"

"Oh—he's, um, not working at the moment."

"At least he has plenty of time to model for you, then."

"Yeah. Look, cheers again. I'll see you on Friday."

"I'll look forward to it."

Actually Bran was looking forward to getting to meet this Euan and finding out for himself about the man's intentions towards Kirsty and, more importantly, his attitude towards Gawen. But when he got to Kirsty's house on the dot of nine on Friday morning, Gawen was waiting by the open front door, shoes on his feet and his small backpack full of whatever odds and ends he felt necessary to make it through a day away from home. Bran barely got to say two words to Kirsty, let alone meet Euan.

Ah, well. It would keep. Meanwhile, he had a nephew to entertain.

He hadn't called Craig. It hadn't seemed necessary after all.

CHAPTER
TWENTY-FIVE

S am didn't see Bran Roscarrock for the rest of the week. He wasn't sure how he felt about that. Relieved, obviously, because it made it a hell of a lot easier to get stuff done. Wary, because it was only a temporary stay of execution. And . . . yeah, if he was honest, guilty too. Sam hadn't meant to victim-blame Bran for being attacked, but he had a nasty feeling Bran had taken it that way. The bloke clearly had his reasons for keeping quiet about his sexuality, and Sam had dragged it right out into the open. Even if he hadn't meant to do that either.

It hadn't exactly been his finest hour.

He found out on Saturday that he needn't have worried about Bran turning up on Friday. Gawen came over for the day, full of excitement and bearing pictures on his phone of the lobster he'd adopted the day before—or rather, the lobster that Bran had paid for him to adopt. Seriously, a lobster? Maybe it was some kind of competition with Mal to find the least cuddly animals to fall in love with.

Gawen was a great kid, but Sam couldn't help feeling like an outsider with him here. Mal, Jory, and Gawen were family, and Sam . . . wasn't.

"Guess I'd better be looking for a place of my own," he said self-consciously as they ate lunch together. "Get out of your hair."

"Nah, more the merrier, innit, JJ?" Mal nudged Gawen in the ribs and made him giggle in the middle of a mouthful of beans on toast.

"You'll give him hiccups," Jory said. "You know how ticklish he is. And Sam? I said you're welcome to stay as long as you want to, and I meant it. It's only been two weeks."

Mal nodded. "Yeah, dude, when we're sick of the sight of you, you'll know it. No more invites to meals, rat turds in your shoes . . ."

Gawen giggled again, and Sam laughed too, but he couldn't help feeling he was taking advantage of their kindness.

Trouble was . . . could he afford to move out? He still hadn't had his first paycheque from the exhibition job, so his bank account was looking sorrier than ever. And the way things were going at work, could he really count on the job lasting?

Sam felt better about himself after spending Saturday afternoon working in the garden with Jory, Mal, and Gawen. They'd cleared a decent amount of the overgrown shrubs and bushes, including a huge tangle of self-seeded brambles, and could actually see the fence on the right-hand side now. Sam's back was aching, his fingers were stained, and he was bleeding from dozens of encounters with thorns that hadn't given up without a fight. Finally, he felt like he was earning his keep at least a little bit.

He didn't check his phone until after they'd had dinner, and when he did, it wasn't encouraging. More messages from the numbers he didn't want to hear from, and another missed call from Mum. She'd left a message too. Sam gritted his teeth and dialled his voice mail. What if something had happened to one of his sisters? Or their kids? No—if that were the case, it wouldn't just be Mum calling him. Still, he held his breath as he listened to the message.

All it said, in his mum's lightly accented tones, was, "Alessandro, will you call me, please?"

Okay. This was bad. Mum only called him his full name when he was in trouble. Although in another way, it was good. If it were a family emergency, he'd have been *Sam*, and she'd have said to call her *now*.

Sod it. He probably *should* call now. She wasn't going to get less pissed off about whatever it was for Sam putting it off.

Knowing he'd put it off indefinitely if he didn't get on with it, he dialled the number.

He had to hang on for six or seven rings. She always left her phone on the table by her favourite armchair so she'd be able to reach it without getting up. But she was never *in* her armchair—at least, not until late in the evening, when she'd sit down to watch *Coronation Street* on catch-up and fall asleep in minutes. Seven rings meant she'd probably been in one of the bedrooms, maybe changing the sheets. She usually did that at the weekend.

"Sam?" She never trusted the phone to correctly tell her who was calling.

"Yeah, it's me, Mum. You all right?"

"I'm fine. Is your new job going well? I was hoping to hear from you sooner."

"Sorry. I've been really busy. Been helping Jory and Mal do up the house—got to pay them back for letting me stay here."

"You shouldn't impose on them too long." Mum had strong views on the difference between friends and family, and what you could expect from each. "Will you be getting your own place soon?"

"Uh, soon, yeah."

"Make sure you give me your address as soon as you do." She paused. "I had a call from someone the other day who was trying to get in touch with you."

"You didn't tell them where I'm living now, did you?" Sam couldn't keep the worry out of his voice. The last thing he needed was his problems following him here to harass his mates.

"No. I didn't like the sound of him, so I just said I'd pass on the message. Sam, are you in some kind of trouble?"

"No, course not. It's just . . . It's probably something to do with my last job. Uh, in Edinburgh, I mean."

"The man didn't sound Scottish."

"Yeah, but neither did I when I worked there."

"I suppose not." She gave him the name and number and, yeah, it wasn't anyone he wanted to hear from right now.

"Thanks, Mum. I'll give him a ring and sort it out." Like hell he would. Why couldn't they give him more time? He was going to pay it back, all of it. But he just didn't have that kind of money right now.

And damn it, if he kept clashing with Bran, he might never have it.

"You know you can tell me if you're in trouble," Mum said, still sounding concerned.

"I'm fine!" He didn't mean to snap—but no, he really couldn't tell her. Mum was all about "Neither a borrower nor a lender be." She was so proud of the fact that she'd never been in debt in her life, even after Sam's dad had died and things had been really tough. How could he possibly tell her he'd run up debts in the thousands from playing stupid games online?

Everything was pressing in on him, suffocating him. "Sorry, Mum—think I heard Jory calling me. I've got to go. You look after yourself, all right?"

"You too."

Sam hung up, and then pasted on a smile to go and join the others in the living room.

On Sunday, Sam, Mal, and Jory went over to the Sea Bell for lunch. Mal was friends with one of the barmaids there, Tasha, and Sam found her fun and easy to talk to. They'd been chatting for ages before he found out she was actually sort of family for Jory and Bran—she and Dev Thompson were foster siblings. Which made her Bran's niece, in a sense, what with Dev being Bea's biological son.

Sam wondered if Bran would see it that way, and if they'd ever met—but no, they couldn't have, could they? From what he'd heard, Bea Roscarrock wanted nothing to do with Dev, so Bran probably never saw him either. And apparently the Sea Bell's landlord had some sort of grudge against Bran, so it wasn't likely he ever drank here.

Sam was introduced to Tasha's dreadlocked girlfriend, Ceri, who called the landlord Uncle Jago but apparently wasn't exactly related. There seemed to be a lot of that about. She had clear white skin, a bunch of piercings, and the scariest resting bitch-face Sam had ever seen, and turned out to be just visiting from Newquay, where she was at college doing something to do with catering.

Ceri hung around through lunchtime and then kissed Tasha goodbye right there in the public bar. And not just a peck on the cheek, either. It was a full-on clinch and ended with lingering looks on both sides. None of the old men propping up the bar batted an eyelid, although a lad so fresh-faced he must have been in here to celebrate his eighteenth birthday pursed his lips like he was about to wolf-whistle and then thought better of it. Sam followed the kid's red-faced gaze to the landlord's granite stare.

"Never thought they'd be so tolerant round here," Sam said in a low voice to Jory.

It was Mal who answered. "What, cos we're in the back of beyond, where men are men and sheep don't go nowhere without half a dozen mates and a can of pepper spray? Nah, this lot are all right. And they seen it all before. Ceri comes over most weekends."

Sam grinned. "So they'd be all right with it if you and Jory ever had a snog in here? Or is it different for blokes?"

"I don't want to push my luck." Jory gave him a wry look. "They *seem* to have forgiven me for being a Roscarrock, but grudges run deep in these parts."

"Yeah, but Jago *lurves* me," Mal said smugly.

Sam raised an eyebrow. "Does Jory need to be jealous?"

"Nah, but I used to live here, didn't I? When I first came to Porthkennack." Mal ran a hand through his hair. "Bit of a shit time, that. Uh, nothing to do with Jago. That was other stuff. Course, then I met Jory." He beamed, his eyes soft, and Sam felt achingly envious of him and Jory all over again.

With his worries over his debts, his living situation, and his job—for which, read Bran bloody Roscarrock—what Sam wouldn't have given for someone to just hold him and tell him everything would be okay.

He thought about it later, when he was lying in bed hoping for sleep to come. Maybe he couldn't do anything about the first two problems until he got paid. *One* source of stress, though, he could do something about.

He had to find a way to get on better with Bran Roscarrock.

Sam put his plan into action the very next day. It'd been the best part of a week since their last argument, which Sam was calling The Battle of Limoges in his head, so hopefully tempers had cooled all round. And he'd come up with an idea that might just help.

Bran arrived at the exhibition centre as Sam was checking the installation of the movie room. It was a small, enclosed area, with bench seating for around twenty, which would show a video presentation about the battle of Crécy starring a sixteen-year-old Edward of Woodstock—yet to be dubbed the Black Prince—in his brutal initiation into the art of warfare. The prince had been beaten unconscious but then emerged, badly concussed, to be covered in glory when the English army literally crushed the heart out of the French by funnelling their attack into too small a space.

At least there was nothing Bran could complain about in *this* exhibit. It was about war, tactics, and teenage courage, pure and simple. Okay, so maybe Sam had added in a few lines emphasising the prince's youth and how his dad had just left him to get on with it, even after messengers were sent to inform the king of all the mortal peril flying around. There was nothing like encouraging modern teenagers to reflect on how different their own lives were.

Still, it seemed as good a setting as Sam was likely to get for making his proposition.

He nodded to Bran. "Morning."

Bran nodded back. Apparently that was all the greeting Sam was getting—or maybe Bran didn't trust himself not to start shouting again if he opened his mouth.

"I'm glad you're here." It wasn't *totally* a lie. "Look, what Jennifer said—she wasn't wrong, you know. This . . . animosity between us—it's affecting everyone." Sam drew in a sharp breath at the way a muscle in Bran's jaw tightened, but for once the bloke didn't say anything, so he carried on. "I've had an idea. How about you and me go out for a meal? Not to talk about the exhibition. Forget about the Black Prince for a night. Just you and me, having dinner."

From the suspicious look in Bran's eye, you'd have thought Sam had asked him to go for a clifftop walk in the pitch-dark with banana skins strapped to his feet. "Why?"

LOVE AT FIRST HATE

"Because every time I see you at work, it seems like, we have a row. I thought . . . maybe if we knew each other better, we'd each know where the other was coming from?"

"And you think we should go out to a restaurant for this?"

Sam *could* have said, *Well, yeah, because throughout history and across cultures, right from when the first amoeba slithered out of the primordial ooze, pointed its pseudopod at a half-eaten bit of bacteria, and said Oi, mate, you going to finish that? sharing a meal has always conferred social obligations. Or in words of one syllable: if you eat with a bloke, it makes it that much harder to be such a pigheaded git to him.* But he didn't. No matter how much he was tempted. "Neutral ground. Well away from the castle, the exhibition centre, and all." It wouldn't help his credit card situation, but sod it. One meal was a drop in the ocean.

And chances were Bran would come over all old-fashioned—correction: *more* old-fashioned—and insist on paying anyhow because he was older and richer. And stubborner. Which, normally, Sam would have had a problem with, but seeing as how it was Bran being such a stubborn git that'd made this meal out necessary, Sam was quite happy to let him pay for it.

"Where did you have in mind?" Maybe not so stubborn after all, seeing as how he'd clearly been won over by Sam's argument. *Result.*

"Not a clue. You're the local—where would you like to go?"

Bran gave him a considering look. Probably trying to decide if Sam could be trusted to know his fish knife from his spork. "Do you like Chinese food?" he asked in the end.

"Yeah, love it." Also, it probably wouldn't be ultraexpensive, which would be handy if Sam did end up having to pay.

"There's a place I know in St. Mawgan. I could make a reservation. When?"

Sam shrugged. "I'm free tonight, if we can get a table." Might as well strike when the iron was hot. And before he had a chance to get cold feet about the whole plan.

Bran pulled out his phone, scrolled through his contacts, and dialled the number. His voice was back to his usual commanding tone as he booked a table for two. Sam wondered if *Roscarrock* was the magic word. Then again, it *was* Monday night. He ended the call and gave Sam a nod. "Eight o'clock," he said curtly, as if Sam hadn't just heard every word he'd said on the phone. "Would you like me to pick you up?"

Sam nearly made a joke of it, like it was a date or something, but he stopped himself in time. If Bran had ever had a sense of humour, he'd since had it surgically removed. Possibly to make room for that stick up his arse.

Struggling to keep his face straight, Sam said, "Yeah, ta, that'd be great. What time?" He wasn't all that sure where St. Mawgan was.

"Seven forty-five. I'll see you at Jory's."

"Looking forward to it," Sam lied, and gave Bran a smile as he left.

Quarter to eight. That'd give him plenty of time after work to get back to Jory's, have a wash, change his clothes, and make a decent start on regretting he'd ever suggested all this.

Sam was already showered, changed, and working a final bit of product through his hair when he glanced in the mirror and realised he'd dressed for a *date*: his favourite dark shirt and jeans blokes always said gave him more than a hint of the bad-boy look. His five-o'clock shadow completed the image. For a moment, he considered changing into something more casual and having a shave—then he thought to hell with it.

If nothing else, maybe he'd find out for certain if Bran was into him.

Sam studied his own expression in the mirror. Did he *want* Bran to be into him? And if so, was it just a matter of having an advantage over the bloke? Or was Sam, maybe, just a little bit into Bran?

His eyes widened in alarm, and Sam turned away with a laugh. Christ, what was he even thinking? Bran wasn't bad looking, okay, and he had the sort of intensity about him Sam had always gone for—who *wouldn't* want that kind of focus, that passion, turned on them in bed?—but he was a total git. And uptight, and closeted, and his *boss*, kind of. Sam had sworn he wouldn't do that to himself again. He'd promised himself he'd never again go out with a bloke who cared more about what other people thought of him than about Sam. Or anyone who had power over him.

On the other hand, at least Bran wasn't married . . .

Christ. Sam ran a hand through his hair, mussing it up and not caring. He was being an idiot. This wasn't a date, and nothing was ever going to happen between him and Bran.

Maybe he'd better go easy on the alcohol tonight, though. Just to be on the safe side.

CHAPTER
TWENTY-SIX

B ran should never have accepted Sam's invitation. He was damned either way—if the evening went badly, it would only worsen their working relationship, and if it went well . . . Bran sighed. It would hardly help him get over the attraction he couldn't help feeling for the infuriating man.

But he'd been right, damn him. Or rather, Jennifer had been right. Things couldn't go on the way they had been. Perhaps seeing Sam outside the context of his work would help him understand the man better.

You have to learn what's important to a man before you can know how to deal with him, his father's voice sounded in his mind. Bran flushed at the decades-old memory. He'd read too much into it, had naively blurted out a shocked query as to whether Father had been talking about blackmail, and had been treated to a lengthy tirade on keeping to the absolute letter of the law lest he bring down shame upon all Roscarrocks living or dead.

Father hadn't been an easy man to read, either. Or maybe it was simply Bran who'd failed at the task. He would have to do better with Sam.

Bran dressed carefully after his shower, in a dark-grey single-breasted suit and a deep-burgundy shirt. After consideration, he left his collar unbuttoned and forewent a tie. Sam had expressed a wish for them to relax and get to know one another. Appearing dressed for the boardroom would hardly show willing.

The taxi driver this time, Bran saw to his relief, was a middle-aged woman who'd driven him before. She always drove carefully and never tried to force him into conversation.

As he sat in the back seat, Bran found himself perversely wishing she would be a little more talkative. His nerves increased the nearer they got to Jory's house, and with their route so familiar he could have described it with his eyes shut, he was left with nothing to distract himself with but the pattern in the weave of her marshmallow-pink hijab.

Finally, the taxi pulled up in front of Jory's cottage, and the driver turned to speak her first words of the journey. "Would you like me to call at the door?"

"No, don't get out, thank you. I'll go." As Bran prepared to heave himself out of the car and knock on Jory's front door, it opened and Sam emerged.

He'd changed since this afternoon, and was wearing a pair of faded black jeans that fit him like a glove, teamed with a black long-sleeved shirt open at the collar. He might have stepped straight from the cover of a magazine, with his tousled hair, wary smile, and lean, good looks.

Bran must look impossibly staid and boring in his business suit, its formality softened only by the removal of his tie. He'd left the house satisfied he was armoured for battle, but now felt more like a rusty knight facing down a modern soldier swathed in Kevlar and armed with an AK-47.

He leaned across to open the car door, stifling a grunt of pain as his ribs protested.

"Taxi?" Sam raised an eyebrow and climbed in.

Bran flushed. "I still find driving uncomfortable." Plus he had a feeling he might be in need of a drink before the evening was out, medication be damned. Sitting in the car next to him, on their way to a restaurant together, Sam seemed somehow far more physically present than he ever had during the working day, and distractingly close. Bran darted a glance over to where the dark denim stretched taut over Sam's thighs, and looked away hurriedly.

"Oh, right. The ribs, yeah?" Now Sam seemed embarrassed as he fumbled with his seat belt. "That must have been rough. Getting mugged in your hometown. Have they got the bastard who did it?"

"No." Bran kept his answer curt, hoping to discourage further enquiry. He needed to compose himself.

But when had Sam Ferreira ever done what Bran wanted him to? "No excuse for that sort of thing. Jory said you got, uh, retrograde amnesia? Must be weird, missing part of your life. Especially something like being attacked on the street. It'd have me jumping at shadows. Not knowing who was a threat." He made a surprisingly sympathetic face. "Uh, sorry. Don't suppose I'm telling you anything you don't already know. Are the police still working on it?"

"So I'm told. Although there are no signs of any arrests being imminent."

"Yeah, I don't expect they had a lot to go on. Hey, did they ask you if you had any enemies, like on the telly when someone gets murdered? It always gets me, that does. Like, who has enemies in this day and age?"

"Apparently, I do." Bran's temper flared. "It must be nice to breeze through life with everyone always thinking well of you."

Inexplicably, Sam flushed and looked away. "Yeah. Must be." He fell silent, his face still turned to the window.

What on earth? Bran felt wrong-footed. It was almost as though *he'd* been the one at fault here, rather than Sam with his careless prying.

The silence grew heavy, its weight pressing on Bran's injured chest. "Do you have family?" he blurted out after what seemed like an age.

"What?" Sam's head snapped back from the window. "Oh, yeah, three sisters. All older than me. They're all married with kids now. And there's my mum, obviously. Dad died when I was little. Heart attack. I don't really remember him. Uh, you?"

Bran blinked under the barrage of information, belatedly registering the question at the end. But surely Sam knew about Bran's family from Jory? Bran found himself answering nonetheless. "Jory and Gawen you know about. And Kirsty, of course. I have a twin sister, Bea. That's it." Apart from a vast tribe of distant cousins he was quite happy to meet only at weddings and funerals.

"How old were you when you lost your parents?"

"Twenty-six." Sam looked at him expectantly, so Bran felt compelled to continue. "My mother was ill for many years. My father's death was . . . sudden."

"Is that 'sudden' as a euphemism?"

Bran's eyes flashed to the rearview mirror, and met those of the taxi driver for a brief, gut-churning moment before she looked back to the road.

"Shit—sorry," Sam was saying. "Forget I asked. None of my business."

No. It wasn't. But to refuse to answer now would only confirm Sam's suspicions. "He was walking on the clifftops behind Roscarrock House. He fell."

"Behind your house? That's got to be rough. Uh, sorry."

Rough? Yes, that was one way of describing it.

Fifteen Years Ago

The *crash* above Bran's head was painfully, terrifyingly loud. Far louder than his father's shotgun, or even the seaward cannon. Not that they'd been fired for years now, not since he and Bea had still been children. The flash came simultaneously, shockingly bright, lighting up the room even through the thick curtains. The power had been out for several minutes and seemed likely to continue so, leaving the house wrapped in darkness so absolute it seemed unreal. As if a blanket had been thrown over his head and he was slowly smothering, trapped in its folds.

School had been a long time ago, though. He didn't jump at shadows anymore, and darkness was just the absence of light, not the prelude to a hateful prank. The storm must be directly overhead. Bran entertained a sudden, vicious hope that lightning might strike and put them all out of their misery.

No. Out of Father's misery.

It'd been four months since Mother died. Father had been . . . Frankly, Bran wasn't sure *deranged* wasn't the right word. He almost wished he could call in a doctor—but since Father would never consent to see one, the question was moot, quite aside from all considerations of what it would likely do to the Roscarrock family reputation and hence its fortunes. Even though Father now took no part in the family property business, leaving it to Bran.

With all the tumult of nature going on above, it was hard to settle with a book, as presumably Bea had done somewhere in the house. Probably she was in her room—she had an ample supply of candles there, and a window seat to read on. Bran found himself wandering the empty halls, the flickering of his candle keeping his pace measured, with a curious sense of having been thrown back in time. How odd it must have been to live in a world of candlelight, as his ancestors had done for centuries in this very house.

Back then, of course, the place would have been bustling with servants even at this time of night. Not silent and still, as if Bran were the only one left alive.

He only went into the study because he saw through the open door that there was a fire lit, and he was curious. Once his father's exclusive preserve, the study had, over the last six months or so, become Bran's domain, and it seemed strange now to find someone else had taken possession. Moreover, the air had been thick and oppressive all day, and although it had cooled markedly now the storm had hit, it hardly merited lighting a fire.

Whether it had been Father or Bea, they weren't there now. Again, that seemed odd—why light a fire, and then leave it to burn down unheeded? Still, the light was cheery in this gloomy night, and Bran drew nearer.

As he did so, he noticed an envelope askew on the mantelpiece, secured at one corner by the antique cannonball Father had used as a paperweight for as long as Bran could remember. The handwritten name on the front wasn't obscured.

Branok Roscarrock

The envelope was addressed to him. Him alone.

Bran stared at it a moment, then stowed his candlestick on the mantelpiece, seized the envelope, and tore it open. The letter inside was handwritten too, in Father's spiky script, and it took Bran a moment in the dim, shadowy light to take in what he was reading.

Oh God. It was an apology.

For their mother's death.

Bran had wondered about it, in the leaden times since she'd died. Her death had come so suddenly, after so many years of inexorable yet gradual decline. Had it really been entirely . . . natural?

"These things happen," the doctor had said, not quite meeting Bran's eye. *"Just comfort yourself with the knowledge she's no longer in pain."* When Bran had voiced his suspicions, Father had flown into a temper and demanded to know how he *dared* accuse Dr. Gibson, an old family friend, of failing in his duty. Had yelled at him to stop sullying his mother's memory with unfounded accusations.

Bran had been silent after that. Because after all was said and done, the most he suspected the doctor of was well-meant collusion—and he hadn't *known* anything had been untoward about Mother's death, had he?

But now he did. It was all down on the page before him, in the strident blue ink from Father's fountain pen. He'd found her suffering unendurable, and had put an end to it at last. He didn't say how he'd done it, only that he had, and that Dr. Gibson was not to be blamed. Father regretted—there was a smudge here, and a word scratched out completely before he'd gone on with strong, confident strokes—that he hadn't allowed her children the chance to say goodbye to her.

Bran stared at the words until they swam on the page. *The chance to say goodbye.* Mother would have insisted on that, wouldn't she? If she'd been able to. Which meant . . . Bran blinked until he could once more read the final lines:

I leave the family and its fortunes in your hands, Bran. I trust you will not disappoint me.

Your father,

Kenver John Roscarrock

Coming without warning, Bea's voice at his shoulder made him startle and crush the letter in unsteady hands. "Oh, there you are. Where's Father?"

Bran swallowed. "Gone."

Bea's forehead creased, the firelight throwing strange shadows over her face. "Gone? Gone where?"

Another crash of thunder, and a flash of lightning lit her features, pale as death.

"I don't . . ." Bran crumpled the letter once more convulsively in his fist. "He just left this note. Saying sorry. Oh God. I think he's gone to . . ." He couldn't say it.

But this was Bea, so he didn't have to say it. She knew. She always knew. "We should check the garage," she snapped at him. "What are you just standing there for? Come *on*."

Bran couldn't move. She meant to save Father. She didn't know . . .

"*Come on*," she repeated, and grabbed his arm, pulling him from the room.

The motion cleared his head—and suddenly he was appalled at himself. "Oh God. Yes. The cars." He ran with her through the house to the kitchen, the candle guttering but miraculously, not quite snuffed—until she flung open the back door to a squall of wind and rain that battered their faces and dowsed their lights, leaving them in darkness.

Bea swore. "Hold on."

She let go of him, leaving him adrift in an inky sea. Lightning struck once more, showing him the way across the kitchen garden to the old stables where the cars were housed. Bran didn't wait. He sprang out through the door, into sheeting rain and a wind that took his breath away. His flat-soled shoes slipped and slid on the uneven paving slabs that formed the path around the tiny garden. Mother's garden; it was weed-ridden and unkempt now in his mind's eye but invisible else, the lightning having ruined his night vision. They should have paved the whole lot over the minute she was in the ground. Christ, what he wouldn't give for a light.

Bran reached the stables sooner than he expected, and slammed painfully into the stone wall. Bruised and rattled, he fumbled his way to the door and wrenched it open against the wind.

No fumes rolled out. One theory dead. Bran took a step forward into the stable, and then another. The relief from the battering of the wind and rain was heady even after so short an exposure, and he struggled to think. If Father had . . . Christ, if he'd, oh God, hanged himself, or used any of the ancient implements in here that could be turned to lethal purpose, there'd be a light, wouldn't there?

Unless he'd done it before the power cut. Bran froze, his thoughts stuttering in horror at the image of himself walking blindly forwards to stumble into his father's corpse. He shivered as an icy trickle of water ran through his hair and down his neck.

Thin yellow light beamed past him. "Is he in here?" Bea asked, her voice raised to carry over the storm and the heavy metal torch in her hand steady as a rock.

"No. I don't know."

She swung the beam across the stables, first high, to the rafters, and then lower down, pausing at each car until it was clear there were no occupants, and no cars missing either.

"Then how would he . . ." Her voice trailed off and although he couldn't see her, Bran knew she had turned to him.

Knew, as he had known so many times as a child, that she was thinking the very same thing he was.

The cliffs.

"We have to look for him," she whispered.

Bran grabbed her arm. It was bare, wet and cold. Her thin summer dress must be soaked through already. "You can't go out on the clifftops. It's not safe."

"Of course it's not safe! It's not safe for either of us. But we can't just not try."

No. They couldn't.

Rain blurred the light of Bea's torch as they hurried out of the stable yard, to the grounds behind the house that ended in a sheer drop. Hundreds of feet straight down to jagged rocks that scythed through an unquiet sea.

Bran and Bea had learned respect for these cliffs almost before they could walk. *"Don't go near the edge; it may crumble. Don't assume a path that was safe yesterday will be safe today. Don't go out in stormy weather; the winds are stronger than you think."* They'd known them so well, back in the far-off days before school and . . . other things had split them apart as if they'd never been almost one person in two bodies. They'd played on the cannon, and crept out at night to watch for smugglers' lights. Later, when Jory had come along, sapping their mother's strength and their father's smiles, they'd taken him out there to threaten him with the loss of a favourite toy if he didn't do as they said.

Once, Bea had even followed through with it, one afternoon when Father had snapped at them to *"For God's sake take that wretched brat somewhere and let your mother have some peace."* Bran could remember

Jory's anguished cry as she'd thrown the teddy far out over the sea, and he'd rushed to the cliff edge to watch it tumble. Bran had been so terrified Jory would follow it over the edge that after he'd pulled him back he'd hit him, all his strength going into an open-handed slap that left a vivid red mark on one baby-fat cheek for hours. Jory had cried for the pain, but he'd cried for his teddy even longer, begging them to go and get him back, as if such a thing were possible. Bran had had to sneak some of Father's expensive dark chocolate from the study drawer to shut him up.

He felt sick, now, with the certainty Father wouldn't be coming back either. Hundreds of yards of cliff edge bordered the Roscarrock lands alone, and the torch beam's feeble light carried only a few feet. How could they ever hope to find him?

Bea tugged at his arm again, urging him on although her voice was lost in the wind.

As he wavered, another crash split the air, and a great fork of lightning crackled in the sky, so close the hairs on Bran's neck stood on end despite being drenched. He could see Bea, her hair plastered to her head and her dress clinging to her thin body. "This is madness!" he yelled. "You'll get yourself killed too."

He grabbed Bea by both arms and pulled her back, away from the cliffs. She struggled and the torch fell, but Bran didn't give a damn anymore. He knew which way the house was and that was where they were going. They stumbled and fell in the darkness, but Bran was stronger than Bea and he didn't care. He was damned if he was going to lose his sister as well.

As they fell in through the kitchen door, feet thick with mud from trampling through that damned kitchen garden, the lights came back on.

Bea stared at Bran, wild-eyed, and wrested herself from his grip to run through the house shouting for Father, as if they might have overlooked him earlier in the darkness.

Nobody answered.

CHAPTER
TWENTY-SEVEN

Present Day

T he cessation of motion was what startled Bran out of his reverie. Although he'd been staring out the window, he'd taken in nothing of their route and hadn't even noticed they'd arrived at the restaurant.

He'd probably come over as appallingly rude, sitting there ignoring his companion. He hurried to get out of the taxi, which was idling in the car park, and paid the driver, only just remembering to add a tip. *Get a hold of yourself, damn it.*

He turned to Sam, who was waiting to one side with a wary look in his eye once more. "I apologise for my taciturnity." It sounded stiff and a little ridiculous in his own ears.

Sam shook his head. "No, my bad. I shouldn't have been so bloody nosy. I kind of forget, sometimes, it's not the same for everyone, dealing with a death in the family. I mean, I regret never knowing my dad, but it doesn't hurt talking about him, *because* I never knew him. So, I'm sorry."

"You don't need to apologise again." Bran took a deep breath. "Shall we?"

Bran resisted the urge to usher Sam into the restaurant with a hand on the small of his back. He wasn't Craig, and this was not a date.

Had it been a bad idea to bring Sam here—a place he'd been to several times with Craig? But he'd been put on the spot, and hadn't been able to think of anywhere else. At least, nowhere he wouldn't risk running into business contacts. If the evening ended badly—and there was every chance it would—Bran would rather any unpleasantness not be witnessed by those likely to hold it over him.

Sam was gazing all around the place. "This is really not what I was expecting."

Unease pricking the hairs on the back of his neck, Bran frowned. "The food is excellent, I assure you."

"No, I'm not complaining. It looks great. It's just not what I'd imagined, that's all."

What *had* he imagined? Bran found himself examining the place with fresh eyes, scoping for whatever seemed to say to Sam that Bran didn't belong here. The restaurant was situated in a former barn attached to the Tinners Rest public house, its ceiling open to the vast pitched roof supported by ancient beams. Too rustic, perhaps? No, that was absurd. Bran was from a family of country squires, for God's sake. Was it, then, too frivolous, with its eclectic collection of English agricultural equipment supplemented with rice flails and paper fans?

Perhaps it was the lighting, which was warm and low. Bran loathed brightly lit restaurants. They were all very well for business lunches and large groups, but when it came to an intimate evening meal, he hated feeling as though he were sitting in a goldfish bowl. He was finding it hard enough to relax as it was.

"Mr. Roscarrock? Your usual table?" The hostess, a woman his own height, elegant in a turquoise cheongsam, smiled to greet them.

Bran managed to smile back. "Yes, thank you."

"Come this way, please."

A gorgeously painted screen divided the restaurant on one side, shielding their corner table from view of the entrance. It was lit by numerous small, shaded lamps, none of them seeming to cast more than a candle's worth of light. The two table settings were at right angles to one another, allowing each diner to sit with his back to a wall, something Bran had never consciously noticed until tonight.

"I guess this answers the question of whether you come here often," Sam said, taking his seat.

Bran gave him a sharp glance. Sam was smiling. Was it mockery?

No. No, he was simply far too on edge. "I prefer to support local businesses in Porthkennack when I can, but sometimes one needs a change." Bran cringed inside at his own pomposity. It was how he might have spoken to a business associate he was lunching with and didn't much like.

But then, of course, he didn't *like* Sam Ferreira, did he? Attraction—and he was forced to admit he was attracted to Sam—didn't necessitate any meeting of souls.

Sam nodded, as if to agree that the antipathy was mutual. "Yeah, I don't feel like I've seen much of Cornwall since I've been here, so it's good to get out of town for me too. I've been spending weekends helping Jory and Mal do up the cottage. And this place looks great. Lots of atmosphere, and not too formal." He ducked his head and opened his menu. "So, are we sharing dishes, or each getting his own?"

"Not too formal." Ah. *That* was why he'd been surprised. "Sharing, if that's agreeable."

"Yeah, why not? If we end up fighting to the death over the last crispy pork ball, then at least we'll know we tried." Sam laughed, and Bran was vividly reminded of Craig sitting there in that very seat, joking that he'd stab Bran in the heart with a chopstick because of something or other. Probably a development in the Constantine Bay dispute that seemed likely to swing things Bran's way.

This was a terrible idea. And there was literally nothing to be done but go through with it now. "Do you have any particular likes and dislikes?"

Sam shrugged. "I'm not fussy. Mum and three older sisters, remember? I ate what I was given as a kid, or I went to bed hungry. But as you're asking, I prefer meat to fish, noodles to rice, and all of them to tofu. And I'll do anything for a decent prawn dumpling."

"Perhaps I should lay in a supply," Bran muttered, perusing the menu, although he knew it well enough by now. He suggested a few dishes, Sam agreed to most and made polite counter-suggestions for one or two others, and they had an order ready for the waitress when she came to their table. Sam appeared happy to accept Bran's recommendation of a German Riesling he'd drunk here before.

If only all things could be decided between them with so little stress.

There was an awkward silence after the waitress departed. "I understand you know Jory from university?" Bran said at last.

Sam's face fell. Did he think Bran was about to interrogate him on his CV? "Uh, yes."

"You were undergraduates together?" Bran persisted. Perhaps he *would* interrogate Sam on his CV.

"No. Postgrads." In Edinburgh, then. Sam's shoulders hunched. "Look, no offence, but . . . I'd rather not talk about that time. Bad breakup."

Bran, who'd been taking a sip of water, all but choked. He avoided a coughing fit by sheer force of will. "You and Jory?" he asked when he was able.

"What? No!"

Thank God. Bran managed not to say it aloud, and was ashamed of the heady rush of relief that swept over him. A bad breakup with Jory would have been a problem only if Bran intended a relationship with Sam himself. Which he most certainly didn't.

Sam's gaze darted around the room, then returned to rest on Bran. "We were never— It was someone else. Bloke, though," he added, his eyes piercing Bran's soul.

There was a challenge in his gaze: *Judge me if you dare.* Or was it a version of *I can tell you're queer because I'm queer too*? Bran's stomach flipped at the thought of being so transparent to Sam, of all people. He'd managed, in the days since their last argument, to half convince himself he'd misinterpreted what Sam had said about being in the closet.

Or did Sam hope Bran might start to treat him as a comrade simply because they had this one thing in common? Although . . . that wasn't all they had in common, was it? There was Edward of Woodstock.

Perhaps Sam was thinking the same thing, as his next question was, "What got you so interested in the Black Prince? I mean, I know there's the local connection, what with the castle, but most people wouldn't spend a fortune setting up an exhibition just because of that. Especially with half the tourist bumf getting him confused with King Arthur's Black Knight."

Thank God for an impersonal topic. Particularly as the waitress had just returned with the wine. Bran went through the ritual of tasting it, then took a larger swallow after she'd filled their glasses and left. "Edward of Woodstock has always been a favourite historical figure of mine. There are so many romantic stories about him—I don't mean that in the modern sense, although his marriage to Joan of Kent appears to have been a true love match. No, the tales of his valour in battle, his respect for chivalry—take his adoption of a former enemy's symbol for his own, as a salute to the man's honour and bravery."

Jean of Luxembourg, the King of Bohemia, had been ageing and almost blind, yet had insisted upon being led out to fight in one last battle, his horse roped to one of his knights'. His ostrich feather emblem, taken from his body on the battlefield by Edward of Woodstock, was used by the Prince of Wales to this day, more than six hundred years later. The fading king could not have hoped for a greater tribute to his courage.

And perhaps Bran had been a little self-deceiving in calling the topic impersonal.

"Jean of Luxembourg's last hurrah, yeah." Sam paused, and Bran silently dared him to either contest the legend or comment unfavourably on its sentiments. But Sam's tone was warm as he said, "I've always thought the Black Prince showed a lot of maturity for a sixteen-year-old."

"Absolutely. His was a baptism of fire, and he came through it with honour. He was very much his father's son—witness them going into battle in unmarked armour a few years later, disguised as ordinary knights, to keep Calais from being recaptured by the French."

"Yeah, but Edward III didn't hesitate to drop the disguise when shit got real, did he?"

Bran frowned. "He was the *king*. There are limits. Edward of Woodstock kept his head, his incognito, and rescued his father." He took a large sip of wine. "And it's a scandal the way he's been slandered through history."

"Rooting for the underdog, then?" Sam half smiled, which Bran counted as a win. "Yeah, I can see that. I had a mate in uni who was totally into Richard III, and you did *not* want to be caught in the crossfire when she got into it with someone over the murder of the Princes in the Tower. She had a real hate-on for Shakespeare. So yeah, a bit like the Black Prince there. Uh, my bad again. We really weren't supposed to be talking about that sort of thing tonight, were we?"

"No."

There was silence for several minutes, as Bran tried and failed to think of a single conversational topic that didn't have to do with Edward of Woodstock. Well, that or the men in Sam's past.

Perhaps Sam was doing something similar, as he eventually coughed and asked, "Did you ever think of becoming a historian?"

"I read history at university. But it was always intended that I'd come home to manage the family properties."

Sam frowned. "Intended by you? Or the family?"

"Both. I've always been quite aware of my responsibilities."

"But didn't you ever want to say to hell with it, and do your own thing?"

Bran gave him a steady gaze. "I wasn't forced into anything, I can assure you. And I'm now in the fortunate position of being able to indulge my interest in history. Although make no mistake, the exhibition centre is an investment and I expect a return."

"So do you do anything that isn't business related?"

An image of Craig flashed into Bran's head. He angrily dismissed it. "I don't spend my every waking hour on work. I go to the gym; I read; I play the occasional round of golf." Although to be honest, the latter was almost entirely work related too these days. "And I spend time with my nephew," he added, feeling on firmer ground here.

Sam smiled. "Yeah, Gawen seems pretty keen on his uncle Bran. He's your heir, right? You seem a bit young to be giving up on the idea of ever having kids of your own. Or do you prefer being able to give them back at the end of the day?"

"I've never imagined being in a position where I'd be able to have a child."

"Why not? There's plenty of gay dads—"

Bran froze. "I'll thank you *not* to make any assumptions about my private life," he said stiffly. "And if you must make them, keep them to yourself."

Sam drew back, both eyebrows raised. "You know they decriminalised it before either of us was born, right? I don't get why you're so—"

"You know nothing about me," Bran snapped, louder than he meant to. Was there a lull in the conversation around them? He glared at his water glass, unwilling to look up and find all eyes upon him.

"You're right," Sam said softly. "Which is why we're here, isn't it? Sorry. I shouldn't have got so personal."

Their food arrived, fortuitously, at that point. As they ate, politeness reigned. Bran talked of other restaurants in the area Sam might encounter—some excellent, some appalling. Sam told a few wryly amusing stories from the time he'd worked at an Indian restaurant in Luton. He didn't mention when that had been. Presumably around the time he'd been a university undergraduate.

Bran found himself warming to the man's self-deprecating humour, and envying his ease in laughing at himself. Bran had always been too worried about giving away his weaknesses. And yet he found himself doing so anyway, telling Sam all about his woeful run-ins with the local council's planning department.

"Someone with a grudge against you there?"

"Apparently they took exception to a letter I wrote to the local paper demanding the council take action on street lighting. In certain areas of town, it's in such a poor state as to be unsafe for residents." Bran frowned. Something about what he'd just said had given him the oddest sense of déjà vu. Hadn't Sally Peters mentioned something like that too?

"Something the matter?"

Bran shook his head. The connection had failed to complete, and perhaps he'd only been imagining it in any case. He took a sip of his wine. "I'm fine. More chicken?"

The food was as good as ever, and Bran relaxed under its influence and that of the Riesling. He ordered a second bottle, as it seemed ridiculous to stint. Sam's face was warmer-toned than ever in the dim lighting, his eyes darker than Bran would have believed possible. He was a remarkably attractive young man, and although it wasn't a date, Bran felt proud to be with him, nonetheless.

Such a shame it couldn't lead to anything more.

"Did you ever feel the urge to move out of Porthkennack?" Sam asked after a while. "Don't get me wrong, it's a great place, but a lot of people I know from small towns, once they went away to uni they never looked back."

Bran shook his head. "I always knew Porthkennack was my home."

"Family tradition, huh?"

"Roscarrocks have been tied to the land here for centuries."

Sam gave a wry smile. "Even Jory came back in the end, right?"

"Never underestimate the power of family." Bran took another sip of wine. Should he clarify? He'd meant that to refer to Gawen, but it could equally be taken as him boasting about his influence over his brother.

But Sam was already speaking. "Tell me about it. Half my family's over in Goa, and I only see them once a year if that, but it's never stopped them banging on about what I ought to be doing with my life." There was a twist to his mouth that suggested their advice hadn't always been welcome.

"Is it just your immediate family who are in Britain?"

"Oh, no. Uncles, aunts, cousins . . . My dad's parents came over a few years after the Second World War ended, and my mum's family a couple of years after that. They ended up going to Mass at the same Roman Catholic church in Luton, and that's how my parents got together. It turned out their families had lived only a few streets apart in Vasco da Gama, but hadn't known each other. Funny how things turn out, isn't it?"

"It is, indeed. My parents grew up together too—in fact, they were almost like brother and sister as children, from what I've heard. Father spent more time at her family's house than in his own." Bran didn't feel the need to expand on Father's likely motives. Bran had never known his paternal grandmother, but his grandfather had been an aloof man with a swift temper who'd terrified him as a child.

"Must be nice, that. Knowing your partner so well." There was a touch of bitterness in Sam's voice.

Bran wondered what it meant. "They were very close. More wine?" Their glasses weren't that low, but it would serve as a way of moving on from a subject that was clearly sensitive for both of them.

"Cheers, yeah." Sam picked up his recharged glass, and raised it with a wry smile. "We should have a toast. Here's to the Black Prince."

"Edward of Woodstock," Bran said, and drank.

There was still food on the table, but Bran couldn't have managed another mouthful. He was content to watch Sam eat, which he did with enthusiasm, leading to thoughts of other activities he might be equally enthusiastic about.

Despite such distracting thoughts, which he did his best to silence, things appeared to be going ridiculously well. Bran wasn't sure if it was the wine, the ambience, or simply the change of scenery, but Sam seemed a different person here. Bran could *talk* to him. He found himself sharing stories from his childhood, and Sam reciprocated, both of them marvelling that two so very different backgrounds could nevertheless have led to them working together. Proof, if any were needed, that Father's views on race and class had been wrong to the point of absurdity.

But Bran didn't want to think of Father again tonight.

They were interrupted by their waitress, who'd come to clear their plates. "Would you like dessert?"

"Not for me," Bran said quickly. "But you go ahead."

Sam leaned back with a smile. "Oh no. I'm stuffed. That was seriously good food."

The waitress smiled. "Coffee, then? Any more drinks?"

Bran raised an eyebrow at Sam. "Coffee and a brandy? We can take it in the bar."

"Sounds good." They took the last of the wine with them to the pub proper, where they found a table in the corner—again—leaving Bran unsure if he was the paranoid one, needing his back to the wall, or Sam was.

Conversation was easy for a while—and then they somehow got back onto the subject of the Black Prince again.

"He was the celebrity of his day," Bran said, leaning forward. "The teenage heartthrob, the rock star—have you seen *A Knight's Tale*?"

"That's the film with Rufus Sewell and all the jousting? Yeah, I've seen it." Sam leaned in so that their heads were almost touching, his elbows on the table. He'd rolled up his sleeves, and Bran couldn't help admiring his lean, muscular forearms.

"Heath Ledger was the star," Bran pointed out.

Sam ran a hand through his hair. "So I've always had a thing for the dark-and-handsome look. And I was at an impressionable age when I saw it on the telly."

"You must have enjoyed the male nudity, then."

Sam laughed, leaning back a little. Despite himself, Bran missed the closeness. "You kidding me? My sisters were in the room. I didn't know *where* to look! I take it you liked the film too?"

"It was completely, *wilfully* anachronistic, of course, but it captured the spirit of the times. Knights were celebrated, adored even, for their valour in battle. Boys would dream of winning their spurs and finding fame and fortune." Bran tapped the table to emphasise his point. A few strands of hair fell over his eyes. He pushed them back impatiently, then looked up to find Sam gazing intently at him.

"And it had a positive portrayal of the Black Prince, so it'd obviously score points with you there," Sam said softly, then gave a wry smile. "So we won't burst your bubble by mentioning infected wounds, battlefield dysentery and coming home to find your family had all died of starvation or the plague."

"But that was the thing—that was *why*." Bran shook his head, aware he wasn't expressing himself well. "Even kings weren't spared the Black Death. Edward of Woodstock lost three sisters to it, and countless friends and companions. Everyone knew they could die tomorrow, so they lived life to the fullest while they could."

"Blitz spirit, and wartime romances," Sam said, nodding. "Like the Black Prince, with Joan of Kent. Seize the day, and go for all the glory you can get."

"Exactly. *Exactly.* I've always thought it sad that Edward of Woodstock never got to be king," Bran mused, swirling the brandy in his glass and enjoying the heady fumes. "It was the job he was raised for, after all. He never quite fulfilled his potential. And he was only forty-five when he died."

"Yeah, once you pass thirty, that starts to look a bit too close for comfort."

Bran snorted. "Wait until you pass forty."

"Hey, you don't look it." Sam leaned towards Bran once more, across the corner of the table, and his soft brown eyes crinkled at the edges in a smile that threatened Bran's composure. "I'd have put you at late thirties, tops. Hope I look as good when I'm your age." He laughed suddenly. "Can't believe you're single, you know? You are single, aren't you?"

"I— Yes."

"Me too." Sam looked down at his brandy for a moment, then lifted his gaze to meet Bran's head-on at point-blank range. "Maybe we ought to do something about that? You know, together?"

Mesmerised by that warm smile, those merry eyes, and the heat from Sam's oh-so-close body, Bran took a while to process Sam's words. Then he froze. Oh God. This couldn't happen. He'd always been *so careful* to keep any liaisons far from Porthkennack. "No. That's absurd. I'm not— It's a ridiculous idea."

Sam drew back, all trace of a smile gone. "Are you going all *no homo* on me? Seriously? Even now?"

"I told you—"

"You told me a load of bollocks. I just don't get you. What's the big deal?"

"That's *my* busi—"

"Funny how you're so keen on a prince who was known for his bravery, when you're too much of a coward to even come out to another gay guy."

"That's not—"

"And while we're talking about the Black Prince—you idolise this guy for his skill at military strategy, his chivalry and his heroism in battle, but you never even think about where all those bloody manly virtues came from, do you?" Sam's voice had risen.

"What are you talking about?"

"All this emphasis on fighting. The Black Prince was brought up macho as hell because his dad was so bloody desperate to distance himself from *his* dad, Edward II. The gay one, remember? Who everyone hated for falling in love with Hugh Despenser and Piers Gaveston. For Christ's sake, even Edward II's death was a bloody hate crime—they sodomised him with a hot poker."

Bran couldn't control his flinch. "That's a ridiculous oversimplification. Edward II was an inept ruler, both in the political and the military sense—"

"Yeah, but you can bet that's not why everyone hated him so much. Kings were supposed to be the peak of masculinity, and he just didn't fit the bill. And you—how can you be so uncritical of the Black Prince? Just because he knew his strategy and he cut a dash on the tournament field? You're like every bloke on Grindr who puts 'masc: UB2' or 'no fems' on his profile."

Bran's blood chilled. "Just what are you insinuating?"

"I'm not insinuating. I'm bloody well saying it. There's plenty of gay homophobes around, and you're one of them."

"I don't know what you're talking about," Bran snapped. "I'm not gay. I told you that before." He had, hadn't he?

"Come off it. I've seen the way you look at women—or don't look, more like. And the way you look at men." Sam leaned closer, invading Bran's space, and his eyes darkened. "I saw the way you were looking at me not five minutes ago. You *want* this. I know you do."

Every nerve ending in Bran's body screamed at the man's proximity. But to back off, to distance himself, would be to lose ground. To admit that there was something to back off *from*. And the reckless side of him, the side he'd tried so hard to quash, was shouting at him. *He already knows. There's nothing left to lose.*

Bran leaned in likewise, his head curiously light while his stomach roiled. He reached out a hand, and was sure Sam was about to take it, inviting the touch—

"You all done with these?" One of the barmaids, collecting glasses.

Bran snatched back his hand, his heart pounding. "Thank you." He waited for her to leave, and then stood. "I'll call a cab."

"Uh, okay," Sam was saying even as Bran strode off. He paid the bill at the bar with barely concealed impatience, then instead of going back to their table, made his way to the door. He hoped Sam would assume he'd done it so as not to disturb other people with his call, because of poor reception in the building—anything but the true reason, which was that he'd had to get away for a moment.

The air outside had cooled considerably in the hours since they'd arrived, but the chill breeze, while a balm to his heated skin, did nothing to clear his head. Pacing by the restaurant entrance, Bran called the cab company and learned to his relief that, as luck would have it, one of their drivers was about to make a drop-off in Newquay, only a few miles away. The journey back was going to be bad enough without an awkward wait for it beforehand.

They'd almost . . . But they hadn't. He'd had a lucky escape. No good could possibly come of anything happening between him and Sam. Any blurring of the line between professional and personal with someone who was, in some sense, his employee was bound to be a bad idea for the exhibition. They didn't even *like* each other, for God's sake—at least, Bran hadn't liked him before tonight, and any change was undoubtedly due to the wine. Granted, Bran admired the man, with his passion for his subject, his refusal to be browbeaten. And it was certainly no hardship to look at Sam Ferreira, with his ridiculously tousled hair and those deep, brown eyes. How much of a hardship would it be to see even more of him, to touch his skin and tousle that hair anew, to be the cause of those warm smiles—and more?

Against all odds, Sam seemed to want him. Unless . . . unless this was a trick? Some way of scoring points against Bran by leading him on to an admission of desire and then rejecting him? Bran didn't think he could bear that humiliation. He'd never be able to face the man again.

Yes, it had been a lucky escape.

What had he been *thinking*?

"Bran?" Sam's voice startled him, despite its softness. "Bit rubbish timing that, wasn't it?"

CHAPTER TWENTY-EIGHT

What are you playing at? Sam wasn't sure—but he was sure he didn't want to stop. Didn't want to let this opportunity pass him by. He was getting through to Bran, he knew he was. Finally breaking down the barriers the guy had been building since childhood. He'd seen a whole different side of Bran this evening—a passionate, humorous, even vulnerable side—and he liked it. A lot.

Sam had always thought Bran was good-looking in an unapproachable sort of way, but when Bran let down his defences and stopped caring so much about what people thought, he was amazing. That moment when he'd been so wrapped up in what he was saying he'd banged on the table, and his hair, usually so rigidly in place, fell over his eyes . . . yeah, that moment put all of Sam's teenage fantasies about dark, handsome actors to shame.

Bran drew back, clearly skittish. "What?"

"Bit rubbish timing, the barmaid turning up like that," Sam said ruefully. "Just as we were gonna—you know."

"I've no idea what you're talking about."

Yes, you bloody well do. They'd been about to *kiss*. And now Bran was trying to backpedal, pretend it'd never almost happened. Suddenly, Sam was sick of it all. Sick of all the arguments, the broken conversation. And especially sick of all the pretending. "Yeah, you do. I know you do. I don't get it—why do you fight it so much? Why not give in and be happy?"

"You think you know what will make me happy?"

Sam laughed softly, without humour. "Pretty sure I know what's making you unhappy."

"And you're proposing yourself as a cure?" Bran's words might be a challenge, but his tone sounded more like a plea.

"Think I might be able to relieve the symptoms for a while, at any rate." Christ, it must be the wine making him bold. Was he risking his job here, making one more gamble he couldn't afford? But God knew, the payout would be bloody fantastic if he won. For everyone—Bran would be a hell of a lot easier to work with if he wasn't struggling with his own desires all the time. But mostly for him and Bran. And didn't they deserve to win, for once? Sam held his breath, and slipped an arm into Bran's.

Bran's whole body tensed, and Sam braced himself for a shove, maybe a blow—and then, slowly, Bran relaxed. He didn't pull away. "All right," he said, and it was the sound of surrender.

Sam's heart clenched. What must it be like to have such a need to be in control that you couldn't even give in to your own desires without a sacrifice? "It's okay," he whispered, then slid his hand down Bran's arm and clasped their fingers together.

Bran squeezed his hand, and how far gone was Sam that such a simple gesture felt like the world? He was afraid to move, afraid to speak, lest he break the fragile detente between them. They stood there together in the dark, by the side of the quiet road. A group emerged from the restaurant, talking among themselves, and passed by Sam and Bran, paying them no more heed than if they'd been statues.

Bran's grasp on Sam's hand didn't falter. He didn't try to escape.

The night was mild, clear, and perfect, pinprick stars glittering down at them and a crescent moon high in the sky. A gentle breeze carried the scent of cut grass, and beneath it, the earthier reek of a nearby farmyard. Sam found himself missing the fresher air of Porthkennack, with its briny sea smells and sudden gusts of wind. He huffed a laugh. He'd gone native, and he hadn't even realised.

"What is it?" Bran didn't sound defensive. Sam liked that.

He waved his free arm. "This place . . . It's really nothing like Luton, you know?"

"I don't know how people can live in cities. Crammed together, on top of one another, with grey walls and barely a glimpse of sky. Never seeing the sea. I'd go mad." Bran's words were soft but heartfelt.

"I lived in Luton for years. Never knew any different. Then I went away, and it all seemed different when I came back. S'pose I was the one who'd changed." Sam laughed, shaking his head. "Christ, that's such a cliché."

Bran's fingers tightened convulsively, then eased, still in Sam's grasp. "Have I changed?"

Sam wasn't sure if he was expected to answer that or not, or what he could possibly say if he did.

Bran carried on. "I always thought I couldn't change. Shouldn't, even. Father always spoke of . . . of continuity. The family, eternal."

"Everything changes," Sam said, squeezing Bran's hand. "And it's not always for the worse." There were so many things he could mention. Gay marriage. Increasing acceptance. High-speed broadband. And okay, yeah, he was still a little drunk.

"Not the Roscarrocks. They never change."

Sam frowned. That was bollocks. Bran's family might be old money, but they weren't stuck in a time warp. Huh—they'd even had a teenage pregnancy. Mal had filled Sam in on the bare bones of the story. "Why did you have to be such a git about Dev? I get it can't have been easy at the time, but after a quarter of a century, isn't it all water under the bridge? Why did you keep trying to pretend he didn't exist?"

Bran closed his eyes against the moonlight. "Because that man ruined *everything*." The words tore out of him like they were taking a part of Bran with them.

Sam gave him a sharp glance. "What, by being born? Bit tight blaming Dev for that."

"No . . . not him. The other man. Devan Thompson's father." Bran's tone was bitter enough to curdle cream.

Too bitter, if it was all about a couple of teens in love who'd got carried away. "What do you mean? Your sister— Did he—" Sam was glad when Bran interrupted him before he had to spell it out.

"At the very least, he took advantage of her. He was older; he knew what he was doing. She was *fifteen*." Bran made an aborted gesture and turned away, his fingers slipping from Sam's grasp.

Christ. Sam tried to imagine anyone *taking advantage* of one of his sisters at fifteen. And, well, he couldn't, because even his youngest sister was three years older than he was and had always seemed incredibly grown-up and sure of herself to him. But he was pretty sure it would've involved whole-family retribution and bodies under the patio. "You don't know what happened for sure?"

"She won't talk about it. Never has. Not even to me."

"Maybe especially not to you?" Sam said tentatively. "You being a bloke, and her brother?"

"We used to share everything. All our lives. Until *he* came along, all sophisticated and charming, with his film-star looks and smiles." Bran scrubbed his face with his hands. "And . . . ruined things."

Sam drew in a sharp breath. He couldn't have explained it, but something made him ask, "Did you want to share him? Dev's dad?"

"I . . . I didn't know *what* I wanted. Not then. I'd never . . . And he was so . . ." Bran shook his head. "I didn't even understand how I felt about him. But *he* did." Bran hugged himself, the fine material of his jacket pulling taut around his shoulders. Sam had hit the nail on the head, all right.

"And he told you to piss off?" Yeah, Sam had been there, done that. Been the one with a hopeless crush on a straight bloke. Course, Sam had already known he was gay at the time, and he hadn't had to deal with his own sister getting knocked up by the bastard who'd broken his heart. "Okay, yeah, I get it. Still not fair on Dev, but I get it. You didn't want him around bringing back all the bad memories."

"It wasn't just me. Bea didn't want anything to do with him." Bran still wouldn't meet his eye. "You think I should have been stronger, don't you? Should have acknowledged him when he sought us out. Have you any idea what a shock it was seeing that face after so many years? He . . . looks just like him, you know."

Sam's heart ached for the guy. For all of them, really. "Hey, I'm not judging. Seriously. I don't know what I'd have done, either."

"I tried to make amends, over the years. When Gawen was born, I did everything I could to make sure he stayed part of the family."

Sam smiled and slipped his arm around Bran's shoulders. Again there was that odd moment of tension before Bran relaxed into his hold. "Yeah. Yeah, you did. From what I hear, you couldn't have been a better uncle to Gawen."

Bran's arm crept around Sam's waist, pulling him closer. "You don't know how much it means to hear you say that. But I don't deserve any credit for it. Gawen's an easy boy to love. He reminds me so much of

Jory, when he was younger, but he's very much his own man. I suppose he's my second chance to make that right too."

Sam made a questioning sound.

"Bea and I weren't particularly nice to Jory when he was a boy."

"That's kids for you," Sam said diplomatically, and then was surprised by a yawn. "'Scuse me. Must be past my bedtime. Heh. I'll be falling asleep at work tomorrow and getting in trouble with the boss."

Bran's shoulders vibrated with silent laughter. "I'm not, actually, your boss. Technically."

"Can I have that in writing?"

"You've already got an employment contract. With the Woodstock Trust."

"Uh-huh. And you're nothing to do with that lot."

Bran drew away slightly to look him in the face. "Sam, I hope you know that whatever might happen between us, it's got nothing to do with your employment. I wouldn't want you to think—"

"Hey, don't worry. Come on—when have I ever worried about keeping you sweet?"

"A fair point." Bran started to say something else, but broke off as a car drew up in front of them. Their taxi.

"We're going to yours, yeah?" Going back to Jory's together was a definite no-no. Bran's shields would go right back up again in front of his little brother.

"We could . . . I've got a place near here we can go to."

Was Sam actually hearing this? Or was he dreaming it all, and he'd wake up in a few hours with a hangover? Did Bran Roscarrock, pillar of Porthkennack, just as good as say he kept a *love nest* round here? "Yeah, okay," Sam found himself saying, because that was so much better than a twenty-minute cab ride and besides, when weird shit like this happened you had to go with it, right?

"It's not far. Just a few minutes in the car."

"You really do come here often, then," Sam said, mostly to himself. Then he started to wonder about it. "Hey, you're definitely not seeing someone, are you?"

The taxi driver revved his engine. Bran tensed again, then stepped away from Sam to open the car door. They climbed in, and Bran gave the address. Newquay. Sam hadn't realised how close they were to the town, here.

He hadn't had an answer to his question. "You're not, are you? Seeing someone?"

"No. I was . . . but it didn't mean anything. It's over now."

Sam frowned. "It wasn't him who put you in the hospital, was it?"

Bran's head spun towards him so fast he ought to have got a crick in his neck. "No. Of course not. Craig would never—" He fell silent, maybe not wanting to give away any further information inadvertently.

"Right. Good. To both." Sam scrubbed his hands on his trousers. "I'm not big on the rough stuff. Or screwing around, for that matter. Just wanted to get that out there."

Bran's gaze darted to the driver, and Sam took the hint and fell silent.

It wasn't far at all to Bran's flat on the outskirts of Newquay. Which was good, because Sam had started to worry the bloke might be second-guessing himself. And yeah, of course Bran had every right to change his mind—but Sam reckoned they'd both regret it if he did. Bran needed to ease up on himself. Let himself have what he wanted for once in his life.

The flat was in a small, modern block, built high on the edge of the cliffs. The rest of the apartments were most likely owned as holiday bolt-holes by people who were absent most of the year, or by young professionals. Nobody was likely to notice or care if Bran brought men here.

Had there been many? Before tonight Sam would have given even odds on whether Bran had ever slept with a man before. Now, he wasn't so sure. Bran might be in the closet, but apparently he liked company there.

They didn't meet anyone inside when Bran unlocked the front door and took Sam through the lobby to the lifts. They got out on the third floor, and Bran ushered Sam into flat number twelve.

A narrow hallway led to a decent-sized living room, with a white-and-chrome kitchenette on the left that didn't look like it got a lot of use. The furniture was all modern, which, like the sleek glass-and-concrete building itself, had to be a change from Roscarrock House. Sam wondered which Bran preferred. He didn't ask. Too-searching questions might have broken this strange, intimate mood between them.

"Nice place," he said instead. "Had it long?"

"A few years. Since it was built." Bran took off his jacket and laid it on the back of the sofa.

Sam stepped through the room and up to the French windows at the far end. "Can I open these?"

"Go ahead."

The key was in the lock, so Sam turned it, opened the doors, and stepped out onto the balcony. Immediately, the sounds of the sea were in his ears, and he smiled. As his eyes adjusted to the darkness, he could just distinguish where the waves, pale moonlight glinting off them, washed up on the beach below. There were few lights visible—they were at the very edge of town here.

In daylight, the views must be spectacular. Bran could make a killing renting it out to holidaymakers, and maybe he did. Although it'd mean restricting his love life to off-season, so maybe he didn't, after all.

"I can see why you chose this place," Sam said, turning back to Bran. "Feels kind of free, doesn't it? Being right on the edge of the land like this."

Bran swallowed, and his gaze intensified. "That's . . . Yes."

It was as if Sam had said something profound. Perhaps he had, to Bran. Sam felt a sudden surge of longing for this deeply private man who only truly let his passion show when talking of a prince six centuries dead. "Will you come outside?"

There were no lights out here. Even if there were anyone nearby, all they'd see would be two silhouettes against the light spilling out from the living room. And yet, it felt momentous when Bran took a step forward, and then another. Sam held out his arms, and Bran first allowed the embrace, then sank into it.

Sam rested his cheek on Bran's hair. He smelled of leather, brandy, and old books. *Eau de gentleman's club*, Sam thought crazily, not that he'd ever been in one or wanted to.

He couldn't stop himself from asking, "Are you sure about this?"

Bran drew in a deep breath. And then kissed him.

CHAPTER
TWENTY-NINE

His head spinning from the combination of alcohol and desire, Bran felt as though he were dreaming. What was happening now would change things, he knew it would, and yet he couldn't make himself stop. Something about Sam made him want to say to hell with his carefully ordered life, where he always did what was expected of him.

It felt like the first time he'd brought someone here. Like the first time he'd been with a man, even. That wonderful feeling of breaking free from self-imposed chains—all with the comforting knowledge deep in the back of his mind that they'd be there waiting for him when he chose to put them back on again.

Except they wouldn't be this time, would they? Sam was part of his life in Porthkennack. Friends with his brother. Things would change. Had already changed. But it didn't matter, because every part of him that touched Sam felt intensely alive, as if the rest of him only slumbered. And Sam's kiss . . . Dear God, those lips, and that tongue. Sam tasted intoxicating, and the heat of him through the thin cotton shirts they both wore was like a cleansing fire.

Bran couldn't have stopped himself from pulling up Sam's shirt if Bea had marched into the flat accompanied by the entire Chamber of Commerce. The urge to feel Sam's bare flesh wouldn't be denied, and he moaned when he reached his goal.

Sam broke the kiss. "Oh God. Get your shirt off."

Some faint remaining traces of a higher thought process reminded Bran they were in the living room, with the light on and the blinds open. There was almost certainly no one there to see, but . . . "Bedroom. This way."

"Now that's a plan I can get behind." Sam emphasised his words with a squeeze to Bran's arse.

Delirious with arousal, Bran half led, half tugged Sam through the door. The light was off, but the moon was high now and shining through the window. In this small room, with bright-white linen on the bed, it was plenty. Bran unbuttoned his shirt with shaking hands, drawing in a gasp as Sam's bare arms slid around his waist. When had he taken his shirt off? Bran didn't care. All that mattered was the glorious, hot touch of skin upon skin, after he finally gave up on buttons and pulled his shirt over his head, wincing as his still-healing ribs protested.

Bran was drawn back into an embrace, and Sam's breath caressed the nape of his neck. "Hey, you okay?" His voice was caring enough that Bran would have been embarrassed to become defensive.

"My ribs. Just . . . be careful."

"Still, huh? Bastard. Let me kiss them better." He began where he stood, kissing first Bran's neck and then moving downwards, kissing Bran's back. "Turn around, and sit on the bed."

Bran did as he was told, and Sam stepped between his legs. Instead of making a move below the belt, Sam kissed Bran's neck and throat, gently like a lover, and then dropped gracefully to his knees and laid a meandering trail of kisses down Bran's chest. It felt like a benediction, as if by kissing over the injured ribs Sam could take away all the hate and the darkness, excise the canker that had grown in Bran's breast since the attack.

It was too much to bear. Bran grabbed Sam's head with both hands and kissed him on the mouth. God, the feel of Sam's hair between his fingers—how long had he wanted to touch that hair? It was softer than it had any right to be, running over his skin like silk. Sam's hands trailed gently across Bran's chest, down his sides, the touch electrifying. Sam's tongue invaded Bran's mouth, taking what he wanted and leaving Bran changed forever.

It was all too much, and not enough. Bran broke the kiss, and they gazed at each other in the dim light of the moon, their breath coming hard and fast. It wasn't a moment for words. Bran let his hands fall to Sam's belt, and he unbuckled it, fumbling not from haste but from strong emotion—what, he couldn't have named even to himself.

Somehow, between them, they managed to lose the last of their clothes, and Sam laid Bran down on the bed so gently he felt as though he might shatter regardless.

"You should be on top," Sam breathed. "I don't want to hurt you."

"It doesn't matter." It didn't.

"Yeah, it does. Come on." Sam lay down on the bed next to Bran, and Christ, how was Bran supposed to resist that invitation? He swung a leg over Sam's slim hips, and let him roll them over until Sam was on his back with Bran on top. The first press of their erections together was a lightning strike. Bran gasped, almost a sob. They kissed again, openmouthed and deep. Sam slid a hand between them to work both their cocks.

It wasn't what Bran wanted. He sat back onto his knees and suppressed a wince at the ache in his ribs as he reached into the bedside drawer. Condoms. Lube.

Bran placed a wrapped condom in the middle of Sam's chest, and reached back to finger himself open. His ribs protested, but it was a dull pain. He could bear it.

"Oh God," Sam breathed, and flung an arm over his eyes, but only for an instant. "Yeah, that's it. Christ, look at you."

Sam tore open the condom and rolled it on himself with a couple of swift, impatient movements of his hand—and then his hands were everywhere, on Bran's chest, his sides, his hips. They glided round to cup Bran's arse, pulling his cheeks apart even as Bran fingered himself. "God, you've got to let me," Sam gasped, so Bran handed him the lube.

A moment later, slippery, deft fingers circled his hole and then pierced inside him, pushing in with confidence. "Jesus, you feel good."

He wasn't wrong. Bran felt wonderful.

"Tell me when you're ready, yeah?" Sam went on, working his fingers in and out and making it hard for Bran to think, let alone speak.

Bran clenched against those invading fingers. "I'm ready." He raised himself on his knees, Sam's fingers slipping out of him, and seized Sam's cock with one hand to line himself up.

Despite the preparations, it hurt to let Sam breach him, to sink slowly down on that hard cock. Bran didn't care. It'd been so long, so very long, and he'd told himself he didn't need this. He might as well have told himself he didn't need food to eat, or air to breathe. He felt full, complete, seared open by this man he'd thought he hated.

Sam grabbed his hips, holding him steady. "God, that's good. So fucking good."

Bran clenched around him, drawing out a moan, then started to move, slowly and deliberately. The angle wasn't quite right so he shifted position—and there, God, yes. That was it. His breathing became harsh, his gasps merging with Sam's stifled grunts.

"C'mon. Faster." Sam's strong hands on Bran's hips added force to his words. Bran resisted for a while, just to show he could, then gave in to Sam's demands. And God, it was worth it for the way Sam's face, clearer now to his dark-adapted eyes but still half-veiled in shadow, contorted with pleasure. Sam's words of encouragement degenerated into incoherency, and he thrust up to meet Bran, his hips bucking uncontrollably.

It felt like flying. Like letting go.

"Jerk yourself off. Wanna see you come on me. Come on." Bran wrapped a hand around his iron-hard cock and worked it feverishly, unable to glance away from Sam's face, more beautiful than ever as he urged Bran to completion. "Aw, jeez, yeah. Come on. *Come* on."

Pleasure shot through Bran and out of him as he painted Sam's chest with his release, its tracks barely visible in the moonlight. Sam's grasp tightened, forcing a last, unlooked-for jet of ecstasy out of Bran, and then Sam gave a guttural cry and convulsed, seemingly forever. Bran floated in a haze of endorphins, alcohol, and exhaustion.

Sam held him up long enough to retrieve the condom, after which Bran collapsed on Sam's chest with a groan of relief. It probably should have hurt his ribs, he thought muzzily, then dismissed the idea as unimportant. Sam's chest, with its sparse, dark hair, was what was important. Bran laid his head on it, not caring about the mess. He probably would in the morning. But not now.

"Uh. Tissues?" Sam sounded as wrecked as Bran felt.

Bran groped for the box he kept on the bedside drawers, and handed it over. Sam lifted Bran's head, gently wiped his cheek, then scrubbed down his own chest with a brisk motion before laying Bran's head down again. Bran floated on a sea of warmth and contentment. "Sleep now," he murmured. And did.

CHAPTER THIRTY

Some godawful racket woke Sam after what felt like about five minutes of sleep. Slapping around blindly for an alarm clock he hadn't owned since his teens, Sam finally realised where the noise was coming from and fumbled for his phone. It took several more rings before he managed to locate it in the unfamiliar surroundings, and then he promptly dropped it on the carpet—onto the used condom, ew—before finally managing to turn off the din.

Bran lay beside him, blinking awake and looking at least as reluctant about it as Sam was. Sam's first thought was a slightly hysterical, *Well, at least the boss can't bitch at me for getting in late today.*

"Time?" There was no clue in that one word as to how Bran felt about finding Sam in his bed in the cold light of day.

"Half past seven. Guess we'd better get shifting." Sam didn't move, though. Bran looked softer, younger with his hair rumpled and morning stubble on his cheeks. He blinked a few times, then frowned sleepily. It was pretty adorable.

"Day's it?"

Sam couldn't hold back a smile. Not a morning person, then. "Tuesday."

There was a pause while Bran processed it. "Ah. Good."

"No breakfast meetings to go to?"

"No."

"That's good." They gazed at each other across the pillows for a moment, Sam wishing he knew if Bran was regretting the previous night. Giving in to an impulse, Sam reached over to brush aside the hair that had fallen over Bran's forehead. "How's the ribs?"

Tension Sam hadn't even noticed was there melted out of Bran at the caress. "Fine. Of course, I haven't tried to move yet."

"Fancy giving it a go?" Sam let the warmth he was feeling show in his voice. "Or shall I come over there?"

Bran drew in a breath. "Come."

Morning sex was always different. Slower, less urgent than the frantic coupling of the night before. More relaxed. Sam could never decide which he liked best. Whichever one he was indulging in at the time, probably. Bran was so fucking gorgeous in bed, like he was a different person to the stuffed shirt he liked to play in public. He could still be demanding—but God, Sam wanted to give in to those demands.

They moved together lazily, just frotting against one another, but somehow it seemed even more intimate than what they'd done the night before. Christ, he'd been *inside* Bran last night. Sam's arousal ratcheted up at the memory, and he increased the pace. Bran responded, and it wasn't long before they were gasping as their jizz mingled on sweaty skin.

The tissue box got another workout, and then they lay there, catching their breath. Still holding one another. Maybe they were both afraid of what might happen if they left this warm cocoon, tucked away from the rest of their world.

It was Sam, in the end, who called attention to the time and suggested that they really ought to be getting back to Porthkennack.

Bran gave a barely audible sigh, nodded, and rose. "I'll have a quick shower. I'm afraid there's unlikely to be anything for breakfast." He padded out of the bedroom.

Sam watched the trim lines of him go with a weird sort of pang, then debated whether to get up and check out the kitchen. Deciding *unlikely* was probably Bran-speak for *the cupboards are barer than my arse right now*, he let inertia carry the day.

He'd almost dozed off again by the time Bran returned—now clad in a towelling dressing gown of the sort spas ordered in bulk— although a glance at his phone told him that Bran really had been only a few minutes.

"There's a towel in there for you," Bran said.

"Cheers." Sam took his clothes with him to the bathroom, although when he got there he found a second, matching robe hanging on the door. It smelled freshly laundered.

Christ. After Sam left here, was Bran planning to wash away all traces of him too?

Sam tried to tell himself he was reading too much into a courteous gesture. His judgement was probably still impaired from all that wine and brandy last night—how many had they had? He didn't feel hungover, precisely, but he wasn't raring to go for a five-mile run in the sunshine either. Good thing neither of them had driven.

Bran didn't put on his jacket when they left the apartment, just carried it over his arm. Sam knew it was a stupid thing to base his hopes on, but it seemed significant, somehow.

He still chickened out of talking to Bran about, well, *anything* besides the weather, for Christ's sake, which he was kicking himself for when they got in the cab. With the taxi driver there, wholesome and motherly in her bright-pink hijab—God, it would have to be the woman who'd dropped them off at the restaurant last night—it was impossible to bring up the subject of whether Bran wanted more than a one-off. Well, two-off, if they counted this morning. She reminded Sam of his *mum*. He pictured himself casually coming out with, "So, great shag, we doing it again?" in front of *her*, and cringed.

They dropped Sam off at Jory's house first. Sam tried to give Bran some money towards the fare, but he waved it away with a curt gesture. It wasn't until Sam was fumbling in his pockets for his key that he realised Bran had paid for everything last night too. Shit.

He really wasn't happy about sponging off Bran now.

When he stumbled into the house, Jory was at work, of course, but Mal was in the living room, buried in a pile of books and notes and tapping away at his laptop.

Right. Exam week. "All right, mate?" Sam braced himself for a round of ribbing about not making it home last night.

Mal glanced up, blinked at Sam, said a vague, "Yeah, good," and returned to his studies.

Sam had never been so thankful for anything in his *life* than that he hadn't mentioned to Jory and Mal who he was going out for dinner with last night. He felt the urge to laugh. *Don't look a gift reprieve in the mouth*, he reminded himself, and headed for a change of clothes.

Sam didn't get into work until nearly eleven, having made a pit stop en route for a large coffee and a couple of Danish. He'd hoped to sneak into his Portakabin and pretend he'd been there since nine, but Jennifer waylaid him with a raised eyebrow as he unlocked the door.

"I was wondering if we'd be having the pleasure of your company this morning. Just as well your lord and master isn't here to see you roll in at this hour." She gave a roguish smile. "Fun party, was it? And on a school night too."

"Uh, yeah. I'd better . . ." He gestured vaguely at the door.

"Don't worry. Your secret's safe with me. I won't breathe a word to anyone named Roscarrock."

Again Sam felt the urge to laugh. Bloody hell, even if he came clean about just what—or rather who—had made him late today, would anyone believe it? "That's, uh . . . Cheers. Listen, I'm in desperate need of caffeine. Talk to you later?"

She rolled her eyes but left, thank God.

Sitting at his desk a while later, blinking at his computer screen as the cursor blinked accusingly back at him, Sam could easily imagine Bran marching in and acting as if nothing had happened between them. It was hard to shake the feeling that he'd let something with the potential to be amazing slip through his grasp. Why the hell hadn't he said something when he'd had the chance? And okay, Bran hadn't said anything either—but Sam *knew* the guy wasn't as confident or as arrogant as he liked to appear. Bran cared about what people thought of him, not that he'd ever admit it, and it made him vulnerable.

He'd probably been waiting to see which way the wind was blowing from Sam. And with all the awkwardness, Sam had definitely not been blowing hot in Bran's direction.

The question was, what was he going to do about it now? He took a large swallow of coffee, then grimaced as he realised how cold he'd let it get. A relationship with Bran wouldn't be easy, would it? Bran had a *lot* of hang-ups about his sexuality—and Sam had promised himself he wasn't going to get involved with any more guys he couldn't be open about.

Did Bran even *want* to get involved with him? Last night it'd felt like he did, with all that carpe diem stuff, and talking about romance—or had it been Sam who'd said that? It'd definitely been Bran who'd brought up the subject. But now . . . Sam struggled to recall the exact words that had been used. Had Bran thought Sam was just being pushy about sex?

And did anything said after that much alcohol count in any case?

Sam slumped back in his chair. The thought of Bran coming in and pretending they'd never opened up to each other, pretending they hadn't spent the night in each other's arms, was a crushing weight on his chest. He'd *liked* Bran last night. Not to mention this morning, waking up in bed next to him. It'd felt like he was seeing the real man, not the starched front Bran liked to show to the world. When Sam thought he might never see that man again . . .

Oh God. This could all turn out to be the most colossal cock-up in the world. Well, since Doug, at any rate. Sam gave a choked-out laugh. Okay, so at least Bran almost certainly wasn't married, hopefully wasn't lying to him, and definitely hadn't publically betrayed him. Yet. *Great standards you've got there, mate.* Would they even be able to work together after this? God, what would happen if Bran decided to let him go? Sam would never be able to pay off his debts—and the chances of him getting another job in his field would be even worse than before. Christ, how could he tell his mum he'd blown this second chance as well?

Would Bran really fire him, though, with so much to be done before the exhibition opened? What if Canterbury used yet another change of curator as an excuse not to lend their relics after all? The grand opening would be a fiasco. But what were the chances Bran would see it that way? If he was that desperate to get rid of Sam, he'd have no problem persuading himself he could do it all on his own.

Could Bran fire him? He kept saying he wasn't technically Sam's boss. Maybe the rest of the Woodstock Trust people—whoever they were—would veto any attempt to sack Sam at this late stage? Relying on that might be wishful thinking, though.

Sam carried on kicking himself for a self-indulgent couple of minutes, then got a grip. Maybe he couldn't have a do-over of this morning, but there was *something* he could do. And hopefully Bran would take it as the olive branch it was intended to be.

Pulling up his proposed wording for the Limoges display, Sam scanned it to see if there were areas of negativity he could, in conscience, tone down for Bran's sake.

He got more than he'd bargained for. Looking at it all with a cool head, he had to admit Bran had a point. Coupled with the other changes he'd made, introducing the point of view of the ordinary people—both English and French—caught up in the Black Prince's military campaigns, it did tend to paint the prince in a bad light.

Sam winced. Christ, he'd had a classic knee-jerk reaction to Bran's partisan worship of the Black Prince, and he'd gone way too far, using a sledgehammer to squash a gnat. He couldn't believe he'd been so blind—how could he not have realised what he'd done?

Because you thought Bran was another Doug, that was why. Sam had leapt to the conclusion, even if he hadn't articulated it to himself, that Bran was doing what Doug had, was trying to paper over the cracks in his research. And yeah, Bran had wanted to put his own spin on the facts, but that didn't excuse Sam gyrating off wildly in the other direction.

Thank God there was still time to make changes. He tweaked a few paragraphs, and gave more prominence to the 2014 discovery of a letter in the prince's own hand regarding the siege of Limoges that detailed far lower casualties among the defenders.

Then he went back to the scripts for the "oral history" recordings and read them through with a critical eye. They were definitely a bit lacking. National pride had been at a real high at the time of the prince's campaigns—he'd been a charismatic leader and a home-grown hero. In World War II, when Churchill said, "We will fight them on the beaches," what he'd meant was, "*You* will fight them." Churchill himself had had a bunker to hide in. But back in the days of Edward III and the Black Prince, leading a battle campaign meant getting on your horse and plunging right into the thick of things. The common folk had respected that. It was like saying, *Okay, my life's better than yours, but I'm willing to die alongside you.*

And Sam had left that aspect out entirely. Where were the fourteenth-century equivalents of the old ladies who sat in their run-down council houses with their collections of royal wedding plates and mugs, telling anyone who asked that the Queen might be the richest woman in the country, but she worked hard and she did a good job, bless her? Where were the citizens of London who turned out to cheer the prince's triumphant return from Poitiers, bringing with him a captive king and, to make sure the cheering didn't die down, having the fountains run with wine instead of water for the day?

The peasants might have revolted in the end, but Sam would bet his PhD a lot of them had had very mixed feelings about it all.

He settled down to make some revisions.

It wasn't until his stomach rumbled that Sam realised just how long he'd been working. He'd missed lunch entirely—fair enough, he'd had a very late breakfast—and it was getting on for five o'clock. Bran hadn't been in touch. Well, okay, that just meant the ball was in Sam's court. Should he call? No, it was too soon. He'd give it a day at least.

Still second-guessing himself, but pleased with the day's work, Sam packed up his things and headed back to Jory's. He lucked out again there—Mal was still in exam mode, and Jory seemed preoccupied. All that was said about the previous night was, "Went well, did it? Good," and later on an awkward reassurance that Sam was perfectly free to have a "guest" stay the night.

After the third time Sam had to repeat himself when talking to Jory, he decided maybe he wasn't the only one who had stuff on his mind. "Are you all right, mate?" he asked cautiously, as he and Jory cleared up after dinner.

"Me? I'm fine."

"Seriously? Because from where I'm standing, you seem like something's eating you." Shit, had Jory somehow found out Sam had spent the night with Bran? Given the obviously strained fraternal relations, that might explain Jory not being comfortable around Sam anymore. "Have you, uh, heard something that bothered you?"

"Oh, it's nothing. Just something Gawen said."

"Gawen?" Huh. Sam always forgot Gawen went to Jory's school, so they presumably saw each other during the day. "Is he okay?"

"He's fine, but I don't think he's been getting on too well with his mum's new man. Gawen said Euan shouted at him over the weekend to leave his effing things alone. And he helpfully pointed out that Euan didn't actually say *effing.*"

"What was that all about?"

"Gawen was looking for something he'd mislaid, and, well, Euan's rucksack was in the living room. Now, Gawen says he only moved it to look underneath, and that he didn't even think of searching inside, which makes Euan's reaction a bit extreme."

"Do you think he's telling the truth?"

"I'd like to think so. Except if he *is*, it's worrying."

Yeah, Sam didn't like to think of any kid getting yelled at for no reason. "Have you spoken to his mum about it?"

"No. I didn't want to overreact myself."

"You wouldn't be overreacting. You're obviously worried, *Gawen's* worried enough to tell you about it, and you don't want to let anything like this escalate. He's your kid too, you know."

Jory was nodding. "Thanks. It's just so hard to judge sometimes, whether I should interfere. I didn't do a great job of being a father for the first years of his life, so Kirsty has every right to tell me to mind my own business."

Sam shrugged. "Just be nice about it, and I'm sure she'll be okay."

"You're right." Jory put down the tea towel. "I'll give her a call now."

Good deed done for the day, Sam thought, and finished clearing up in the kitchen.

Later, as he was going to bed, Sam checked his phone. Still no message from Bran, but then he hadn't really expected one. It was going to have to be him making the first move, wasn't it? Maybe it was a bit soon, but then again, best to make contact before Bran had a chance to turn up at the castle and pretend nothing had happened.

If Sam wanted last night to be the start of something more, that was. When he asked himself that question, he was almost surprised to find he really, really did. He'd been wrong about Bran, dismissing him as just another repressed corporate type with a stick up his arse. Okay, maybe he'd been right about the repression, but Sam got the feeling that was something he'd struggled with all his life. The way he spoke about his family—particularly his dad—made Sam think a lot of Bran's issues had been caused by his upbringing, and that he'd be only too happy to lay them to rest.

It gave Sam a warm feeling, to think he might be able to help with that. And it wasn't just altruistic. Bran with his hair down was a man Sam wanted to spend a lot more time with. His stomach fluttering, Sam fired off a quick text, then shut his phone down for the night.

CHAPTER
THIRTY-ONE

B ran had never been good at mornings after. He generally found
it impossible to gauge whether a partner intended their liaison
to be a one-night stand, or the start of something more regular. Much
of the time, of course, Bran had no desire for a repeat performance—
but making this clear generally went a lot better when the other party
was on the same page.

One thing Craig had been good at was articulating what he
wanted. Which was probably why he'd lasted so much longer than
any other men in Bran's life.

Sam, now . . . Last night it'd all seemed so simple. Earth-shattering,
yes, but also simple. Sam and he were embarking on a relationship,
and they weren't going to hide it. Bran had made the momentous
decision to change everything about his life. But this morning, with
its awkward conversation and nervous glances, had left him uncertain
whether anything had changed at all.

Alone in the kitchen of Roscarrock House, Bran stared into
his coffee cup and tried to see some wisdom in its depths. Did he
want things to change? The thought of it was terrifying—but also
exhilarating. To be openly in a relationship with Sam . . .

The idea fluttered in his stomach. He felt as though he were
standing at a crossroads, and to choose the road ahead would take
him . . . where, he didn't know, but there would be no coming back.
But the roads on either side led nowhere he hadn't been before. And
he was sick and tired of trudging the same old paths.

Then again, it might not be his decision. Would Sam still want a
relationship with him, in the sober light of day? This morning hadn't
exactly been reassuring in that regard, at least, not once they'd got out

of bed. Perhaps Sam had already been regretting his choices of the night before.

This was pointless. Bran would find no answers here, and he wasn't about to hurry over to the castle like a lovesick idiot, begging Sam to tell him where he stood. Bran drank the last of his coffee and rose. Time to get some work done.

Bran settled down to work with his old vigour, and by the time Bea came home, he was well satisfied with his day's progress, especially given the late start. He came out of his study to meet her in the hall. "We should go out to eat tonight."

Bea cocked her head. "Are we celebrating something?"

"Can't I just want to take my sister out for a meal?"

"To make up for not coming home last night?" she asked with unsubtle emphasis.

Bran frowned. "You were all right, weren't you?"

"Of course I was. Don't be silly. I'm a grown woman. And we don't need to eat out. I brought some food home."

Bran had somehow failed to notice the bags by the door, although he realised now there was an enticing aroma of garlic coming from that direction. The bags turned out to contain a varied selection of delights from a local delicatessen. "Feeling hungry tonight?" he asked, surprised.

Bea coloured faintly. "I felt like making an effort, that's all."

"In that case, I'll open a bottle of wine. Pinot grigio?"

She nodded, looking pleased. "That would be nice."

Forking up some rather good pasta salad ten minutes or so later, Bran decided now was as good a time as any to sound her out a bit. "Bea . . . how would you feel about me seeing someone?"

Bea stilled for a moment, but then carried on dissecting her chicken. "Why should I have any particular feelings about it?"

She could be so bloody difficult, sometimes. "If I were to have them to stay at the house, for example?"

"Why are you asking me? Have you met someone you'd want to do that with?"

"I . . . was speaking hypothetically." Bran flushed, even though it wasn't a lie—nothing was settled with Sam, for God's sake.

"Is it a man?" she asked coolly.

She'd known. Of course she'd known. "Would it make a difference if it was?"

Bea put down her fork. "Possibly. To some people, definitely. Whether that would have a material effect on the family's interests—"

"Damn the family's interests. I meant to *you*." Bran took a swallow of his wine. "Your opinion matters. It always has."

"Why wouldn't I want you to be happy?" She didn't meet his gaze.

Bran knew, then, that something was wrong. "Are *you* happy?"

Bea's mouth twisted, and she placed her knife and fork neatly together on her plate.

It had the impact of a drumroll. Bran put his own cutlery down and gave her his full attention. Perhaps, finally, he was going to find out why she'd been so . . . distant these last few weeks. "Are you?" he prompted.

She took a deep breath. "I'm thinking of moving to London."

It was so wholly unexpected Bran couldn't speak for a moment. "Why?"

"I've been offered a job. A good job. And if I don't go now, I never will."

"But do you *want* to leave Porthkennack?" Bran couldn't imagine it. Not for himself, and not for her either. Exchange the wild freedom of the Cornish coast for a life hemmed in by skyscrapers, with the din and reek of constant traffic?

And would Porthkennack be the same without her? They'd always been together, he and Bea. *Always*, apart from when they'd been at school.

Everything changes, Sam had said last night.

"I should have left a long time ago," Bea said harshly.

"Why?" Bran was stung.

Bea stood, shoving her chair back. She didn't walk away, though.

Bran stared at her in silence, fearing any word from him might put her off, might persuade her to keep her thoughts to herself.

"It's never like you imagine it will be, is it?" she said softly.

Bran matched his tone to hers. "What isn't?"

"Life." She paused. "When you were attacked . . . it made me think. I realised that if you died, I'd be all alone. I don't want that. I *hate* it, but I don't."

"You'd still have Jory and Gawen."

She gestured dismissively. "You know Jory and I have never got on. And Gawen's a child."

She'd never been good with children, Bran recalled. Even when she'd been one.

"That's why I've got to go," she went on. "I don't want to sit alone in this old house going mad from the wailing of the wind." *Like Father.* The unspoken words were wrenchingly clear. "I need to make a life for myself. Somewhere else."

"Away from me." Bran felt frozen inside.

"Oh, don't look at me like that! Gawen likes *you*. And you've got your . . . whoever. *Hypothetically*. You've always had your men." She said the last quietly, as though it were something to be ashamed of.

Then again, he'd always acted as if it were, hadn't he?

Bea walked out of the dining room. Bran's appetite went with her, but he forced himself to finish his plate. He was still healing, after all.

The wine he put in the fridge. Perhaps she'd want it later. Bran cleared away the plates and wrapped up the remains of the food to put in the fridge as well. Had she bought all this with her revelations in mind? A figurative last supper for the two of them?

He struggled to decide how he felt about her coming departure. Hurt, yes—she'd made it sound as though she were desperate to get away from him, and how could that do anything *but* hurt him? But no, this was about her, not him. It was a struggle to comprehend, though. He'd always thought Bea sufficient unto herself.

It was both reassuring and unsettling to hear that she'd known all along about Bran's men, despite the fact they'd never talked about the subject. Perhaps they should have. Well, that would change. He wouldn't exclude her from his relationship with Sam—if, that was, Sam agreed that they should embark upon one.

When he plugged in his phone charger before bed, he found he had a message. From Sam.

Heart thumping, he opened it up. *Can you come to the castle tomorrow? I've got something to show you.*

Bran stared at it for a long time before sending a quick, affirmative reply. So, he'd find out tomorrow where he stood with Sam. And it boded well that Sam had asked to see him so soon.

Didn't it?

His emotions riding a switchback between excitement and fear, it took him a long time to find sleep that night.

CHAPTER THIRTY-TWO

The next morning, Bran forced himself to wait until midmorning before going down to the castle to see Sam. Sick of taking taxis everywhere, he decided on impulse to take his BMW for its first outing in . . . how many weeks? Bran didn't like to count. The car didn't seem to resent his neglect, or perhaps was simply happy to be in use once more, as it started readily and purred all the way across town. Even his ribs, still achy, didn't protest as much as they might have at the unaccustomed exertion.

Bran hoped it was a good omen. His heart rate sped as he got out of the BMW. He wasn't at all sure what would be the outcome of this meeting with Sam, and couldn't help remembering the awkwardness that had descended between them after they'd left the Newquay flat. Still, Sam had said he had something to show Bran—not the dreaded *We need to talk*. It was at least cautiously optimistic.

Having found the Portakabin empty, Bran walked over to the exhibition centre. Sam was in the reception area, talking to Roarke. He used wide, open gestures while Roarke nodded, face impassive, apparently impervious to the lively charms of the man in front of him. Although he would be, wouldn't he? Roarke had been married twenty years and, as far as Bran knew, had never looked at another woman, let alone a man.

Bran's stomach fluttered anew. Given the choice, he would have much preferred to have met Sam without witnesses. Should he have waited in the Portakabin? No, that would have been ridiculous. Still—

Sam glanced over and smiled.

Bran's chest was tight, but it was a good tightness. Not painful. He found himself smiling back, and took a moment to compose himself before striding over to Sam. "Good morning. You had something to show me?"

"Yeah. Yeah, I did."

"I can wait if—"

"No, no. We're done here." Sam turned back to Roarke. "Okay, so we're clear on that?"

Roarke nodded. "Will do. Morning, Mr. Roscarrock." He hesitated for a moment.

"Carry on," Bran said quickly.

Roarke nodded again and walked away, leaving Bran with the oddest feeling that the man had hovered in case Bran might be in need of protection. *From Sam?* No, that was absurd.

"The display case for the funerary achievements has arrived, and they're about to start installing it." Sam huffed a rueful laugh. "I wanted to make sure they knew just how important it is to get it right."

"God, yes." Bran couldn't help following Roarke's retreating figure with his gaze. Should he have a word with the man himself? No, he trusted Roarke—and he trusted Sam, too, to have given all necessary instructions. Still . . . "Did you remind him it was custom-built, and the Canterbury conservators will want to inspect it soon?"

"Yeah, not to worry. I made a point of telling him just how much that thing cost too. Was that a Canterbury requirement? I mean, it's only going to be in use for a few months, and I'd have thought you could have got something off the shelf a good few thousand quid cheaper."

Bran shrugged. "Nothing that would have fitted in with the style of the other display cases. It was well worth the extra expense."

"I guess." Sam had an odd expression on his face.

Bran gave up trying to interpret it. "Was it the display case you wanted to show me?"

"Oh, no—I thought you'd prefer to see that once it's in situ. No, come back to my office." Sam looked happier than Bran had ever seen him. It was attractive—and contagious. "Um. Coffee? We can get one on the way."

"No, I'm fine." Bran's nerves needed no extra stimulation this morning. "What did you want to talk about?"

"I, uh, well, I've been working on some of the displays. Again. I've redone the one on Limoges, and I think you're going to like—"

Bran stopped dead, a void opening up in his stomach. "You've done this because of . . . because of what happened?" This wasn't what he wanted at all. Not from Sam. If Bran won an argument, he wanted it to be because he'd *won*, not because Sam felt— What? The need to please him?

"No! I mean, yeah, kinda, but . . ." Sam ran a hand through his hair. "I realised you had a point on some of it. So yeah, maybe it's because of . . . you know, in a way, but only because we had this whole clash-of-heads thing going on. And, um, now we don't."

Sam stood there on the grass, halfway back to the castle, looking impossibly young with the wind fluffing up his tousled hair and an uncertain expression on his face.

"I see." Bran wasn't at all sure he did. He cleared his throat. "Then we should . . ." He gestured towards the Portakabin.

Once inside, the door closed behind them, Bran wasn't sure how to deal with the new intimacy between them. From the way he held back, Sam was equally at sea. They stood there for a moment, gazing at each other—then Sam's face creased into a smile, and all at once they were both laughing.

Bran desperately wanted to touch him, to hold him. But they were in the workplace. And besides, although he now had even more reason to be hopeful, he didn't have definite proof that a touch would be welcome.

"Bit weird, isn't it?" Sam waved vaguely around. "You and me, meeting in the office, after, uh, Monday night."

Bran nodded. "We should probably keep things professional. While we're here." He held his breath, but Sam didn't take the opportunity to correct him, to say that he'd reconsidered and now thought things should remain professional between them in all spheres.

Sam just smiled and said, "Definitely. Right, uh, I'll show you what I've done. Come and see." He gestured for Bran to follow him around the desk, and sat in his chair to bring up his work on the computer.

Bran stood behind him, looking over his shoulder and struggling to resist the urge to put an arm around him. It didn't help that Sam had pushed up his sleeves *again*.

Things became easier once Bran was able to focus on the exhibition, and it was paradoxically reassuring to see the limited changes Sam had made. He'd by no means gone as far as Bran might have wanted him to—there was still an emphasis on presenting different views, but somehow the whole feel of the displays was more positive. Celebratory, even.

For the first time, the exhibition felt like something they'd created together, not work for hire done under protest. Bran suggested a few minor alterations of wording here and there, and Sam agreed in some cases with an airy, *Yeah, why not?* In others, he stood his ground. When Bran argued his point, discussion was spirited, but somehow they managed to avoid the animosity of the past. More than that— it was fun. The differing viewpoints were still there, but there was something new too. Respect for one another. Their first meeting, with Bran in pain and feeling undermined, his authority usurped, had done more harm than he'd guessed.

Looking back, Bran could scarcely believe that a scant few days ago, presenting Edward of Woodstock in a positive light had been all-important to him. As Sam had said, what did it *matter* if not everyone shared Bran's view of the man as a national hero? He didn't need their validation.

Hadn't he already accepted the impossibility of pleasing everyone in his private life?

"We should have lunch," Bran said almost before the thought had fully formed in his head.

"Now?" Sam glanced at the time displayed in the corner of his screen. "Whoa. When did it get this late?"

Bran felt similar shock to see it was after 1 p.m. "Do you like Italian food?"

"Who doesn't?"

"Funnily enough, my sister's never been much of a fan." But then she'd always seemed to view eating as more of a chore than a pleasure.

Sam gave one of his easy, irresistible smiles. "Good thing you've got me to eat it with, then."

Yes. Yes, it was. "I'll give Gente di Mare a ring." Bran dialled the number and was reassured that of course there was a table free for Mr. Roscarrock and his guest.

Sam looked at him quizzically when he hung up. "Does anyone ever say no when you ask for a table?"

Bran blinked. "Not for a midweek lunch, no. But for Friday nights and special occasions, I book ahead like anyone else."

Sam grinned. "Just checking."

Gente di Mare was a small, family-run restaurant situated in a Porthkennack side street. Bran had first eaten there because he liked to encourage local businesses, and had returned since for the relaxed atmosphere, continuity of staff, and decent, no-nonsense food. The window tables were already occupied when Bran and Sam got there, and they were shown through an archway to a table towards the back of the restaurant.

A curious blend of relief and disappointment washed over Bran. Having decided to take the leap into a relationship with Sam—and he was almost certain, after this morning, that Sam still wanted that, wanted *him*—it felt like an anticlimax not to sit in the window together for all to see. Although in fact there was nothing about the two of them to indicate that they were anything more than acquaintances—friends, at most. Nothing to betray that they'd spent Monday night in bed together, touching one another intimately, again and again. Bran's breath caught at the memory.

"All right?" Sam glanced up from his menu. His eyes shone with warmth. Bran found himself captivated all over again.

"Fine." Bran gave a rueful smile. "I suppose, as it's a workday, we shouldn't order wine. Unless you'd care to make an exception?"

"Love to, but I'm thinking we'd probably better have this conversation sober."

"A fair point. So, ah, we should probably order."

They each chose pasta dishes, salads and, regretfully, mineral water. Not that Bran *needed* the help of alcohol, but, well, it wouldn't have gone amiss, either.

He was still wondering where to start when Sam broke the brief silence. "You eat out a lot, don't you? Cos I've got to tell you, I don't know how you manage to stay so trim on it."

Bran tried not to look too pleased at the compliment. "I exercise. And meals at home aren't generally all that inspired, I'm afraid. Neither Bea nor I enjoy cooking."

"No? I find it kind of relaxing. You don't have to be all finicky and exact with food—just throw in a few ingredients and see what comes out."

"Garbage, in my case. And I thought that was why there were recipe books?"

"My mum taught me to cook, and she never uses recipes. At least, not written-down ones. She just cooks stuff she learned from her mum. Or she gets ideas off the telly. She does a wicked roast lamb."

Bran tried to imagine himself in the kitchen with his mother, receiving instruction on preparing a meal, and actually sparked a long-forgotten memory of baking with her. Something sweet, he thought—for a moment the remembered aroma of vanilla overpowered the scent of garlic and basil that pervaded the restaurant. It must have been before Jory had come along and she'd been too ill and tired all the time to bother with that sort of thing.

"I've always thought lamb makes the best roast, if it's done well," he said, mostly to cover the confused emotions that memory had inspired.

"Yeah? Hey, me too. And seriously, you'd sell your own grandmother for the way my mum cooks it. It never quite turns out the same when I do it. I mean, Jory and Mal thought it was great when I made it for them, but I could tell, you know?" Sam lowered his voice, his tone seductive. "I could cook it for you, sometime."

Bran's heart rate increased. "I'd like that." He was considering whether to reach across the table to take Sam's hand when the waiter returned with their drinks, breaking the charged atmosphere.

How would the waiter react if Bran did it anyway? Would he care? He was a young man, early twenties at most. Did any young people care these days if they saw two men holding hands?

More to the point, why should Bran worry about what a young man who knew him only as a customer thought? Wild recklessness seized him again, and he almost acted on his impulse—but Sam had pulled out his phone and was tapping at it. The moment had passed.

"Sorry about that. Message from Jennifer." Sam made an odd expression, then held out his phone. The text read, *Need a rescue?* "I think maybe we were seen leaving together?"

"Ah." Bran hesitated, this reminder of the outside world, and its probable reaction to them being together, dampening his mood. "What will you tell her?"

"I, um, well. I thought we'd talk about that?" Sam ran a hand through his hair. "So, uh— Oh, looks like this is us."

Their food arrived moments afterwards. Bran was seriously reconsidering his policy of always leaving a tip.

"Ever go out for pub lunches?" Sam asked, forking up his spaghetti with an expert twirl.

"Occasionally the Hope & Anchor. Their food is excellent, although I'd warn you, it's hardly pub-grub prices."

"Not the Sea Bell, then?"

Bran winced at the challenge in his tone. "You've heard about the Gerren Ede business, then."

"Uh, no, I was thinking of your, um, nephew? Mal's mate, Dev. Who's Gerren Ede?"

"An old friend of the landlord of the Sea Bell. And of most of the regulars. He was a popular man—volunteered on the lifeboats for years. He used to rent his house from me."

"And?"

Bran suppressed a sigh. This was *not* what he wanted to be talking about right now. "He was a nightmare of a tenant. No, that's unfair, but he certainly wasn't easy. I'd been trying to get him to let me modernise that house for years—the kitchen in particular was in a shocking state, and there was damp in the bathroom—but he kept coming up with excuses not to let the work go ahead. Consequently, when he passed away, there was a great deal to be done and we needed vacant possession."

"Why didn't he want the work done?"

"He complained to all and sundry that it wasn't fair to expect a man of his age to deal with all the upheaval." Bran scowled. "As I eventually found out, it was more like he didn't want to have to move his pot plants, or risk anyone finding them."

Sam laughed. "You mean pot as in hash? Seriously?"

"Apparently he suffered from arthritis." Bran concentrated on his pasta, unable to meet Sam's gaze. "I . . . may have overreacted a little at that point. It felt like adding insult to injury, finding illegal drugs on the premises, plus I had the contractor on my back saying they could do the work either now or in six months' time, and I certainly couldn't re-let the property without the renovations . . ."

"So you told the old boy's family to clear out?"

"A little more abruptly than might have been compassionate, given their recent bereavement, yes. I'm not proud of having let my temper rule me." Bran stared at the flower vase in the middle of their table, its solid blue and white stripes comfortingly familiar. He'd far too often let anger be his default response to any perceived threat. That was going to change, starting now.

"Hey, we've all done stuff we're not proud of." Sam leaned across the table and placed a warm hand on Bran's arm, but only for an instant. So that no one observing them would notice anything untoward, presumably. It was thoughtful of him, although unnecessary, and Bran wished the touch had lingered.

He was beginning to suspect Sam was a far better man than he was. "I can't imagine you doing anything unworthy."

"Believe me, I've had my moments." Sam ducked his head.

"It can't have been anything too bad."

Still not meeting Bran's eye, Sam drew in a shaky breath and let it out again.

Concerned, Bran put down his fork. Whatever it was, it clearly troubled Sam to admit it. The words *No, you don't have to tell me* were on the tip of Bran's tongue when Sam spoke. "I . . . well, I used to have a bit of a gambling problem."

"Gambling?" That was the last thing Bran would have expected. And was that all? He had thought Sam about to confess to something terrible. Bran took a mouthful of pasta in relief.

"Yeah. See, after that bad breakup I mentioned the other night, I . . . kind of needed something to distract me. And, uh, I was unemployed at the time, so a little easy money would've gone down nicely. Don't worry—I've stopped now. Made a clean break from it when I came down here."

"That's very commendable." Bran knew only too well how hard some habits were to kick.

Sam grimaced. "Haven't paid off all the debts yet, but I'm going to."

"But if money was tight, why waste it on gambling? You're an intelligent man. You must know the odds are against you." Bran made a helpless gesture with his fork. "I don't mean to berate you. I'm just trying to understand."

Sam shot him a wary glance, then took a breath. "It's . . . it's a rush, I guess. Those few moments just before you find out if you've won or lost, everything else goes away, and you just focus in on the gamble. I mean, don't you ever . . . I dunno, buy houses at auction?"

Bran blinked. "Sometimes, yes."

"And don't you get that buzz when you win?"

"I . . . Maybe?" Bran thought back. "In the beginning, I suppose I did. Yes. But after a while, it all became routine."

When had he lost the joy in what he did? The thrill of a successful venture? Was this why the Black Prince exhibition had come to mean so much to him? Because the rest of his life had become empty?

No. No, that wasn't true. He had his family. Gawen in particular.

Whom he'd been grooming to take over the reins of the family business. Was Bran just setting up his nephew for a life of chasing profit while finding no real satisfaction in the capture?

"Bran?"

"Sorry, what?"

"You, uh, spaced out a bit there. Is everything okay?" Sam sounded anxious.

Bran nodded slowly. "My apologies. These debts—how large are they? Have they been passed on to debt collectors?" Guilt surged as he recalled his earlier blithe comments about a few thousand extra pounds being a small price to pay for perfection.

"It's nothing I can't deal with."

"I meant—I know what debt collectors can be like." Bran flushed. "I've had to employ them upon occasion. I thought . . . I could make you a loan."

"No."

"Why not? I can afford it."

"*No.*"

"Because I'm in some sense your employer?" Bran huffed. "We've been through all that. But if it bothers you, look at it this way: anything that's causing you stress is likely to impact your performance at work. It would be beneficial for all concerned—"

"I said no, all right? It's not . . ." Sam ran a hand through his hair. "I don't want you lending me money."

"Why not?"

"Because . . . because it'd change our relationship. And I don't want that."

"Our relationship?" It was what he'd wanted to talk about all along, and yet he found himself woefully unprepared for the sudden reappearance of the subject.

"I meant . . . professionally. As friends, even." Sam gazed earnestly at him across the table. "We are friends now, aren't we?"

"Are we?" Bran's mouth was dry. Was he about to be let down gently after all?

He wasn't sure he could bear it.

Sam glanced down, and then away. "Look, I think we got on okay the other night. Better than okay. And—cards on the table—I'd like us to be more than friends. If that's what you want too."

More than friends. Bran's heart swelled with a wild joy he didn't think he'd ever known before. When he put a hand on Sam's arm, they both tensed, and Sam breathed in sharply but didn't move away. "Yes," Bran said, his voice tight and hoarse. "I'd like that."

They should have kissed then. It was a moment for a kiss. But they were in a restaurant, in public, in the middle of the day, and they were British. So instead Bran took a deep breath and tried to convey with his eyes how very much he would like that.

"Ground rules, though. I'm not going to be anyone's dirty little secret." Sam's voice was strained. "Been there, done that, got the scars to prove it."

"The bad breakup you spoke of?"

"Yeah. You remembered. So . . ." Sam swallowed, the workings of his throat mesmerising.

"I . . ." Bran took a deep breath. Today was his day for being reckless, wasn't it? "I accept those terms."

Sam gave a curt half laugh. "Wanna have your lawyer run up a contract? Shit, no, sorry, don't get uptight. I'm a bit on edge."

"But you do want to . . . be in a relationship. Openly. With me." Sudden doubt made Bran queasy.

Sam dug his fingers into his hair again, but he was smiling, and the sight of that warm, honest expression made everything all right. "You drive me fucking crazy, you know. Yeah. Let's give it a go. Christ knows how we'll explain it to Jory and Mal—or even *Jennifer*, bloody hell—but yeah."

CHAPTER
THIRTY-THREE

S am hadn't got a lot of work done this afternoon. For a start, he'd been late back—very late. He and Bran went for a walk along the sea front after they'd eaten, and Bran shared stories of growing up in Porthkennack, plus a couple of anecdotes from his schooldays that made Sam fervently glad he'd been a state school lad. Sam told him about family holidays in Goa, feeling way more British than he ever did back home, and trying to remember which auntie was which when he only saw them once a year.

It was good. Really good. Bran was open, and clearly happy, in a way Sam had worried he might never see again. Some blokes were just like that: all over you for a night—and even for the morning after— but then they acted like they barely knew you the next time you met. Sam was glad they hadn't gone for the wine at lunchtime. At least now he knew for sure it hadn't just been the alcohol that'd got Bran going the previous night.

It was him. Sam got a warm feeling just thinking about it.

They parted with a kiss—right out in public—and a promise to have dinner together in a couple of nights' time. Sam couldn't wait. And later that afternoon, just before he was about to leave work for the day, he got an email from Bran. Sam wasn't sure what to expect— would Bran be up for romantic *can't stop thinking about you* type messages? Or would he be the sort to keep it strictly businesslike?

In the end it was neither. Or both, maybe: Bran had sent him a tactful couple of lines along with links to government debt advice and the Citizens Advice Bureau. Which . . . okay, Sam was still cringing a little from Bran knowing about the hole Sam had dug for himself, but on the other hand, what could say clearer that Bran was thinking about him? Sam had been on tenterhooks, telling Bran about that, but he'd felt he owed it to the bloke, wanted to show Bran he wasn't the only one who cocked stuff up now and again. And after all his worry, all Bran wanted to do was help him out. It was just as well it was the end of the day. Sam wasn't sure he could have concentrated on work if his life had depended on it.

Should he mention the new state of affairs to the people he was living with? Yeah, he really, really should, he decided as he let himself into Jory's house that evening. Before they started coming up with their own explanations for him going around with a soppy grin on his face all the time.

Sam waited until they were eating that evening, plates on their laps in the living room, to bring up the subject of Bran. For one thing, it was the only time Mal didn't have his nose in his laptop or his notes. And for another, it made it easier to naturally work the conversation round to it.

Well, that was the theory, anyhow.

What actually happened was every time they got even close, either Jory or Mal would veer off at a tangent. Sam was seriously starting to think the meal would be over, and Mal would be back to his books, before he got a chance to say anything.

He decided to make one last-ditch effort. "Listen, about Bran—"

"Yeah, why do we keep talking about that git?" Mal shoved a forkful of food in his mouth.

Sam cringed inside, and then went for it. "I'm, um, seeing him. Bran. We're together."

Mal choked.

Jory thumped Mal's back, but it was Sam he stared at. "You . . . and *Bran*?"

"Uh, yeah."

"Is he even into blokes?" Mal's face had gone an unattractive red, and his eyes were watering. "Or, like, people? At *all*?"

"I thought you hated him?" Jory's voice had gone up about an octave.

"We just had a personality-clash thing going on." *Great, Sam. Way to convince them it's a match made in heaven.* "I mean, before we got to know each other."

Jory's eyebrows made a bid for flight. "So when did you *get to know* each other?"

"Uh, the other night."

"Uh-*huh*." Mal took a gulp of water. "So, we're talking biblical sense here, are we?"

"That night you didn't come home . . ." Jory looked horrified.

Sam was starting to get a bit pissed off with this. "Look, he's a grown man, okay?"

"Trust me, mate, not the issue," Mal muttered just as Jory came out with, "He's *Bran*."

Jory coughed. "Are you sure he feels the same way?" It was the same tone of voice he might have used to ask one of his schoolkids if they were sure the Empire State Building was on the planet Coruscant and not in, say, America.

"*Yes*. We had lunch today at that Italian place in town and, you know, talked. About being open about it, and all."

Jory stood up abruptly and walked out of the living room. A clatter from the kitchen suggested he'd deposited his half-eaten dinner in the sink, and none too gently at that. Footsteps sounded on the stairs.

Sam felt cold. Beside him, Mal stared down at his plate and sighed.

"What the hell?" Sam struggled to work out what was going on. "I thought he and Bran were getting on better these days? Why's he being such a—"

"You don't wanna finish that sentence, mate. Trust me." Mal took a last regretful look at his dinner and put his plate on the floor. Then he stood up, rubbed the back of his neck, and grimaced. "Look, it's just . . . Bran gave Jory all kinds of shit about being gay, that's all. Telling him he should suck it up and stay married to Kirsty for the good of The Family." Sam could hear the capital letters. "And now he's gonna . . . Ah, fuck it. Don't worry, mate. Not your fault."

Mal disappeared up the stairs, presumably to go comfort Jory.

Fuck.

Sam ate another forkful, but his appetite had gone. He cleared up the plates—covering Mal's in case he might want to finish it later—and washed up. It seemed like the least he could do.

Then he googled the nearest cinema and took himself out for the evening. That also seemed like the least he could do. And the latest action movie sequel was mindless enough.

It wasn't until he'd snuck back into the house and was getting ready for bed that Sam noticed Mum had left a message on his phone for him to call her. Sam glanced at the time, but he already knew it'd be too late to call now. He'd have to leave it until tomorrow. It almost certainly wasn't anything dire—when Uncle Alessandro, whom he'd been named for, had died, Sam had had messages from all three of his sisters as well as his mum and his auntie.

No, it was nothing to worry about. Sam got into bed and lay there, thinking about Bran. Christ, he was so different when you got to know him properly. Still had that fire, that passion—but he was a lot more sensitive than Sam reckoned anyone gave him credit for. Yeah, he made mistakes, but he owned them afterwards. He'd even taken Sam's confession about the gambling debts totally in stride.

Should Sam tell him about the Joan of Arc paper, and how it'd got him fired? His stomach clenched. It felt dishonest not to—but then again, maybe it'd be better to hold off until the exhibition opened, and Sam had proved he could do a bloody good job? He wasn't sure. If Bran was preparing to come out and be honest about them being together, shouldn't Sam show the same honesty to him?

Sam yawned. Tomorrow. He'd sort everything out tomorrow.

CHAPTER THIRTY-FOUR

After saying goodbye to Sam following their extended lunch, Bran made his way home in something of a daze. He'd done it. He'd committed to a proper relationship—and to being open about it.

He should be terrified. In fact, judging by the feverish churning of his stomach, he *was*. But more than that, he felt wonderfully, joyfully *free*.

Why hadn't he done this years ago? Bran snorted. For a start, he hadn't met Sam then, had he? He couldn't help thinking of Craig. They'd been together—for a given value of *together*—for nearly a year, and Bran had never, until very recently, seriously considered being open about their relationship. What was it about Sam Ferreira that had him agreeing to take that step after a single night?

Or did it say more about Craig—or rather, the way Bran had felt about him from the start? He'd been honest with the man, hadn't he? Told him from day one that he wasn't interested in romance. But the length of time they'd been together might easily have led Craig to assume Bran had changed his mind.

Bran hadn't meant to lead him on. But the stab of guilt that pierced his bubble of happiness told him he'd probably done just that.

He should apologise, and the sooner the better—certainly before Craig heard about Sam from any other source. Bringing up Craig in his contact list, Bran sent a quick text. *Can you meet me this evening?*

The answer came within minutes. *Dinner at Tinners Rest?*

God, no. Not after his evening there with Sam, and all that had followed. Bran texted back with the name of a wine bar in Newquay they'd been to before and which was convenient for Craig to get to after work, and a time: 6 p.m. It was highly unlikely Craig would want to draw out the evening after he heard what Bran had to say, and Bran certainly didn't intend to make a night of it.

He had a few hours in hand now. Plenty of time to start looking for possible help with Sam's debt problem. Sam might not want to accept money from him—but hopefully he wouldn't take offence at some advice. Bran smiled, and opened up his web browser.

Bran arrived in Newquay for his meeting with Craig a little early, which was how he liked it. The wine bar was brash, modern, and impersonal, with chrome fittings and a tiled floor that magnified the din of the after-work hubbub. Men and women in suits mingled with others in more casual business attire, most of them far closer to Craig's age than Bran's.

Bran took a stool up at the bar and ordered a bottle of sauvignon blanc. He'd barely taken more than a sip of it before Craig arrived.

"Bran. Lovely to see you." Craig slid onto the stool next to Bran's. He was wearing a pale-grey suit with an eggshell-blue shirt Bran had always liked. Strange, how it left him cold today. Craig's carefully tousled hair was perfectly in place, a tribute to whatever expensive product he was using to excess, and didn't move a millimetre as Craig took off his jacket, folded it carefully, and placed it on the bar. Having first, of course, checked to ensure there was nothing spilled there. His appearance was impeccable, but it only made Bran want Sam, with his easy smiles and casually pushed-up sleeves, all the more.

"Wine?" At Craig's nod, Bran poured him a glass.

"Thank you." Craig took a gulp, then put his glass down with a sigh. "You know, I'd almost given up hope of hearing from you again, let alone seeing you."

"I thought I should speak to you in person," Bran began.

"You thought you *should*? That doesn't sound hopeful."

Wishing he'd had the time to drink more of his wine already, Bran pushed on. "I owe you an apology. I . . . didn't treat you very well."

Craig's gaze narrowed almost imperceptibly, but then his forehead smoothed. "All forgiven now, I assure you."

"That's decent of you."

"So what brought this on?" Craig played with his glass, swirling the wine around to form arches.

"I'm seeing someone." Bran forced himself to look at Craig as he spoke, and didn't miss the little moue of hurt that formed for an instant, then vanished as if it had never been.

"A woman?"

"A man." Bran gave a nervous laugh. "I've finally taken your advice to be more open about . . . that sort of thing."

The expression that spread across Craig's face could not have been more different from one of Sam's spontaneous smiles. "Wonderful. And who is the lucky man?"

"His name's Sam Ferreira. He's a friend of Jory's, from Edinburgh University. A historian, a very talented one."

"Ferreira? Spanish?" Craig raised an eyebrow. "Dark and handsome, I presume? You always did have a thing for exotic beauties."

Bran frowned. "He's not *exotic*. He's a British man of Goan descent. He's curating my exhibition."

"Your . . .?" Craig frowned as if puzzled.

"The Black Prince exhibition," Bran said, keeping his voice even. He'd mentioned it to Craig often enough before. But he was supposed to be apologising here; he could allow Craig his petty digs.

"How lovely that you have a shared interest." Craig tossed back his wine and stood. "Well, I mustn't keep you. I'm sure you and Sam have plenty to do together." He had his face under control now, and his voice was light and carefree.

Bran stood. "I'm sorry. I never meant to hurt you."

Craig laughed. "Oh, my goodness. Is that what you're worried about? Don't worry. You're hardly the only fish in the sea." His smile tightened as he put his jacket back on, paying attention to the lay of his cuffs. "You never were."

That rankled, but Bran held his tongue and watched Craig leave. After a few minutes, he ordered some tapas to go with his wine. The food here was good; might as well make the most of what was likely to be his last visit for a very long while.

When Bran got back home an hour or so later, there was a message from Craig on his phone. Bran sighed, but clicked on it. Best to get it, whatever it was, over with.

The email was surprisingly short. A single line: *I hope you're aware of your curator's public reputation*, followed by a couple of links. Then another line: *No doubt he's entirely trustworthy in the personal sphere.*

For God's sake. Had Craig gone directly from the wine bar to his computer to try to dig up some dirt on Sam? Bran's exasperation turned cold as he reread Craig's words. What precisely did he mean about Sam's reputation? His trustworthiness?

The first link was to a page from the Edinburgh University site. It took Bran to a university publication, showing a thumbnail picture of Sam and, underneath it, the name *Dr. Alessandro Ferreira*. His hair was shorter and he looked younger, but there was no mistaking that face. Bran couldn't find anything noteworthy about the information, although it was disconcerting to realise he apparently hadn't known Sam's real first name. Bran frowned and clicked the second link.

What he found chilled him to the core.

CHAPTER THIRTY-FIVE

Sam's stomach roiled queasily as he parked his car at the castle. Breakfast this morning had been awkward as hell. Jory had clearly still been upset over Bran's . . . hypocrisy, Sam supposed it must look like, but Christ, wasn't a man allowed a change of heart? God knew Bran hadn't found it easy to get to where he was now—couldn't Jory see that?

But no, he probably couldn't, could he, because Bran and Jory, they didn't bloody *talk*, did they? Not about emotional stuff, anyhow. It seemed a shame, what with them being brothers and all—but then, when had Sam's sisters ever come crying on his shoulder about their love lives? There wasn't as big an age gap between Sam and Maria as there was between Bran and Jory, but even so, the thought was a mix of ridiculous and horrifying.

Mixed feelings were pretty much all Sam had right now. He felt bad about Jory—but he couldn't help resenting him just a bit too. Then he felt guilty about *that*, because he owed Jory a lot.

So at any rate, while Sam was glad Bran had responded to his text of *Can we talk?* with a short and snappy *Your office 9 a.m.*, he wasn't sure how the conversation was going to go or even how it *should* go. He felt torn between wanting Bran to acknowledge how his actions had hurt Jory, and wanting to defend the bloke. Fuck it, maybe he should just lock them in a room together and let *them* talk it out.

Except he really wanted to see Bran himself, because, Christ, he'd got it bad and he'd been missing him already. Sam couldn't help smiling when he saw Bran waiting for him outside the Portakabin. His expression faltered as Bran very much didn't smile back.

"Is everything okay?" Sam asked as he unlocked the door. Shit, had Bran been thinking Sam had got him here to break up with him? "Look, when I said I wanted to talk, it's nothing major, honest."

"Isn't it?" Bran's voice was so frigid Sam turned to stare.

"Uh, what?"

"Inside."

Shocked, Sam waved Bran ahead of him and followed him into the Portakabin. He shut the door behind them. "What's wrong?"

"Oh, nothing *major*." Bran's tone dripped bitterness. "Simply that you've lied to me from day one. About your past, about your credentials—about your *name*, for Christ's sake, Dr. Alessandro Ferreira, late of Edinburgh University. Late and, I might add, very much unlamented. As you're doubtless aware. Well done; it made it harder to pick you up in an internet search. But not impossible."

Oh. Oh *Christ*.

Bran knew everything.

His knees weak, Sam sank against his desk. Why hadn't he told Bran all about it earlier? *Jory knew*, he wanted to say. But he couldn't, because what kind of a shit would make relations between the brothers even *worse*? "I didn't lie about my name," he said shakily. "*Sam's* just a nickname. My youngest sister, Nat, when I was born she couldn't say *Alessandro*, and she just called me *Sam*, and it stuck."

"But the rest?" Bran's face was as cold as ever he'd seen it. It was like the shutters had come back down. As if the guy he'd laughed with on the beach had never existed.

And it was all Sam's fault. His chest hollow, Sam hung his head. "It's complicated, all right?"

"Not really. Or at least, not as I see it. Were you, or were you not, fired from your post at Edinburgh University when it came to light that you'd falsified the research behind one of your papers?"

"Yeah. Yeah, I was. But it wasn't how it sounds." Sam's voice came over as desperate in his own ears. Pleading.

"Then how was it?" Bran's tone was clipped. Disbelieving.

Bastard. Sam's temper flared as he took in that closed-off face. "Do you even want to hear what I've got to say? Is there any point to all this, or should I just go straight over to Jory's and pack my bags and save us both the aggro? Because you giving me a fair hearing? I'm not getting that. Not from the way you're looking at me now." His fist had clenched all on its own. Sam forced himself to straighten out his fingers.

Bran's eyes narrowed. "How the bloody hell do you expect me to look at you? As if I'm happy the exhibition I've been planning for years, have invested a considerable amount of my own money in, has been irretrievably ruined, its credibility utterly undermined? I'm going to be a bloody laughing stock. All because of what you did."

"Nothing's been ruined! That paper was on Joan of Arc, not the Black Prince." Sam ran a frustrated hand through his hair. "The Black Prince had been dead for fifty years by then, for Christ's sake."

"You really think that matters? Why should anyone believe a word you say anymore? Why should *I* believe you?"

"Why should *you* believe me?" Fuck, that was a low blow. "Because I thought we had something. I thought you— Fuck it, I thought you were actually starting to care about me."

"Apparently the man I may have been starting to *care* about doesn't actually exist."

"Jesus, Bran, I'm still the same person. I made a mistake, that's all."

Bran's tight-lipped expression didn't soften, and Sam's hopes crumbled. "Deliberately falsifying research isn't a *mistake*. It's fraud."

"Christ, if that's how you feel, why not call the bloody cops? So this is it, then? You're going to tell me to fuck off for something that happened before we even met? Fine. Tell you what? Don't bother. I'm going. Have a nice exhibition. Have a nice sodding *life*."

His hands shaking, Sam wrenched open the door of the Portakabin and launched himself through it.

Bran didn't say a word.

Sam drove almost blindly, away from the castle and out into the countryside with no idea where he was going. When he saw a sign to a clifftop viewpoint he took the road—little more than a track—and drove up to the far end of a small car park. The few other cars there were clustered around an ice cream van near the entrance. Sam was alone, which was how he wanted it.

He stood in the stiff breeze that was blowing up from the sea, gazing down over crags and rocks to the churning water below. Was he *never* going to escape his past? Was one moment of weakness always going to count more than all the years of study and hard, hard work before it?

This was supposed to be his fresh start. And for fuck's sake, he hadn't lied about anything. He'd checked that Jory knew all the facts before he took the job, hadn't he? So how come he was apparently still in the wrong?

Bran had looked at him like he was *nothing*. Like he wished he'd never set eyes on Sam. He hadn't even given him the chance to explain—he'd had Sam tried and convicted before Sam could say a word in his own defence. That was Bran all over. Leaping to judgement. Seeing everything in black-and-white. Nobody was wholly good or bad, were they? Not the Black Prince, and certainly not Bran himself, the self-righteous bastard.

The wind was making his eyes sting, and Sam blinked furiously. It wasn't fair . . . except it was, wasn't it? He'd brought all this on himself. The Edinburgh thing would never have happened if he hadn't been so bloody naïve. If he hadn't wanted what he shouldn't have. And Bran . . .

That was worse. Sam had *known* he ought to tell Bran about his past. He'd known how important the exhibition was to Bran, and he still hadn't disclosed information that Bran would absolutely have wanted to know. He'd pushed it aside, told himself it didn't matter so long as he'd been honest with Jory—Jory, who was nothing to do with the exhibition or the Woodstock Trust. He'd just done a favour for a brother he didn't like all that much.

Even after they'd slept together, Sam had been too busy living in the moment. Seizing the day, because tomorrow the axe might fall.

It'd bloody well fallen now.

The breeze freshened, and Sam wrapped his arms around himself, although the sun was still shining. Christ, how could he have done that to Bran? Undermined the very thing he held most dear—well, maybe not, because God knew the guy loved his nephew, and Sam was fairly sure he was fond of Jory too under all that big-brother posturing, but still, the Black Prince was Bran's passion. Had been all his life, pretty much. And Sam had lied—by omission, at any rate—about a threat to that passion.

Christ, he was a dick.

Seagulls swooped and whirled around the rocks below, their cries sounding over the crashing of the waves. How far down were they—a hundred feet? More? Life must be so bloody simple for seagulls. Catch fish. Eat fish. Maybe steal some poor sod's ice cream for dessert. Rinse and repeat.

"Are you all right, mate?"

The voice startled Sam, and he whirled. A middle-aged white bloke in walking gear was standing there with a worried look on his face. "Uh, yeah, fine."

"The wife and I were just about to get a cup of tea." He nodded to a plump lady standing a few yards away, holding a grinning Staffie on a lead. "You'd be very welcome to join us."

"I . . . No, I'm good, thanks." Sam mustered up a weak smile. Christ, he must look worse than he felt. "Not a jumper. Just came up here to think, you know?"

"Sure?"

"Yeah. I'm fine." Sam moved away from the edge to show willing, and the guy visibly relaxed. "Going to head back down in a mo."

He did end up having tea with the couple, because they looked so worried about him. Roger, the bloke, bought him a doughnut to go with it and told him all about getting made redundant a few years ago and thinking his life was over at fifty, but then he'd met Asha waiting at the deli counter in Tesco's (she'd smiled at that) and got a new, better job—less money, but less stress too—and now they were in Cornwall celebrating their anniversary.

Sam didn't say a lot. He didn't have to. He felt better while he was with them, and a little of it lasted as he waved them off on their walk, but then the bleakness settled back over his soul like a sea mist, chilling his heart.

He climbed into his car and checked his phone out of habit. There was another message from Mum—again, just telling him to call her. Suddenly, talking to his mum sounded like a really, really good idea. At least she'd never stop loving him.

He dialled her number. "Hey, Mum."

"Alessandro, what is going on?" Her voice was sharp.

Sam's chest tightened, and the chill slid deeper. This might not turn out to be the comforting chat he'd been hoping for. "Uh . . . what do you mean?"

"Why have I had bailiffs at my house?"

Oh. Oh *crap*. "Mum, you didn't let them take anything, right? Christ, I'm so sorry."

"Of course I didn't let them take anything. I told them you don't live here, and if they didn't go away I would call the police. And I repeat, Alessandro: *What is going on*? What trouble are you in now?"

Sam winced at the *now*. "It's . . . a misunderstanding."

"Then you don't owe anyone any money?"

"I do, but . . . I told them I'd pay it back. They just need to wait." Crap. He'd meant to get in touch with them, tell them he'd definitely start paying once he'd had his first salary cheque, but with everything else going on, he'd forgotten. How could he have forgotten?

"How much do you owe?"

"It's not that much. I'll pay it off in a few months." Except how was he going to do that with no job? Christ, his life was a mess.

"*How much*, Alessandro?"

Sam cringed at her tone. Reluctantly, he named the figure.

There was a shocked silence. "Why do you owe so much money?"

Suddenly it was all too much. Sam squeezed his eyes shut against the too-bright light coming through the windscreen. "Because I'm an idiot. It's . . . Mum, I'm sorry, but it's gambling debts."

"Gambling? How could you do something so foolish?"

Sam hunched in on himself. "I told you I'm an idiot. It was just supposed to be a quick flutter. Something to help me relax, but once I started . . . I'm sorry, Mum. I tried to stop—I *have* stopped now, I promise. I haven't placed a bet since I got this new job." His voice cracked on the last word.

"Oh, Sam." Her tone was softer now. "Why didn't you tell me you had money troubles?"

"How could I? I knew you wouldn't be happy. And it wasn't so bad at first. But then the interest kept racking up . . ."

"And it still is, hmm?" She sighed. "I'll send you the money. You need to pay this off straight away."

"Mum, where are you going to get that kind of money?"

"The mortgage is paid off. I can get a loan—"

"*No*. You're not going to put your home at risk."

"It won't be at risk because my son will pay me back."

"And what if I don't?" Sam drew in a shaky breath. "What if I . . . What if I lose my job?"

"Sam? Is there something you're not telling me? Is everything all right?"

It was too much. First the guy on the cliff, now her . . . Sam's eyes were stinging again, and there wasn't any breeze to blame it on in the car. "Mum? I've made a real mess of things."

"Then tell me about it, and we'll fix it."

Sam wasn't sure it could be fixed. But the telling . . . Yeah. It was about time he stopped trying to sweep stuff under the carpet.

CHAPTER
THIRTY-SIX

B ran sank into Sam's desk chair, desperately wishing he were at home but not yet trusting himself to drive. He'd hoped . . . He wasn't sure what he'd hoped for, but it wasn't for Sam to admit to everything. To acknowledge he'd come here under false pretences, with a reputation in tatters—and that his disgrace had been deserved.

Damage limitation. That was what was needed. Bran would have to distance himself from Sam—no, Ferreira—immediately. Make sure everyone knew he was outraged to discover the man's tarnished credentials. The exhibition should not be allowed to suffer. Perhaps he could get hold of another historian? And this time, *not* via Jory.

That betrayal hurt almost as much as Sa—Ferreira's. Jory knew how important the exhibition was to Bran, and yet he'd let him place his trust in a publicly disgraced curator. Did Jory really hate him that much? He'd thought things had been getting better between them.

And Sam . . . Oh God. Bran had actually been prepared to brave public opinion and enter into a relationship with him. Openly. Never mind all the snide comments and unfunny jokes there had been about Jory and his boyfriend after they'd set up house together. No one had said anything in front of Jory—of course not—but Bran had heard, at the golf club and at drinks parties. He'd known only too well what certain people would think about him if he took that step with Sam. But he'd been ready to face it—and for what? A man who'd deceived him. Had attempted to deceive the academic world.

How could he trust anything Sam had told him now? Bran's chest ached more fiercely than at any time since he'd been attacked.

It was almost a relief when his phone rang—at least, after the surge of disappointment that crushed Bran despite himself when he saw it was Kirsty, and not Sam somehow calling to make everything okay again.

"Bran? Can you come over? Now, if possible?"

"Is something wrong?" Oh God, Gawen—

"No, but I need to talk to you, and the sooner the better."

If Gawen was all right, what could possibly be so urgent? But at least it was something to think about other than the disaster his life had become. "I'll be right over."

The short drive from the castle to Kirsty's house took well over ten minutes, and Bran cursed at every delay caused by slow-moving tourists on the road. The dejected apathy with which he'd greeted her request had been replaced by a tight knot of concern. Was this about Gawen after all? Kirsty had said nothing was wrong, but then why the urgency?

It was a school day, he reminded himself. If anything had happened to Gawen, Jory would be right on the spot, and it would be him Bran had heard from, not Kirsty.

Nevertheless, he was heartily relieved to reach her front door and have her open it with a smile, however tight-lipped. "Is everything all right?" he couldn't prevent himself from asking.

"Fine. But come in, yeah? Euan's got something to say to you."

"Euan?" What on earth could *he* have to say to Bran? They'd never even met.

"Just come on in, will you?"

Perplexed, Bran followed her into her living room.

The man who stood there waiting for them was tall and well-built, with dirty-blond hair tied back into a loose ponytail. He wore faded, ripped jeans, an equally distressed T-shirt and a scowl. Bran wouldn't have trusted him as far as he could throw him, and he wasn't at all happy about someone so disreputable looking being around his nephew. No wonder Kirsty had made sure they hadn't met—until now.

Or had they? The more he looked at the man, the more there seemed to be something vaguely familiar about him. Bran still couldn't see what on earth Euan could have to say to him. Unless . . . An uneasy feeling churned in his stomach. Kirsty was divorced from Jory now—which meant she could remarry any time she wanted to. Did Euan want her to move away from Porthkennack? Take Gawen away? "I'm told you've got something to say to me," he all but snapped, unable to bear the tension any longer.

A muscle twitched in Euan's scruffy jaw, and he looked away for a moment before putting a hand in his back pocket and pulling out a wallet. He handed it to Bran, who took it automatically, confused.

Then he blinked. This was *his* wallet. The one stolen from him the night he'd been attacked. He opened it in a daze and found its contents, unbelievably, intact. The picture of Gawen, the credit and debit cards he'd cancelled and replaced, even the cash. "Where did you get this?"

Euan gave a bitter laugh. "Where the hell do you think? Shit, you don't remember me at all, do you?"

"You were there when I was assaulted?" Bran's pulse thudded in his ears.

"How about earlier? That afternoon, when you chucked me out of your gaff. Came over all lord of the manor and told me to sling my hook after I took a wrong turning in your precious stately home. Like the fact your ancestors licked the right arses and robbed the right ships makes you better than everyone else."

"Euan." Kirsty's tone was a warning. "You're supposed to be apologising, remember? Or do you want to go to prison?"

Bran wasn't sure if the pain in his suddenly tight chest was real or just a memory. "You. It was you who assaulted me." He took an involuntary step back on legs that were appallingly shaky. "Kirsty, call the police."

Euan folded his arms, his very stance belligerent. "Oh, for fuck's sake. I told you he'd be like this."

"Sit *down*, both of you," she snapped. "We're going to talk about this like adults."

Glowering, Euan sat down on the sofa. After a pause to make it clear that it was *his* decision, Bran took an armchair. He managed not to make it an undignified collapse.

Kirsty nodded and sat next to Euan, although with a noticeable gap between them. "Right. So, Euan, are you going to tell Bran what we talked about? Finally? And leave out all the class-warrior bullshit. Or I will call the police."

Euan scrubbed his face with both hands, then turned to look at Bran squarely. "I'm sorry, all right? I just lost it for a minute. Been drinking, hadn't I? Down the Sea Bell." He gave a harsh laugh. "I'd watch your step round there if I were you. Not one of the locals 'ave got a good word to say for you."

Bran felt hollow inside. Was he really so hated? "Why?" he asked hoarsely.

"Why have they got it in for you? Cos you screwed half their families over, from what I heard. Or do you mean why did I lay into you?"

"You said . . . But for God's sake, all I did was ask you to keep to the public areas of Roscarrock House!" Bran flushed as he said it. Perhaps he had been a little harsh with the man—but it'd hardly merited a violent attack.

"It was just everything, all right? First you practically set the bloody dogs on me, then Kirsty here tells me I can't come over that night cos she's got you visiting, so I goes down the pub—"

Where he'd presumably spent the evening nursing his grievance and marinating it in alcohol.

"Then," Euan went on, his voice increasing in volume as he spoke, "when she *finally* tells me I can come and have my dinner, cos Lord bloody Roscarrock's pissed off at last, which by the way was a good two hours later than she'd let me think it was going to be, I see you walking down the street towards me. Taking names and addresses from the sodding street lamps for dereliction of fucking duty. Then you look up and give me the evil eye like you're going to have the law on me for walking down the bloody street. I just lost it."

"And he took your wallet so it'd look like a mugging," Kirsty said quietly, into the silence that'd followed Euan's tirade. She sounded exasperated. As if the attack which had landed Bran in hospital twice and left him in pain even now were nothing but a minor misdemeanour.

Bran's temper flared. He could have *died*. If he'd hit his head harder; if the pneumonia had been more severe . . . He opened his mouth to say so.

"Have you counted your money?" Euan interrupted defiantly. "I didn't take a penny of it."

As if that mattered a jot. He sounded like a sullen teenager. Bran wondered how old he actually was, beneath the unkempt hairstyle and the weathered skin of an outdoorsman. Younger than Kirsty, he was certain. But then Bran could hardly throw stones on that count.

"Bran?" Kirsty asked with unusual hesitance.

"What do you expect me to say? That I understand perfectly, these things happen? What do you expect me to *do*, even?"

"I'm asking you to not come down too hard on him, now he's owned up to it," she said, looking him in the eye. By her side, Euan stared at the floor.

"Why the hell shouldn't I? I could have *died*."

Euan stood up explosively. "See? I told you he'd be like this. Waste of bloody time!"

"Then don't let us keep you." Kirsty's voice was firm. "You've done your bit anyhow."

"Fine. *Fine*. You know where to find me." He stomped out of the living room, and a moment later the front door slammed.

Kirsty let out a long breath. "What were we saying? Right. Look, we both know you've got a lot of clout round here. If you tell them to chuck him in jail and throw away the key, then that's what they'll do. And God knows you've got reason, but . . . I'm asking you to just think twice first." She muttered something afterwards that Bran didn't quite catch, but which might have been *Christ knows why*.

Bran would like to know too. "Why?"

"Because he's never been in trouble with the law before. Because Gawen likes him, and it's gonna upset him enough already to know Euan's the one who hurt his favourite uncle. Because we've all done something we've regretted after a drink or two." She gazed at him earnestly. "And I know it's not been easy for you, getting over the injuries and the illness. But I don't reckon going all out for revenge is going to make that any better."

Revenge? Bran would have called it justice. But she was probably right. Bran could have died, perhaps—but he *hadn't*. And he remembered, now, that incident with Euan at the house, and while the punishment had been out of all proportion to the crime, it didn't show Bran in any good light. In fact, he was appalled at himself. Or perhaps more honestly, he was appalled at the thought of anyone he cared for—of *Sam*—ever finding out he'd acted that way.

Even after discovering Sam's deception, Bran still cared for his opinion. The realisation left him heartsick and breathless from the pain in his chest. Had he been asleep, all these years until now? Dwelling in a dream world, where nothing he ever said or did was wrong, and fooling himself into thinking it was reality? Waking from his delusions was brutal—and well overdue.

After all, what was Kirsty even asking him for? Merely to refrain from taking undue advantage of his privileged position here in Porthkennack. A position Bran only held because of an accident of birth. Who was to say if, born into the same circumstances as Euan, and as bitterly aware of social injustice, Bran might not have let his temper get the better of him and landed on the wrong side of the law?

Edward of Woodstock had always given due honour to his enemies. Surely Bran could show mercy to his?

He made his decision. "I won't press charges."

Kirsty's eyes went wide. "What? I wasn't asking you to let him off altogether."

"I know you weren't. But I . . . I've become aware, recently, that my past conduct has not been wholly blameless, and I can see how I might have contributed to the situation. It only seems fair to allow Euan, too, a chance to change his ways." She opened her mouth, and Bran hurried on to forestall her. "I have some conditions. First: Euan goes. I don't want Gawen spending time with someone with a proven capacity for violence. If you want to keep on seeing him—"

"Not a problem. He's had his marching orders already. He told me he never meant to hit you that hard, and I told him, I believed he hadn't meant it. And I did believe it. But one day, who's to say it wouldn't be me or Gawen who got on his wick, and he wouldn't mean to hit us hard either? But it'd be too late. And I told him straight, I'm not risking that."

Bran took a deep breath. "Good. You deserve better. Although I suppose I should give him some credit for admitting his crime to you."

She snorted. "Not a lot else he could do, was there? Not once I'd found your wallet shoved down the bottom of his rucksack. Christ, I thought it was drugs, you know?"

"What?"

"Jory didn't tell you? S'pose not. He had Gawen crying on his shoulder over Euan getting in a snit cos Gawen touched his stuff—so when he told me, I thought, what's Euan got to hide? So that's when I searched his bag. A bit of weed's one thing, but I'm not having the hard stuff round my lad."

"And you found my wallet. Why on earth didn't he get rid of it?" Bran was more concerned at this evidence of Euan turning his temper on Gawen. Thank God he wouldn't be around to do so any longer.

"That's what I said." Kirsty rolled her eyes. "Think he was hoping if he ignored it, it'd go away by itself. Right, what's the rest of your conditions?"

"There's just one more. I realise I can't enforce this, but . . . tell him to get some anger management help, for God's sake. There must be something available on the NHS, if he can't afford private. And make sure he knows that if I ever hear of him being violent again, I won't hesitate to inform the police of what really happened here." Bran hesitated. "Are you all right here on your own? I suppose he'll be coming back for his things. Do you want me to . . ." Bran wasn't sure how to end that sentence. See him off the premises? Round up a West Country posse to run him out of town?

Kirsty shook her head. "He's not an axe murderer. Just an idiot. I'll be fine."

"Call me, after he's gone for good."

"I'll be *fine*." She flashed a sudden smile. "It's a well-kept secret, isn't it?"

Bran frowned, puzzled.

"You. Bran Roscarrock. I've always known you had a heart in there." She jabbed a finger at his chest, thankfully without making contact. God knew it ached enough already.

"Don't spread it around. I wouldn't like my reputation for ruthlessness to be tarnished."

Kirsty folded her arms and gave him a long, hard look. "Wouldn't you?"

And that was the question, wasn't it?

Bran drove himself back to Roscarrock House, lost in thought.

CHAPTER
THIRTY-SEVEN

S am had driven home from the cliffs with nothing resolved, feeling like a wrung-out dishrag. He'd persuaded his mum to give him a few more days to sort out the money mess before she did anything drastic like remortgage the house.

And he'd promised to look up those debt-advice links and ring the Citizens Advice Bureau the next day, despite how thinking about the way he'd felt when he'd got Bran's email—Christ, only yesterday—was like a knife in his heart.

Was it really the only way to get his finances straight? He could win it all back if he only got lucky . . .

No. He wasn't going down that route again. Not ever.

It might not have been the worst day of Sam's life, but it was right up there with the day he'd found out what Doug's corner-cutting was going to cost him.

Jory was already in when Sam got back to the house. Sam waved a quick hello and ducked into the kitchen to make a sandwich.

He really wanted a sweet chutney one like his mum had used to make when he was a kid, but Jory and Mal didn't have any fresh coriander or grated coconut. Or any green chilli—in fact, the only ingredients they had were bread and sugar.

Which wasn't to say Sam didn't consider it for a moment. He settled on jam, and as he was spreading it, Jory came in and cornered him with the air of a bloke determined to get something off his chest.

Sam looked up warily.

Jory took a coffee mug off the mug tree and fiddled with it. "I, well, I'm sorry I reacted the way I did when you told me about you and Bran. I should have been happy for you. Which I am, obviously. Happy."

Yeah, right. Happy people always went around moping like someone had just shot their dog.

Sam sighed. "You don't have to be."

"Yes, I do. It's good that you've found someone. And that Bran has. That you've found each other." The handle was going to come off that mug if Jory didn't watch out.

"No, I mean, he's dumped me." Saying it out loud brought a sharp twist of pain in Sam's gut.

Jory almost dropped the mug. "What? I mean, why?"

"He found out about me getting sacked from Edinburgh. Doug's dodgy research—everything."

"But that wasn't your fault!"

"Not the way Bran sees it. So I'm out of a job, and out of a . . ." Sam's voice cracked, and he hung his head, blinking hard.

Strong arms slid around his shoulders, startling him even as they drew him in to Jory's warmth. Christ, he didn't deserve this comfort. But it was so bloody nice, even though he didn't know what the hell to do with his hands, one of them still holding a knife covered in strawberry jam.

Jory's voice rumbled in his ear. "I'm so sorry. This is all my fault."

What? Sam broke the hold and took a step back. "No way, mate. Are you serious? After everything you've done for me?"

"I told you not to tell Bran everything. If we'd been honest with him from the start—"

"He'd never have let me in the door, and you know it."

"How did he find out?"

Sam shrugged. "Stuff's there on the internet for anyone to find. S'pose I should be surprised he hadn't checked up on me before now."

"It's odd that he should do it just after you two get together."

"Is it?" Sam huffed a bitter laugh. "Not short of a few trust issues, your brother. Not that I've helped on that count."

Jory looked away. Yeah, he was probably feeling guilty too. "And he told you you were fired?"

"He didn't have to. Came at me, all guns blazing. Said I'd ruined everything."

"That's rubbish. He's overreacting." Jory's jaw firmed. "I'll talk to him."

"You don't have to. It's my mess—"

"And he's my brother." Jory's tone softened. "Go and eat your sandwich before the bread gets all dry. I'll put the kettle on."

Sam admitted defeat and took his snack into the living room, where he found Mal sprawled on the sofa. When had he come in?

Mal looked up with a grin. "You two finished having a cuddle? Cos I could murder a cuppa."

Shit, had he seen Jory with his arms round Sam? "Uh, whatever you saw, it wasn't—it didn't mean anything. Uh, there's nothing going on— Okay, you can stop laughing now."

Mal didn't. "Jesus, your face. Yeah, I worked that out all by myself, ta. For a start, Jory's never been into kinky stuff involving food and cutlery—" He ducked as Sam threw a cushion at him.

They were both really nice to him all evening. Sam couldn't help feeling he'd done nothing to deserve it.

Friday morning, Sam didn't bother going into work. What was the point? He'd probably find the Portakabin padlocked and Roarke's entire team of construction workers under instructions to see him off the premises. Preferably with extreme prejudice.

And, okay, that last bit was unlikely on a lot of levels, but Sam couldn't have faced going in.

Instead, he gritted his teeth and looked up the nearest Citizens Advice Bureau. *Before* his mum could send him a text reminding him to do it. He'd missed the day for drop-in advice this week, but telephone advice was available. While he was holding, waiting for an advisor to be free, he looked up all the debt advice he could find on their website.

In a way, it was reassuring. For a start, it brought it home to Sam that a lot of people had it way worse than he did. There was a link to click on called *What to do if you're about to be evicted*, and advice on prioritising your debts. At least Sam wasn't juggling court fines, utility bills, and unpaid rent with his credit card debt. The website laid out simple, step-by-step instructions on what to do and how to do it, with sample letters to send to creditors asking them to hold off debt collection and freeze interest and charges.

In another way it was totally depressing. The information was written so a five-year-old could understand it, and here Sam was, with a PhD to his name, having to face the fact that he hadn't even managed to come up with these simple steps on his own. It was obvious, when he thought about it, what he should have done from the start. But that was the key phrase, wasn't it? *When he thought about it.* He'd been doing everything he could to *not* think about it.

Thank God Jory and Mal weren't around to overhear his pathetic, stammering call once the advisor finally connected—or the one he made afterwards to his credit card company. Sam felt hot, and stupid, and small. The woman on the line was perfectly polite and businesslike, but she'd wanted to know when he'd be able to pay his debt, and with the way his job was going—had most likely *gone*—he hadn't been able to give her a good answer. But with the tourist season starting, he ought to be able to find *some* kind of work in Porthkennack, even if it was worse than the job he'd had in Luton. There had to be plenty of crappy jobs no one would take unless they were desperate—cleaning seagull shit off the prom, or mucking out taxis after hen nights, maybe—and after all this, Sam had to concede he was desperate.

He still nearly wept when she finally agreed to hold off collection and freeze the debt. He put the kettle on for a cup of tea feeling light-headed—hell, light-bodied as well. He wasn't even sure it was a *good* feeling, what with one problem sort-of-solved making way for another that most likely didn't have a solution.

Okay. One thing at a time. Sam opened up his laptop and started looking for jobs.

CHAPTER
THIRTY-EIGHT

B ran couldn't face going down to the castle on Friday. Too many painful associations. Instead, he hid himself in his study from the visitors invading his house, and tried to concentrate on work that had nothing to do with the exhibition.

It was getting on for lunchtime, when the door opened. Bran frowned up at the interloper, a blistering tirade on keeping to the public areas already on his lips. It died unspoken when he saw Jory.

Anger at his brother's betrayal crashed head-on into shame that he'd been so ready to repeat the mistake he'd made with Euan, leaving Bran tongue-tied. Jory didn't speak either as he came in and shut the door behind him.

Bran found his voice at last. "Shouldn't you be at school?"

"I've got a free period, and I'm not on duty over lunch. Plenty of time to come up here for a word." Jory folded his arms and stood with his feet hip-width apart, as though bracing for a storm.

Bran fought the urge to snap at him to sit down and stop looming. He leaned back in his chair and tried to ignore the crick in his neck. "And?"

"Sam told me about . . . you and him. That you're together. Lovers." Jory flushed bright red.

"We were." Bran's throat was tight. *Damn* this. "Did you know about Sam's past? The circumstances under which he left Edinburgh?"

"Yes." Jory's colour deepened, and his stance was no longer so steady. "He, um, he made sure I knew."

And neither of them had so much as mentioned it to Bran. "Yet you still brought him here? To take charge of *my* exhibition? What the hell were you thinking of?" He'd stood up almost without realising it, the better to look his brother in the eye.

It was at times like this that he hated their very obvious physical differences. Jory was a head taller than he was, and broader as well. It shouldn't have mattered—neither of them was at all likely to resort to blows, for God's sake—but somehow it did.

Jory's chin went up. "Maybe I was thinking he deserved a second chance. It wasn't fair, what happened to him—at least, it shouldn't have to follow him around his whole life."

"He falsified research!"

"He didn't falsify anything. It was the lead author on the paper who did it. Sam was coerced into going along with a fait accompli."

"Coerced? By whom?"

"By the man he was in love with, who was effectively his boss, and who lied to him about both the relationship and the research." Jory took a step towards Bran's desk, and lowered his voice as he leaned on the front, bringing his head down to Bran's level. "Sam's not the villain here. Maybe he did wrong in letting it slide, but just how easy do you think it would have been to speak out against his supervisor? The man he loved? And he's been punished for it enough—for God's sake, he took the whole blame for something that was only peripherally his fault. He hasn't had a decent job since it happened—until now."

"Because nobody wants to employ someone they can't trust." Was it true, though, what Jory had said? Was Sam really more innocent than he'd appeared? Bran knew only too well that just because Sam had convinced Jory his spin on the matter was true didn't mean it actually was—but he desperately wanted to believe it.

He should have let Sam explain himself. Listened, instead of shouting him down with a mind already closed to any reasons or excuses.

"You can trust Sam," Jory was saying. "I know him—he's a good man."

"But what about his reputation? Even if this story is true, Sam's name attached to the exhibition is bound to tarnish it."

Jory pushed off the desk with an impatient gesture. "Outside academia, who even cares? How many of the tourists who'll go to the exhibition do you think will even bother to notice the name of the curator?"

"But what if they do?"

"Then you tell them what I told you. That everyone deserves a second chance."

When had Jory got so grown-up? Become so unafraid to speak his mind in front of his big brother?

"You owe it to him," Jory went on. His eyes narrowed. "And you owe it to me too."

"To you?"

"Yes. For all those years you made me feel being gay was something to be ashamed of."

Bran felt it like a blow to the heart. He made to move away from behind his desk, but stalled after the first step. "I never said—"

Jory stepped back with an angry gesture. "You didn't have to say it! Father said it for you, and you never once disagreed with him. Anytime the subject came up, you'd get that look on your face, as though you'd rather . . . I don't know, eat slugs or something, than talk about men loving other men."

Bran clutched the back of his chair. Was that really how it'd been? He hadn't wanted to think about it, that was true. After the humiliation of Devan Thompson's father . . .

He'd felt he'd deserved it, Bran realised. He'd told himself Father must be right, that being gay was something shameful and could only lead to unhappiness. It had been so much easier not to fight it, not to risk any further pain. To follow the path that Father laid out for him, narrow though it was.

It hadn't even occurred to him that Jory, so much younger, had been taking note of his behaviour. Bran stepped around the desk, towards his brother.

Jory hadn't finished. "And then with Kirsty—insisting I marry her."

"That was for *Gawen*."

"And because you were hoping once I was tied to her I'd decide I might as well be straight after all." Jory stood below the portrait of Edward of Woodstock, his posture just as stiff and resolute as that of the long-dead prince.

Bran shook his head. "No. It was for the family."

"You never stopped trying to push me back towards her."

"I may have applied some gentle pressure, but I think you'll find I stopped all that after I found out you had a lover in Edinburgh."

"Even then, you never made me feel it was acceptable. You certainly never invited Rafi down to stay." Jory's frown softened into hurt.

Oh, for God's sake. "Because that would in no way have embarrassed your wife and child."

"Kirsty wouldn't have given a toss."

Bran opened his mouth to protest that the reality of their relationship didn't matter, that it was *appearances* that mattered—but the words died on his tongue, unuttered. Christ, had he really used to believe that? "No." He cleared his throat. "You're right."

"And—" Jory broke off and stared, his mouth open as if Bran had just gut-punched him. "What?"

Bran took a deep breath and met his gaze from a scant few feet away. "There were . . . things you didn't know about, and they may have affected how I behaved to you . . . I'm sorry."

"Oh."

Jory looked as though he wanted to ask what those things were, so Bran hastened to head him off. "I honestly had no idea you were gay. Not until you made that announcement about having a male lover and being uninterested in women. And in the circumstances, I think it's understandable that I had some trouble believing you were sincere."

"Oh."

Bran held his gaze for a moment longer, and then turned away. The clock on the mantelpiece stood slightly askew, and Bran raised a hand to straighten it—but changed his mind and let it stand, crooked and proud. "I'm sure you'll find this almost impossible to believe, but I was entirely wrapped up in my own problems at the time."

"Oh." Jory shook his head, as if to shake himself out of the verbal rut he'd fallen into. "I always thought—you know. That you were trying to make it clear you disapproved."

"It was never aimed at you." Bran's throat was dry. Should he tell Jory the whole, shameful truth? *Could* he?

"You realised you liked men," Jory said slowly. "And you weren't comfortable with it."

Bran nodded, relieved beyond belief to be spared a full confession. Then guilt pierced him. Didn't he owe Jory more than this? "I . . ." Oh, Christ. "Did you ever have a hopeless crush on a straight boy, in your teens?"

Jory blinked at him. "Um, no. I mean, there were boys I liked, but . . . no, not really."

"Good. I can't recommend it." There was a pause. Bran stared into the unlit fireplace and hoped he hadn't gone as bright red as Jory had.

"Anyone I know?" Jory said at last.

Oh, bloody hell. "No, but you've met his son. Devan Thompson," he added, because if he was going to rip this plaster off he might as well do a thorough job.

Bran turned back to his brother, oddly light-headed for having finally got it all out in the open.

"Oh."

"You know, for a teacher your vocabulary is sadly lacking." Bran gave Jory a twisted smile. Yes, he was definitely light-headed.

Jory looked as though it might be contagious. "My pupils, believe it or not, rarely manage to shock me into monosyllables. Well done on that."

"Yes, well, I'm hoping not to make a habit of it."

"Thank God. Um." Jory glanced towards the window, his shoulders hunching just a little. "So what are you going to do about Sam?"

For a moment, Bran wasn't sure. The deception still hurt—but Jory was right. He owed Sam another chance. Odd, though, how Bran had found it so much easier to be magnanimous to Euan Mayhew, who'd broken his bones, than to Sam, who'd . . .

Bran swallowed. "Do you think, if I asked Sam to come here to talk, he would?"

Jory frowned. "I think so—but wouldn't neutral ground be better?"

"No. I think he should come here. It's past time."

"Father will be spinning in his grave," Jory said drily. "His eldest son and heir, bringing a male lover into the house?"

"Father can go to hell, if he isn't there already." Bran knew from Jory's shocked expression that he'd gone too far. But Jory didn't know everything, did he? *He killed our mother.* Bran couldn't bring himself to say it. The old instinct to protect his younger sibling—no matter how much Bran had resented it in the past, and probably Jory too for that matter—was too strong, and feelings were too raw right now. He took a deep breath. "Don't you think he's ruled our lives long enough?"

Jory nodded slowly. "You're going to call Sam?"

Bran hesitated. "I'll write. I don't want there to be any possibility of misunderstanding." He returned to his desk to scrawl a brief note, slipped it into an envelope, and stood to hand it to his brother.

"I'll give it to him this evening. And, um, maybe put in a good word or two. I'd better be getting back now." He made a move towards the study door, then stopped. Stepping around Bran's desk, he enfolded him in a hug.

Bran froze, then awkwardly returned it, patting Jory's back.

Jory stepped away again, his face pink. "I'm really glad we had this talk," he said, and left.

Bran sank into his desk chair, absurdly overcome.

CHAPTER THIRTY-NINE

I t nagged at Bran, what Jory had said about Father spinning in his grave. Already unable to settle as he waited to hear from Sam—or not—Bran couldn't put Father out of his mind. He thought about visiting his parents' grave, but if Father lingered anywhere in this world, surely it would be here, by the house that bore his name, not in St. Ia's churchyard where they'd laid him to rest?

The cliffs behind the house. That was where he had to go. Bran made his way out there before he could lose his nerve, the path an odd mix of the familiar and the strange. He'd rarely come this way since Father's suicide, and his memories of it were all from childhood—and that awful night of the storm. Against all logic, the way seemed to have lengthened, the path taking more turns from the straight line to the cliff edge.

It was a warm afternoon, but the breeze was blowing up stiffly from the sea, whisking away the scent of wildflowers to leave only the ever-present brine. Bran shivered as he reached the edge of the land, careful not to tread too near. Gulls swooped and called above the waves far below, their raucous cries muted by distance. The tide was up, and the beach at Big Guns Cove overcome by the water. *"Full fathom five thy father lies"* ... No. It wasn't any truer for Bran than it had been for Shakespeare's prince. They'd recovered Father's body.

"Father?" he said softly. If anyone was there to hear him, a whisper would be as good as a shout, and Bran wasn't about to go yelling his private affairs out in public. "I don't know if you can hear me, but ..." He fell silent. No, he wasn't going to start off being uncertain. Either Father would hear him, or he was beyond all that, in which case it didn't matter anyway. "Father? I can't be what you wanted.

I don't want to be. I have to be my own man. You were wrong, you know. About so many things. And I was wrong to listen to you, to try to please you. People . . . shouldn't be put into boxes. Everyone deserves respect, and the right to choose how to live their life. You . . . you should have given Mother a choice too." Bran broke off then, his throat clogged and the wind stinging his eyes, and it was a few minutes before he could speak again. "I'm gay, and I deserve to be happy, and I'm not going to be afraid to bring my lover to my own house any longer."

Bran turned and strode back to the house with the same sense of scoured-clean, giddy lightness he'd felt talking to Jory, although it trembled perilously close to nausea.

A much-needed cup of tea later, Bran remembered another duty and gave Constable Peters a call. "I need to talk to you about the assault."

"Have you remembered something?"

"I have some further information." Bran thought it best to leave it at that over the phone. "Could we meet up?"

"Tell you what—are you at home? You work from there, don't you?"

"Yes. To both."

"I'll come over, then. Be there . . . ooh, about half past three?"

"That will be perfect. Just tell them at the door you're here to see me, and they'll direct you to my study. I'm afraid we'll still have volunteers and, quite likely, visitors in the house until after five."

"I'll see you soon."

It was nearer four o'clock when Bran heard the knock on his study door, and he half hoped it might be Sam calling instead—although he had no idea what time he might expect to see Sam, if indeed he'd come at all. Perhaps he'd be offended at having to make the running?

Bran should have suggested they meet somewhere neutral, as Jory had said. There would have been time enough for a symbolic opening-up of hearth and home later—*if* the first meeting went well. Too late now, though. Bran took a steadying breath and opened the door.

It was, of course, the constable. Bran was surprised to find her out of uniform, wearing a summer dress that showed off her warm brown skin and made her look younger and prettier.

"It's actually my day off," she said with a smile. "But I wasn't busy, so I thought why not?"

"That's very kind of you." Bran gestured for her to come into the study, fighting not to let the queasy mix of relief and disappointment show in his manner. "Should I call you Ms. Peters, as this isn't an official call?"

"Sally, please. Thanks for inviting me," she said, glancing around at the house. "Always meant to come and take a look at this place." She grinned suddenly. "Hope you're not going to charge me the visitor's fee now I've said that."

"That would hardly be fair, as you're here at my invitation. And you'd have to put up with a very inferior guide."

"Oh? Are you telling me you don't know your family's history forwards, backwards and sideways? I'm sorry, sir, I believe you're being economical with the truth."

"Should I call my lawyer before I say another word?" Bran couldn't help smiling. "I may know all the stories, but I'm afraid I'm not the best at telling them."

"Don't sell yourself short. There's nothing like the personal connection." She returned his smile with a warmth that lit her face.

Sam would like her, Bran thought with a pang. "I'll get you a drink. Sherry?"

"Don't mind if I do, seeing as I'm not on duty. Dry, if you've got it."

Actually, dry was all they had. Both Bran and Bea loathed sweet drinks. Bran poured them each a glass.

"This is where you work, is it?" Sally gazed up at the portrait of the Black Prince. "The royal family were a lot better looking in those days, weren't they? I bet his military bearing brought all the girls to the yard."

"I've always thought so." There was a pause. Bran could feel her eyes upon him, and wondered what she saw.

The truth, apparently, as her smile softened. "It's a lot to live up to."

Bran didn't ask her what she meant. "Won't you take a seat by the fireplace?" He gestured at the leather armchair, and after she'd sat down, he moved his desk chair closer to the hearth and joined her.

She sat gracefully in the old armchair, leaning back with evident pleasure, and raised her glass as if in a toast. "Oh, this is luxury. Do you light the fire in the winter?"

Bran nodded.

"You must feel like you're in a Charles Dickens adaptation. One of the nice ones, not the ones set in debtor's prisons or anything."

"Believe me, for six months of the year this room is just as draughty as the Marshalsea ever was. As a listed building, we have to get approval for any modernisation to the heating system—and I wouldn't even dare ask about fitting double glazing."

"And you're right on the tops, here. No shelter from the storms. Hm. I guess inheriting a pile like this has its downside." She cocked her head. "Is that why you open the house up to visitors? Is it a requirement or something?"

"If we want to keep the estate intact, yes. It exempts us from inheritance tax. Without that break, there'd be nothing left to pass on a few generations down the line."

"Thought it must be something like that. You've always struck me as a very private person." She took a sip of sherry. "Do you ever think of handing it over to the National Trust and letting them worry about it all for you?"

"Never. There have been Roscarrocks in this house for over five hundred years."

"And you're hoping there will be for another five hundred, as well? Quite a lot to place on the shoulders of a young lad, that is."

She wasn't wrong. Bran swallowed. "I was twenty-six when my father died. Not so young."

"Young enough. But I was talking about the next generation. Your nephew."

Oh. Gawen. And of course she would know that he was Bran's heir. Anyone investigating the attack would have been criminally remiss not to have considered who might benefit in the event of his death. Although as they'd just discussed, the inheritance was a two-edged sword, wasn't it? Would Gawen thank him for it in the end? Bran couldn't bear the thought of being remembered less than fondly by the boy.

But he should be getting down to business, not second-guessing himself over his long-held plans for the estate. "Cons—Sally. I'm sure you're aware I invited you here for a reason. I want to speak to you about the assault case. Off the record."

"Go on."

Bran took a fortifying sip of sherry. "You can close the case. There's no need for any further action."

Her eyebrows raised sharply, then lowered. "You know who attacked you."

Bran nodded. "I don't wish to press charges."

"Technically, we don't need you to. We can prosecute for grievous bodily harm without the victim's say-so." She gave him a direct look. "Having that sort of power can be useful in, say, domestic assaults. Or any other situation in which the injured party might be coerced into dropping charges."

"That isn't the case here."

"Have you considered that it's not in the public interest to let a violent offender walk around unpunished?"

"I'm satisfied the matter was . . . personal. There's no danger to anyone else."

"What about further danger to you?"

"No. The . . . individual will be leaving Porthkennack."

Sally pursed her lips for a moment. "I'm going to need a little more information than that, I'm afraid. You understand it's not my decision whether to drop a case or not."

"I do understand that." In fact he'd considered going straight to the top and still would if necessary, but the thought of going over her head hadn't sat well with him. "I'm sure, though, that your recommendation will be listened to. After all, you're the officer with the most connection to the case."

"So convince me."

"The individual who assaulted me was . . . inebriated, and had a grudge against me. The attack was on the spur of the moment, and was later regretted." Actually he doubted Euan had regretted a single thing until he'd been caught out, but Bran had promised Kirsty he'd smooth this over.

"And the theft of your wallet?"

"It's been returned to me. Including its contents."

"Still, it's hardly no harm done, is it? Are you sure—" Sally broke off as the study door opened.

Bea took a step inside, then stopped short. "Bran, I— Oh. Sorry. I didn't realise you had company." She glanced from Sally to Bran, and raised an eyebrow.

"This is Constable Sally Peters, who—"

Bea cut him off. "I know. We've met. But this doesn't look like an official call."

Sally uncrossed her legs and stood. "Bran was kind enough to invite me up here for a drink. But I should be going now."

"No, please stay. I was just surprised, that's all. Bran didn't mention you were coming."

He hadn't, but then again, neither had Bea mentioned she'd be home from work this early. "It wasn't prearranged," Bran said.

Bea cocked her head at him but didn't comment. She turned to Sally. "You mustn't let me disturb you."

"Thanks, but I ought to go. One sherry on an empty tum's my limit."

Sally was deaf to further entreaty, and Bran saw her to the door through a hallway now blessedly empty of visitors and volunteers alike. "Can I count on your discretion?" he asked as they said their goodbyes.

She gave him a searching look, then nodded, following it with a rueful smile. "It's not like we'd have a case without your cooperation, anyway. So yes. Subject to the higher-ups agreeing, obviously."

"Thank you."

Bran closed the front door behind her, and turned to see Bea gazing at him curiously. "Was I wrong?" she asked.

"About what?"

"I didn't think you were interested in women. She is attractive, though, isn't she?"

Bran blinked. "I'm not—this was a professional visit. Anyway, why are you home so early?"

"I had a meeting cancelled. And don't change the subject. It makes it seem as though you've got something to hide. A professional visit, in that dress?"

Trust Bea to jump to the right conclusion—albeit about the wrong person. Then again, *did* he still have something to hide concerning Sam? Only time would tell. Time, and the man himself. "It's her day off. Surely she can wear what she likes? There's nothing going on between me and Sally."

"Then what did she have to say? Have they caught the man who attacked you?"

"No." He hesitated. "There isn't going to be an arrest."

Bea took a step forward. "You know who did it. You remembered?"

"No, but I have my wallet back, and the person who took it won't be a problem again."

"You're just letting it go? You could have *died*. Have you got any idea what it was like, seeing you so battered, so ill?" Colour rose in her face as she stalked up to him.

"I doubt it was worse than suffering through it directly!" Aware he'd raised his voice to match hers, he made an effort to get himself under control. "Bea, I haven't made this decision lightly. It's for the good of the family."

She subsided, as he'd hoped she would. A moment later, though, she flashed back into anger. "Tell me it wasn't Jory."

"No—Christ, no." Bran took her hands. "Jory would never do anything like that. It's no one we care about, I promise."

Bea looked momentarily confused, then her face smoothed. "You're sure this is the right way to go about things?"

Bran nodded. "I am. We'll never see him again."

"Good. God, I need a drink." She dropped Bran's hands and walked back down the hall—missing his startled realisation that they would, after all, be seeing Euan Mayhew again. He was the model for Kirsty's sculpture. They'd be seeing him every time they went to the exhibition.

Oddly enough, Bran found himself more wryly amused than annoyed.

He went back into his study and checked his phone. No message from Sam. Bran wondered if Jory had spoken to him yet. Would he come? And if he did, would it be tonight? He might want to sleep on it before making a decision.

Bran was tempted to call him—but no. He'd made his overture, and hounding Sam about it wouldn't help. He would just have to bear the uncertainty. For as long as it took.

CHAPTER
FORTY

Jory didn't get back from school until gone five—he had an after-school club he supervised on a Friday, which Sam reckoned was true dedication.

"I talked to Bran today," Jory said without any preamble when he walked into the living room, where Sam had taken his laptop and his job search. "He wants to see you."

Oh God. Sam couldn't face that. "What, so he can give me my P45 in person? No, thanks. He can spring for a stamp, the tight bastard." Christ help him, he still felt disloyal, talking about Bran like that.

"It's not about the job. It's about *you*." Jory looked earnest. "I think he really cares about you."

"No. No, he doesn't. I fucked it up, didn't I?"

"*No*." Jory bit his lip. "This is my fault. I should have—"

"No! Seriously, mate, this isn't on you. You and me both knew we weren't telling Bran the whole truth. And you did it to give me a chance. To give me a job doing what I love. So don't go blaming yourself for it going wrong. You did the best you could for me."

"I'm not sure I did. But I tried." Jory rubbed the back of his neck. "Will you talk to him? Please?"

Did he have any idea what he was asking? Sam shook his head. "There's no point. He'll just shout me down. Tell me again how I've ruined his life."

"I don't think so. He wrote you a note." Jory handed over a crisp white envelope.

Christ, that was Bran all over, that was. Fondness stabbed Sam painfully in the heart. Anyone else would have texted, but Bran preferred to send a proper letter. Sam took a deep breath, ripped open the envelope, and slid out a folded slip of paper.

The message was short. And not at all what he'd been expecting.

Sam, I deeply regret not giving you a fair hearing. Please forgive my hasty speech, and accept my invitation to Roscarrock House. Yours, Bran

It messed with his head. Was Bran saying he was still Sam's? Or was it just formality? But the way he'd written the note, with *deeply* and *please* . . . Sam looked up. "There's no time. Or date, even."

He hadn't even known until he spoke that he was going to accept the invitation.

Jory shrugged. "He wants you to come whenever you can. Will you go?"

Sam hedged. "I thought you were mad at him. How come you're so keen on him getting his way?"

"We talked. It, um, it turns out I might have got the wrong impression about a few things."

Yeah, it seemed there was a lot of that about. "I'll go." Sam scrubbed his hands on his jeans. Should he get changed? No, this wasn't a date. His T-shirt was presentable enough—it was the black one Maria had given him for Christmas, with the George Santayana quote on it: *Those who cannot remember the past are condemned to repeat it.* And he hadn't spilled his food down himself today, thank God.

Christ, his gut was churning with nerves. Best get it over with.

Walking up to the front door of Roscarrock House felt like turning up at Buckingham Palace on spec to ask if the Queen fancied a cup of tea and a natter. It wasn't just the cannons on the lawn, facing out to repel boarders. The house itself was intimidating—big, grey, blank-faced. It'd stood here for centuries before any of Sam's family had set foot in England. What would Sir John Roscarrock, who'd built the place back in the sixteenth century—Sam had looked it up, so sue him—have thought of an Indian immigrant turning up to court his great-times-many-grandson?

Actually, come to think of it, the bloke had been a privateer, hadn't he? Which was a fancy way of saying a government-sponsored pirate. There was a good chance neither Sam's gender nor the colour of his skin would have been an issue for him. Buoyed by this thought, Sam knocked on the door.

Bran opened it himself. Sam's breath caught. He looked . . . vulnerable.

Sam swallowed and shoved his hands in his jeans pockets to stop them reaching out of their own accord. "Hi."

"Thank you for coming," Bran said, watching him closely from the doorway. It was cool, now, high on the cliffs with the breeze getting up and the sun going down, and Sam shivered. Bran stepped back immediately. "Come in."

"Thanks." Sam looked curiously around the hallway. It was a little bare, without any personal touches. Sam supposed that was to be expected. He knew the place was open to visitors some days, but he'd never had a chance to come. Once he'd got to know Bran, it would just have been weird to turn up at his place like a tourist.

"Come through to my study." Bran led the way to a smallish room that housed a large, expensive-looking antique desk. A comfy chair in red leather stood by a tall fireplace, above which hung—Sam smiled—Burnell's portrait of the Black Prince.

"It's a copy, but not a bad one," Bran said. "Can I get you a drink?"

"Uh, yeah, thanks. Just a small one. I drove." Sam didn't really want a drink, but he didn't want to seem standoffish, either. And it'd give him something to do with his hands.

Bran poured them each a brandy from a crystal decanter. "Please sit down." He gestured at the comfy chair.

That was a measure of making himself at home Sam wasn't ready for. Not yet, and maybe not at all, depending on what Bran had to say. "Thanks, but I'm good. You wanted to talk?"

Bran nodded and swirled the brandy in his glass. Already the rich aroma was filling the small study, taking Sam back to the drinks they'd shared at the Tinners Rest. "I'm sorry," he said at last. "I didn't give you a chance to explain yourself before."

"No. No, you didn't." Sam swirled his own brandy, mostly so he could take a fortifying whiff of it before he spoke. "It's— I'm not saying I'm blameless. I cocked up. I know that. But it wasn't— I didn't set out to defraud anyone."

"Jory said you were coerced."

Oh God. He really was willing to listen. Hope flared in Sam's breast, but he tamped it down. They still had a way to go yet. "Not sure I'd call it that, but Doug begged me not to say anything. I didn't know until after we'd sent the paper off, and then . . . I know I should've got them to pull it, but he'd been under a lot of stress—his wife was ill, and he was under pressure from the university—and he said no one would ever find out." Christ, he was explaining this badly.

"Doug?"

Sam leaned against the wall by the door, all the energy drained out of him. "Dr. Douglas Craignton. He was my supervisor, and the lead author of the paper. I was just down as coauthor."

"And you're saying he was the one responsible for the lies? The falsified research?"

"Not lies. Not really. He—he cut corners. Didn't adequately verify the authenticity of the papers we were using to support his theory. I guess he just *wanted* it to be right. But I was reading through some other sources, just out of interest, and I realised the key document we were relying on had to be fake. I told him at once, obviously, and he . . . he told me to bury it. Let the paper stand. He said it didn't *disprove* his theory. It just didn't actually prove it. And what people didn't know wouldn't hurt them."

"And you just agreed?"

"I didn't *just* anything. I told you it was complicated. We were . . . we'd been having an affair." Sam took a gulp of brandy.

"You said he was married."

"Yeah. I know. Shitty thing to do. Maybe I deserved what I got. But I . . . Shit, I loved him. I thought he loved me. When he said he was planning to leave his wife, he just needed her to get well first, I believed him. I even swallowed the whole *We haven't shared a bed for years* line. And he was desperate. He hadn't published anything for so long, and this was going to get his name right back out there, you know? He seemed so certain no one would call us on it." Sam swallowed, his gut churning at the memory of that anxious time. He'd barely slept, agonising over whether they'd get away with it. If they even *should* get away with it. It'd almost been a relief when the shit had actually hit the fan—until he'd realised just how bad it was going to get. "Course, he was wrong about nobody catching on. As soon as the paper was published, the emails started coming. The paper was attacked in the press and ... well."

"You were both sacked?"

Sam gave a bitter laugh. "Both? No. He blamed it all on me. Told everyone he'd trusted me with the verification, and I'd assured him all due diligence had been applied. He tried to justify it to me afterwards, you know? He said he had so much more to lose—his position, his income, his family's home, all that." So basically, Sam hadn't been worth shit to Doug, set against all that. Sam had never come so close to hitting a man in his life as he had at that moment.

Bran had gone pale. "You must have thought I was just like him."

"*What*?" Sam took a step towards Bran. "Why the hell would I think that?"

"Because I put my own reputation above your welfare."

"That's not the same. I betrayed your trust. You had a right to be angry. He—Doug was a coward. You're not the same." His chest tight, Sam put his drink down on Bran's desk and took Bran's arm. "You're nothing like him."

The light coming in through the study windows had that jewel-like quality Sam had always loved about early evenings in the country. Bran's dark eyes met Sam's gaze for a long moment, then flashed away. "More than you think, perhaps. I ... I've been questioning my values, lately. Wondering if the way I've lived my life has been a mistake. There have been consequences I hadn't foreseen. That I hadn't even been aware of until now."

Despite everything, Sam laughed. "Jesus, Bran, you're talking to *me* about mistakes having consequences?" He gave Bran's arm a squeeze. "Coming here, to Porthkennack, was supposed to be my fresh start."

"And has it been?"

Sam thought he knew what Bran was asking. "Yeah. It has been. If you can forgive me."

"Can you forgive me?" Bran countered.

Yes would have been Sam's instinctive answer, but he forced himself to remember how hurt he'd been. "Can you promise me, next time we have an argument, that you'll at least listen to my side of the story before flying off the handle?"

"I . . ." Bran glanced away for a moment, then looked Sam straight in the eyes. "I'd like to. I wish I could, but I don't want to lie to you. I can promise I'll try my utmost, and that if I fail, I'll know it, sooner rather than later, and I'll be deeply sorry for it, and do my best to make it up to you."

Sam's heart melted at Bran's honesty. God knew it was a quality Sam could do with a bit more of. He hadn't been honest with Bran— hell, he hadn't even been honest with himself, hiding his head in the sand and hoping his problems would just go away by themselves.

"Can't ask for more than that, can I?" he said, his voice hoarse. "And me too. I mean, I promise that too."

Sam reached out, and Bran came readily into his arms.

CHAPTER
FORTY-ONE

It was so natural to slip his arms around Sam and pull him closer—so different from the awkward embrace he'd given Jory earlier. Bran breathed in the scent of him, basked in his warmth, and felt whole for the first time since the storm had broken. He could admit, now, that he'd overreacted. Had lashed out at the sting of betrayal.

It still hurt that Sam and Jory had colluded in, if not actively deceiving him, then certainly keeping him in the dark. But if they hadn't . . . what then? Bran would have vetoed Sam's appointment. Would, in all likelihood, have tried to take on the job himself, while still racked with ill health and juggling his other responsibilities. He'd have made a godawful, ill-conceived hash of it. And more to the point, he'd never have met Sam.

A sharp taint of anger soured his dizzy joy at their reconciliation. Had Bran thought himself betrayed? That was nothing to what this *Doug* had done to Sam. For a few moments, Bran indulged himself with some vicious revenge fantasies.

Then Sam kissed him, and all other thoughts fled. Sam was here, in Bran's home, warm and solid, tasting of brandy and hope for the future. Banishing the faint ghost of Bran's father which had always lingered in this room. Bran manoeuvred them until Sam half fell into the red leather chair by the fireplace, and then he clambered onto Sam's lap, straddling him, kissing him all the time. Hands delved into clothing, and matters swiftly escalated.

It was as though it was their first time again, only minus the alcohol and the secrets.

Afterwards, they sprawled, boneless, in the chair. Odd—it had never seemed too big to Bran before, but it somehow seemed the perfect size for the two of them now.

Sam glanced up at the portrait of Edward of Woodstock. "Gave him a bit of an eyeful, didn't we?"

Bran followed his gaze. "He doesn't seem too put out about it."

"Heh, maybe he had more in common with his grandad than we thought?"

"Three words: Joan of Kent."

"What, so he couldn't have been bi?" Sam's stomach gurgled loudly, and he laughed. God, he was gorgeous. "Oops. Could be time to get some food. Gotta keep our energy up, haven't we?"

"I like your thinking." Bran hadn't realised until now how absolutely ravenous he was. He stood, dislodging Sam gently. "There's probably some pizza in the freezer."

Sam made a face. "All right, but first birthday you have? I'm buying you a cookbook."

"Fine, as long as you'll promise to eat whatever travesties I manage to produce from it."

"Hey, it can't be any unhealthier than all that frozen crap." Sam got out of the chair and adjusted his clothing, now sadly wrinkled, although fortunately otherwise unscathed. "Um, is your sister at home?"

"I think so. But we probably won't see her." It was a large house, thank God.

"Shouldn't we ask her if she wants to join us?"

"I'm not sure she'd thank us."

"But—" Sam shook his head. "No, fine. She's your sister."

Bran managed to locate pizza, and even found some leftover salad in the fridge to go with it. Sitting at the kitchen table with Sam, eating their simple meal, felt domestic in a way Bran hadn't even known he'd missed. It brought back memories of his mother, serving up food when he'd been a child. Before she'd become ill. There had been life in Roscarrock House back then. It'd been absent for far too many years.

Whatever Bea was doing, she stayed out of their way. Had she realised what was going on? Or was she simply wrapped up in her own world, making plans for her future far from Porthkennack? Whatever the reason, Bran was grateful not to have awkward introductions spoiling the mood.

He worried Sam would make his excuses and leave after the meal. But Sam simply stayed, as if there had never been any question of him leaving. And at the end of the evening, they tumbled into Bran's bed and made love again, slowly this time and savouring each moment, every touch.

Even after they'd both reached their climax, Bran couldn't seem to stop touching Sam. They lay in the dark of Bran's bedroom, holding one another. "Is this the room you had when you were a kid?" Sam asked idly. "There's no sign of teenage you."

"At the age I am now, I should bloody well hope not. And I was never sentimental about childhood."

"Yeah? Go on, admit it. You've got an attic full of old toys you can't bear to part with."

Bran stroked Sam's chest, enjoying the lightly furred dip between his pectorals. "No. All my outgrown toys were passed on to Jory. I'm not sure any of them survived the experience."

"So am I the first bloke you've had up here?" Sam asked, his voice teasing. "Or did you use to sneak boys in all the time when you were in your teens?"

"God, no." Bran shuddered, unable to stop himself.

Sam lifted himself up on one elbow to gaze down at Bran, his eyes wide and black in the dim light. "Parents not supportive? Or did it just take a while for you to grow into your looks?"

"Father had strong views." Going into detail about those views would only pain them both. Bran paused, uncertain—but here, in his bed, curtains drawn, it finally felt safe to admit it. "And it took me a long time to get over . . . Devan's father. And yes," he added in a determinedly lighter tone, "it took me a while to grow into my looks. I was well into my twenties before people stopped assuming I was Bea's much younger brother, not her twin."

"Think she'll be okay about you and me?" Sam's voice was soft.

"I think so. Yes, she'll have to be." He stroked Sam's hair, marvelling anew at its silky texture. "She's decided to make some changes in her own life, so she can hardly begrudge me mine."

"Good," Sam said drowsily. "So I'm okay to stay the night?"

"Yes." Bran drew him closer. "Stay."

Sam seemed to have an insatiable appetite for morning sex. Bran wasn't complaining—having woken up enfolded in strong arms, with a tousled head nuzzling into his neck, he had quite an appetite for it himself. They came together lazily at first, and then with more urgency, hands and tongues getting involved, ragged breaths turning to stifled moans.

Not so stifled, by the end. As Bran came down from his high, he found Sam looking at him sheepishly. "It's just gone nine. Your sister will have left for work already, right?"

Bran struggled to get his brain sufficiently in gear for speech. "Possible. It is Bea. But unlikely, seeing as it's Saturday."

"Huh. So it is."

"We are open to visitors today, however."

Sam's eyes widened. "Shit, are they here now? Do you think they heard us?"

Bran laughed. "We don't open until ten thirty. So no."

"Oh. Good." Sam relaxed back into Bran's arms for a moment, then raised himself up on an elbow. "If someone sees me here, is it gonna be an issue?"

Bran gazed at him, taking in the tiny crease between those soft, dark eyes. He couldn't imagine, now, wanting to hide what this man was to him. "No. It won't be an issue."

It was a while before they made it out of bed. In the end, it was rumbling stomachs that got them up and sent them downstairs for breakfast, by which time, as Bran had half expected, Mrs. Castilla was there. A widowed lady in late middle age, she was one of their keenest volunteers. She looked nonplussed at seeing Sam with Bran, but recovered well, wishing them a good morning and then bustling off with a mutter about checking the flower arrangements.

Bran sent Sam a rueful smile. "I'm afraid we're going to be the topic of conversation all over Porthkennack by nightfall. Mrs. Castilla doesn't believe in keeping things to herself." And if he felt a flutter of nerves in his stomach at the thought, he was fairly sure he managed to keep Sam from noticing.

Sam grinned. "Hey, you think I'm bothered? I snagged the most eligible bachelor in town. You think I'm gonna keep quiet about that? Uh, you don't *want* me to keep quiet—"

Bran laughed, somehow at ease once more. "No, I don't. Come and see if we can find something for breakfast."

With visitors potentially arriving, Sam clearly didn't feel comfortable staying at Roscarrock House after breakfast, so Bran exacted a promise to see him for dinner and let him out through the kitchen. When he made his way back upstairs, he met Bea outside her room.

She'd apparently been waiting to talk to him. "Who was that?"

"Sam Ferreira."

"Your curator?"

"Yes."

Bea gave him a searching look. "So things are changing around here too. I want you to know I'll be leaving for London in August. Probably for good. I've spent too long trapped in this house with memories and ghosts."

Trapped? Bran could never see Roscarrock House, or Porthkennack itself, in that light. This was his *home*. "There are good memories too, aren't there?" he asked, stung.

"Perhaps I'll remember them better when I get away." She hesitated. "You and your curator . . . it is what I think it is, isn't it?"

Bran's heart fluttered in his chest. It was a terrifying thought, but a liberating one too. Preparing to tell Bea that he was planning to be open about being gay, that he and Sam were in a relationship, felt very like readying himself to step off a cliff—

And that was another thing, wasn't it? "Bea?" he said, his voice gentle. "Let's go into your room. I've got a few things I need to tell you. The first one is about Father. And Mother."

EPILOGUE

Five Weeks Later

The grand opening of the Black Prince exhibition might not have gone off without a hitch, but in Bran's experience, things rarely did. At any event, all last-minute crises fell well within the boundaries of what he considered acceptable.

Bran had a feeling those boundaries were considerably more relaxed than they had been only a few months ago. Sam had borne all their shared stress with patience and good humour, and Bran had done his utmost to appear to be doing likewise. At least the biggest hurdle had been cleared some weeks previously, with Canterbury Cathedral giving their secular blessing to the arrangements for the loan of the funerary achievements.

To Bran's irritation, people had spent far more time gazing at—and photographing themselves in front of—the vividly coloured replicas of the prince's armour displayed in the entry hall than they had examining the actual precious relics themselves. "For God's sake," he'd muttered to Sam. "That surcoat was worn by Edward of Woodstock."

Sam, who'd been infectiously giddy all day, had only grinned. "Yeah, but you've got to admit it was in a lot better nick back in those days. And the dim lighting"—a condition of the loan, so as not to further damage the delicate fibres—"makes it even harder to see the detail. Just look on it as a good omen for when we have to give the real ones back."

Bran had had to concede he had a point. And admittedly it'd made policing the "no photography" rule for the relics somewhat easier.

After the public opening, with jousting and other medieval delights courtesy of English Heritage, there was a reception for press and local dignitaries at the exhibition centre. Speeches were made, although mercifully short, and canapés and prosecco served. Kirsty's sculpture was unveiled, while she stood serene and proud, Gawen by her side. He seemed more subdued, but that might just have been discomfort with the public attention. Certainly he was back to his normal self as soon as he was out of the spotlight.

Bran had half wondered if Craig might turn up to disrupt proceedings, like a jealous ex standing up at a wedding to voice his objection, but there was no sign of him. Probably he was entirely over Bran already. Sam and Bran had discussed what to do if anyone brought up the discredited paper, and were confident they could handle it, but it was a relief not to have to deal with that sort of thing.

There were one or two other absences, none of which surprised Bran. He'd been able to predict with remarkable accuracy which of his former social circle, such as it was, would react negatively to news of him and Sam. What was even more astonishing, however, was how little he cared. Weighed against his happiness with Sam, what were a few old fogies who no longer wished to partner him for a round of golf? He'd never liked the game all that much anyway. Or certain players, come to that.

Dr. Banerjee had of course been invited. Bran had been a little surprised, although gratified, that she'd accepted, and looked out for her. She arrived late, pushing a wheelchair in which sat an ill-looking man of her own age.

Bran strode over to greet them. "Dr. Banerjee, I'm so glad you could make it."

"Thank you for the invitation. This is my husband. Sanjay, this is Mr. Roscarrock."

Bran shook the dry, trembling hand that was held out to him. "Delighted to meet you."

"I'm glad it all came together," Dr. Banerjee said. "I felt so guilty leaving you in the lurch, but with Sanjay's health . . ." She made a two-handed gesture of helplessness.

Bran's chest ached. Life, and love, could be so very fragile. But . . . *she* felt guilty? "I'm so sorry. If I'd known your circumstances—"

"I should have told you, perhaps. But when he had the attack—and such a bad one—it was very hard to think clearly. And in any case, I think leaving was the right decision. For more than one reason."

He couldn't help glancing over to where Sam was talking animatedly to a reporter from the local paper. When Bran looked back at Dr. Banerjee, she gave him a knowing smile.

He was *almost* certain he didn't blush. "I must introduce you to Sam, when we have a moment. Dr. Ferreira, that is. We're planning a book on the prince, once the exhibition is running smoothly, and we were hoping you wouldn't mind us using some of the work you undertook during your time here. We'd credit you, of course."

"Writing? I always thought you were too busy for anything like that."

"I was. But my priorities have changed." Again, Bran's gaze flicked to Sam as if of its own accord. "Please, take some time to think about it."

"I will." Her smile broadened. "And I'll look forward to speaking with your Dr. Ferreira."

It was immensely satisfying to see the surprise on the face of Jennifer Solomon as she drew near and took in Bran and Dr. Banerjee talking civilly. *There* was someone always ready to believe the worst of him. He wondered how Dr. Solomon had taken the news that he and Sam were together—then decided that on reflection he didn't really want to know.

Bran exchanged a few more words with Dr. Banerjee and her husband, then left her to the presumably more welcome company of Dr. Solomon. There were plenty of other people he needed to make nice with, but eventually, the promised introduction was made and Sam and Dr. Banerjee seemed to hit it off immediately, to Bran's mingled pleasure and mild chagrin. At length, the event began to wind down. Bran was free to rejoin Sam, now relaxing with his family.

Only two of Sam's sisters had made the trip from Luton with his mother to attend the opening—the eldest, Maria, and the youngest, Nat. Bran, having braced himself for the dragons of Sam's description, had found them to be charming, erudite women who clearly relished an outing without their children (and, perhaps, their husbands). He'd been a little more nervous about meeting Sam's mother, and she'd given him a thorough examination both visually and verbally, but he'd apparently passed muster. At least, she'd started scolding him for not eating enough, which Sam had whispered was a sign of approval.

"We're going to be heading off now," Maria said when he rejoined them. They were staying in a hotel, which Bran had insisted on paying for, as having guests at Roscarrock House during peak visitor season wouldn't have been ideal. "I need to call the kids or they won't go to sleep. But it's been a lovely day." Sam winced as she dug him in the ribs with an elbow. "You did good, baby brother."

"Oi, less of the *baby*."

Mrs. Ferreira wrapped her arms around Sam, standing on tiptoe to kiss him on the cheek. "I'm very proud of you. We'll see you for lunch tomorrow." She then, to Bran's pleased discomfort, hugged him too. "Look after my son. And don't let him make any more bad decisions."

"*Mu-um.*"

"I'll do my best." Bran tried not to smile too much at Sam's expression. At least she hadn't mentioned the debt problem explicitly. Bran had offered a loan again, and been refused again. But Sam had agreed to a payment plan and was sticking to it.

Sam sighed as they waved his family off. "Why is it that even when you're in your thirties, mums still treat you like you're a spotty teenager?"

Bran thought, with a pinprick of conscience, of Jory. "It's not just mums."

"Yeah, tell me about it. Older sisters too. You have no idea how lucky you are."

"I have an older sister," Bran pointed out. "Bea is ten minutes older than I am."

"Yeah, but that's . . ." Sam cocked his head. "Okay, fair point. I mean, obviously I like her and everything—she's your sister . . ."

Bran took his arm. "Probably best to end that sentence there. I know she can be a little intimidating." Not to mention, there was still bad feeling over the Devan Thompson affair.

Bran hadn't said anything to Sam yet, but he was planning to write to Devan Thompson. To apologise for the way he'd behaved on meeting him. He wasn't sure it would bring about a reconciliation—nor would he blame the man for that, after how he'd been treated—but he hoped at least they'd be able to end any active animosity. After all, with Mal being his close friend, it was quite likely Devan would be in Porthkennack again.

Another thing he hadn't mentioned to Sam was the donation he'd made to the lifeboats in memory of Gerren Ede. He'd thought long and hard about whether to make it openly, in the spirit of an olive branch, but had decided in the end to remain anonymous. He didn't want to appear to be trying to buy goodwill.

As the last guests drifted away, Bran turned to gaze at the exhibition centre. A trick of the setting sun enriched the wood of the structure into beaten copper warmth, and the reflection of salmon-pink skies blazed from the plate glass windows. To one side, the standard of St. Piran, with its white cross on a black background, fluttered lazily in the warm evening breeze. Out in front, aloof and alone and larger than life, stood the Black Prince himself, carved from local timber. Rough-hewn at the base, the figure sharpened into focus, its features clearly—at least to Bran's knowing eye—those of Euan Mayhew.

Sam followed Bran's gaze. "Does it bother you that it's him?"

"Mind reading as well? Is there no end to your capabilities?" Bran spread his hands, and smiled as Sam captured one of them to hold in his own. "No. To be honest, I thought it would, but it doesn't. He . . . he didn't win, in the end."

"Got away with it," Sam said darkly. "After nearly killing you."

"But it was my choice not to press charges. That makes a difference. The worst thing about the attack was feeling so . . . powerless. Vulnerable. I don't feel like that anymore. Mayhew's well away from here now, and hopefully he'll think twice before letting his fists do the talking in future." And hopefully Kirsty would think twice about the sort of man she was with before she let the next one into Gawen's life. But Bran had to resign himself to there being some spheres over which he had no control.

Sam raised Bran's captive hand to his lips and kissed it. "Still think he got off lightly."

Sally Peters, who had lingered for some reason, joined them at that point. "Very effective, that sculpture. Reminds me of someone."

Don't you start. "The model left Porthkennack a couple of months ago."

She nodded. "So I heard. Euan Mayhew, wasn't it? I'll look out for him. In case he ever decides to pay another visit."

"I doubt he will."

Sally raised an eyebrow, but said nothing. Then she glanced over Bran's shoulder, and smiled. "Bea. I wasn't sure if you were still here."

"I came with Bran." Was it Bran's imagination, or was there more warmth in Bea's tones than he'd used to hear?

"Ah, so you've been stuck here waiting for the men. Well, I was about to head off, so if you like, I could give you a lift."

"There's no need—" Bran began, but Bea interrupted him. "Thank you. That's very kind."

He and Sam stood and watched the women walk away, their figures gilded by the setting sun. Sally, much the taller, moderated her stride to accommodate the more petite Bea, but still there seemed an odd asymmetry between them.

"It's nice those two are friends." Sam's tone spoke louder than his words.

Bran laughed. "No, I didn't see it coming, either. Bea doesn't really have friends. Still, maybe she's changing." After all, he had. "I don't know what'll happen when she moves away next month, though." Maybe befriending Sally was simply a practice run for building herself a social circle in London.

Or even, perhaps, a way of making sure she'd hear how Bran was faring in her absence? With Bea, one really never knew.

Bran couldn't say he was sorry to see her go. He'd miss her, but it was past time they lived their own lives, instead of relying on each other for everything. They'd isolated themselves in their clifftop stronghold, and it hadn't done either of them any good.

And when she moved out, Sam would be officially moving in.

It was time for Roscarrock House to be a real family home again. One where the occupants were bound not just by history, but also by love.

Explore more of the *Porthkennack* universe:
riptidepublishing.com/titles/universe/porthkennack

a PORTHKENNACK CONTEMPORARY

Wake Up Call
JL Merrow

Junkyard Heart
Garrett Leigh

Broke Deep
Charlie Cochrane

Tribute Act
Joanna Chambers

House of Cards
Garrett Leigh

One Under
JL Merrow

Foxglove Copse
Alex Beecroft

a PORTHKENNACK HISTORICAL

A Gathering Storm
Joanna Chambers

Count the Shells
Charlie Cochrane

Contraband Hearts
Alex Beecroft

Dear Reader,

Thank you for reading JL Merrow's *Love at First Hate*!

We know your time is precious and you have many, many entertainment options, so it means a lot that you've chosen to spend your time reading. We really hope you enjoyed it.

We'd be honored if you'd consider posting a review—good or bad—on sites like **Amazon, Barnes & Noble, Kobo, Goodreads, Twitter, Facebook, Tumblr,** and your blog or website. We'd also be honored if you told your friends and family about this book. Word of mouth is a book's lifeblood!

For more information on upcoming releases, author interviews, blog tours, contests, giveaways, and more, please sign up for our weekly, spam-free newsletter and visit us around the web:

    Newsletter: riptidepublishing.com/newsletter
    Twitter: twitter.com/RiptideBooks
    Facebook: facebook.com/RiptidePublishing
    Goodreads: tinyurl.com/RiptideOnGoodreads
    Tumblr: riptidepublishing.tumblr.com

Thank you so much for Reading the Rainbow!

RiptidePublishing.com

RIPTIDE
PUBLISHING

ALSO BY
JL MERROW

The Plumber's Mate Mysteries
Pressure Head
Relief Valve
Heat Trap
Blow Down
Lock Nut

Porthkennack
Wake Up Call
One Under

The Shamwell Tales
Caught!
Played!
Out!
Spun!

The Midwinter Manor Series
Poacher's Fall
Keeper's Pledge

Southampton Stories
Pricks and Pragmatism
Hard Tail

Lovers Leap
It's All Geek to Me
Damned If You Do
Camwolf
Muscling Through
Wight Mischief
Midnight in Berlin
Slam!
Fall Hard
Raising the Rent
To Love a Traitor
Trick of Time
Snared
A Flirty Dozen

ABOUT THE AUTHOR

JL Merrow is that rare beast, an English person who refuses to drink tea. She read Natural Sciences at Cambridge, where she learned many things, chief amongst which was that she never wanted to see the inside of a lab ever again. Her one regret is that she never mastered the ability of punting one-handed whilst holding a glass of champagne.

She writes across genres, with a preference for contemporary gay romance and mysteries, and is frequently accused of humour. Her novel *Slam!* won the 2013 Rainbow Award for Best LGBT Romantic Comedy, and her novella *Muscling Through* and novel *Relief Valve* were both EPIC Awards finalists.

JL Merrow is a member of the Romantic Novelists' Association, International Thriller Writers, Verulam Writers and the UK GLBTQ Fiction Meet organising team.

Find JL Merrow on Twitter as @jlmerrow, and on Facebook at facebook.com/jl.merrow

For a full list of books available, see: jlmerrow.com or JL Merrow's Amazon author page: viewauthor.at/JLMerrow

Enjoy more stories like *Love at First Hate* at RiptidePublishing.com!

www.ingramcontent.com/pod-product-compliance
Lightning Source LLC
Chambersburg PA
CBHW030646020726
47493CB00006B/1889